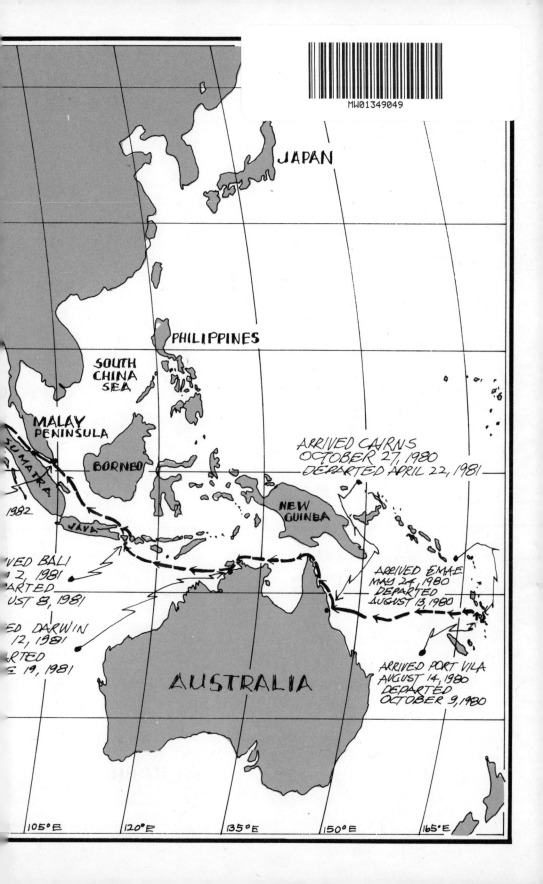

THE OCEAN WAITS

BOOKS BY WEBB CHILES

Storm Passage: Alone around Cape Horn
The Open Boat: Across the Pacific
The Ocean Waits

THE OCEAN WAITS

by Webb Chiles

W·W·Norton & Company · New York · London

Copyright © 1984 by Webb Chiles
All rights reserved.
Published simultaneously in Canada by George J. McLeod Limited, Toronto.
Printed in the United States of America.

The text of this book is composed in Avanta, with
display type set in Bernhard Modern Bold. Composition and
manufacturing by The Haddon Craftsmen, Inc.

First Edition

Library of Congress Cataloging in Publication Data

Chiles, Webb.
  The ocean waits.

  1. Chiles, Webb. 2. Chidiock Tichborne (Boat)
3. Voyages and travels—1951– . I. Title.
G530.C4774 1984   910.4′5   83-8040

ISBN 0-393-03286-8

W. W. Norton & Company, Inc., 500 Fifth Avenue, New York, N.Y. 10110
W. W. Norton & Company Ltd., 37 Great Russell Street, London WC1B 3NU

1 2 3 4 5 6 7 8 9 0

I dedicate this book to my friends:

> Louise Bleakly
> Robert Reed
> Terence Russell
> Ralph and Martha Saylor
> Howard and Susan Wormsley

who helped me through the worst of this voyage, "the alien nights in harbor."

Contents

~~~~~~~~~~~~~~~~~~~~~~~~~~~

    Charts   9
    Acknowledgments   11
    Apologia   15
1. The Resurrection of *Chidiock Tichborne*   21
2. A Gift of the Coral Sea   32
3. Cruising the Ghost Coast   42
4. Sea Snakes and Shallow Seas   55
5. The Proper Storm   64
6. The Battle of Bali   73
7. Dire Straits   90
8. In the Middle   101
9. Another Start   109
10. Pirates of Malacca?   121
11. The Longest Passage: A Specimen Day   131
12. The Longest Passage: Landfall   142
13. "She Is Dying"   150
14. The Red Sea Backwards   155
15. Going Home   169
16. A Shipwreck of the Spirit   176
17. The Shipwreck That Wasn't   186
18. Arabian Prisons: Rabigh Gaol   197
19. Arabian Prisons: Jiddah   210
20. Poems of a Lone Voyage   231

Charts

~~~~~~~~~~~~~~~~~~~~~~~~~~~~~~~~~~~~~~

1. Emae Island to Rabigh   Endpaper
2. Emae Island to Port Vila   23
3. Port Vila to Cairns   35
4. Cairns to Cape York   44
5. Cape York to Darwin   60
6. Darwin to Bali   66
7. Bali to Singapore   92
8. Singapore   114
9. Malacca Strait   124
10. Singapore to Rabigh   133

    Plans for the *Bounty*'s launch   51

Acknowledgments

~~~~~~

Although I sail the course alone, I have come increasingly to realize that this voyage would have been much more difficult and perhaps impossible without the generous help of others. I cannot mention all of those who helped me. Some, such as the Swiss sailor who rowed a pot of tea and a freshly baked cake over to me as I slumped in *Chidiock*'s cockpit, feverish and exhausted after anchoring in Port Sudan, I hardly knew. But I do thank them all, particularly, in addition to those to whom this book is dedicated, the following: the people of Emae Island; Brian, Barbara, Tony, and Danielle Voller; Yves Cadiou; Brian Mander; my fellow prisoners in Rabigh Gaol; Fernando Sanchez and the staff of the American embassy in Jiddah; Burnett and Katherine Radosh; A. Barry Jones; Jack Scarritt of Voyageur's; Luke Churchouse and Rich Huffnagle and the men and women of Honnor Marine.

Parts of this book have appeared in *Sail; Cruising World; Sea;* the *San Diego Evening Tribune; Modern Boating* (Australia); and *Voiles* (France). The photographs are by Webb and Suzanne Chiles.

"You are mad," shouted Angus, who had learnt to cherish his own limitations as a sure proof of sanity.
—Patrick White, *Voss*

With my dying strength I will bite the lips of the jaws of death.
—Yuichiro Miura, *The Man Who Skied Down Everest*

Live passionately, even if it kills you, because something is going to kill you anyway.
—Webb Chiles

Apologia

~~~~~~

There are things in this book not usually found in books about voyages.

To me a voyage is essentially an act of will and a testing of the human spirit. If a sailor doesn't learn anything more important from the sea than how to reef a sail, the voyage wasn't worth making.

One of the pleasures in setting out on a voyage is not knowing where the sea will lead. On a voyage a sailor is at risk. On a voyage a sailor knows he is truly alive. A voyage is not an escape from life; it is a reach to life. The sea may take the sailor anywhere and bring him anything: joy, pain, love, marriage, divorce, exotic islands, shipwrecks, safe harbors, despair, death, human kindness, human stupidity, even a prison cell in the desert.

A voyage is a struggle against wind and wave, and time and chance, and sometimes of the spirit against itself.

Everything in this book is about that kind of voyage.

There are many reasons why you make such a voyage, among them simply that you like to sail. But mainly you go because you must. There are strengths and talents that by their very existence demand use and testing. In his sonnet "On His Blindness," Milton wrote, "And that one talent which is death to hide / Lodged with me useless." As I set sail on my first attempt at Cape Horn, I wrote, "I was born for this."

The spirit of adventure probably exists in all men, but it is overwhelming in some. That this is so has survival value for the species.

It is the spirit of adventure, the desire to explore new lands, to sail new seas, to find new facts, to discover new ways, that has taken man from the cave. The spirit of adventure is a means by which the species provides for change and adaptation. Someone must go ahead to point the way for the rest of the tribe to follow.

Other sources of values are also needed. The adventurer, the explorer, the scientist, the artist, are not enough. They are disrupters, although necessary disrupters. The species also needs those who stay behind and provide stability. In any age, great parents are probably as rare as great artists, and certainly as useful.

The adventurer, and the pure scientist, and the artist, have no responsibility that their work be of specific value to the rest of mankind. By definition the explorer cannot know what he will bring back from the unknown. We are all experiments, and most of us who are the most radical experiments will prove to be unsuccessful. The only duty of the man who is compelled to go beyond where other men have gone is to go and struggle and bring back what he can, whether he goes to the depths of his spirit, or to a test tube, or across a new continent or sea. Time alone can determine if the exploration had practical value.

But in addition to possible practical value there is surely value in living a life of example, in saying: Here is my goal, and nothing, no suffering, no obstacle short of death, will keep me from struggling toward it; of proving with my life that man can do more.

Voyages are objective. People can like my poems and books or not. People can like me or not. People can think this voyage was worth-while or not. But I have made it. Thinking you can do things—sail, write, love—is not enough. You must do them.

In an open boat I have done what no sailor has ever done before. Not the ancient Phoenicians, nor the Greeks, nor the Arabs, nor the Polynesians, nor the Vikings, nor the seamen of the East, nor the great navigators of the West. I have explored an uncharted coast of the human spirit. I am proud of that, and I do not apologize for my pride.

This is not all ego. You form an image of yourself and make statements partially as a means of forcing yourself to live up to that image and those statements. Several years ago, the French magazine *Voiles* commissioned a drawing of me. It was based on a photograph taken while I was sailing. Although you can't tell from the drawing, I am looking up at the trim of the sails. I am smiling. It is a portrait of vitality and joy and confidence. This painful year I hung it on a wall to remind myself of what I was and must be.

I have continued to struggle despite storms and calms and imprisonment and illness and betrayal. I have sailed and written truly. Those are not bad things to know about yourself.

I wish all our lives could be voyages of such adventure. But without the capsizes.

Man can do more.

San Diego, California
December 28, 1982

THE OCEAN WAITS

1

The Resurrection of *Chidiock Tichborne*

A day made for sailing. A steady ten-knot trade wind. Sunshine. Blue sea, shading from turquoise in the shallows to dark blue on the horizon. Tan sails fluttering as they are raised, then filling as the sheets are drawn home. Tan triangles arching up and out beyond my mind.

But not on September 8, 1980. The only sails arching up from *Chidiock* that day were in my mind. The sails themselves had been left on the dock in Noumea, 300 miles south, where they and the masts and the floorboards and the rudder and the other pieces needed to make *Chidiock Tichborne* more than a hulk at anchor had been sitting for almost a month, since their arrival from England. Three times the *Captain Kermadec*, the ship that was to bring them up to Port Vila, had been delayed. That morning at last the *Captain Kermadec* had arrived and I had trotted down to the shipping office, clutching the bill of lading in my hot little hand, only to be met with a shrug, a bored "You know, the tropics," and a halfhearted gesture of appeasement: "Perhaps on the *Rodin* at the end of the month."

Suzanne knew to make my sunset drink a bit stronger than usual that night, and as I sat sipping it aboard *Chidiock* and staring morosely out the pass, I tried to tell myself that I was lucky to have a boat left to repair. If they thought they could wear me down this easily, they were wrong. I would outlast them, and sooner or later they would give in and bring the parts up from Noumea. Sooner or later. Sometime. Surely. I told myself.

Chidiock and I had come apart at midafternoon on Saturday, May 24, when I cut the lines securing the inflatable dinghy to her. It was our fourteenth day adrift after the little yawl had been swamped halfway between Fiji and what were then the New Hebrides. Once apart, we fell, each with our own momentum, through time and space, coming together only briefly the following morning after we had each made our separate way over the reef at Emae Island and been found by the natives. There *Chidiock* stopped, but I spun off again a thousand miles through a veil of fever and starvation, by airplane to a hospital in Port Vila, then to a hotel room, by other airplanes to Noumea and Auckland, a reunion with Suzanne, and a room at her parents' home, and finally by automobile a hundred miles east to a quiet house at Cook's Beach, where I came to rest and began to mend.

In those first days ashore, I spent most of my time asleep and was fed up with the sea when awake, but still I trusted that someday I would want to go sailing again, however unlikely that seemed at the moment, and took some positive actions toward that end. On the suggestion of Fred Timakata, the main chief of Emae Island, I gave the villagers who had found *Chidiock* floating upside down in the lagoon 20,000 New Hebridean francs, about $300 U.S., as a "gift" for finding the boat and for watching over it in my absence. On my own initiative I obtained a letter stamped by both the British and French immigration services permitting me to return to Port Vila without an onward airline ticket because I would be leaving on my yacht. I stumbled through the shops in Port Vila seeking nautical equipment, and found very little. And I wrote to *Chidiock*'s builder, Luke Churchouse, the president of Honnor Marine in England, asking if he would send the needed replacement parts to me in Port Vila.

Luke Churchouse's response came by return telegram. Somehow he had managed to get everything onto the first ship heading for the western South Pacific from Europe, the *Cora Bank*, due to reach Noumea in mid-August. This was the first good news I had had since coming ashore, the firm fact that made a continuation of the voyage this year possible. There was *Chidiock*'s bare hull resting at a small village on a tiny island in the Pacific; there was I beside a cold and beautiful bay far to the south; and there were the parts on the ship steaming toward us from half a world away. All I had to do was recover my health and the will to bring the three of us purposefully together. And in the meantime, when I was able, I had to settle down to my typewriter and earn the money to pay for the other things necessary for the voyage.

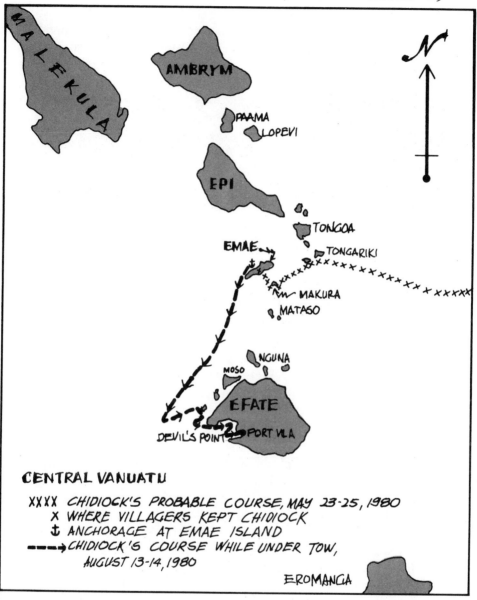

CENTRAL VANUATU

XXXX CHIDIOCK'S PROBABLE COURSE, MAY 23-25, 1980
X WHERE VILLAGERS KEPT CHIDIOCK
⚓ ANCHORAGE AT EMAE ISLAND
---→ CHIDIOCK'S COURSE WHILE UNDER TOW, AUGUST 13-14, 1980

Even with a small boat, shipwrecks are expensive. How expensive I would soon learn, for without extravagance I was to spend nearly *Chidiock*'s entire cost when new in 1978 before she was back together again in 1980. British Admiralty charts went from $7 to over $10 each while I was in Auckland. The Admiralty pilot for the Australian coast was $27.50. A plastic sextant cost more than $100; a fifteen-pound CQR anchor, $134; foul-weather pants, $55. And on and on, with the topper being a final tally, including various shipping and handling and storage charges, of $300 for some spares for my Boston Whaler inflatable dinghy, which were sent to me in New Zealand, where I was told by the shipping company that they could not be given to me, even if I paid the duty, unless I first obtained a special import license. "And where do I get an import license?" I naïvely asked.

"Oh, you can't. They've all been granted for this year," came the prompt reply.

Eventually the parts were transshipped with me to Port Vila.

I had left the condominium of the New Hebrides, but I returned to the Republic of Vanuatu. Because I did not know how long I would be there, and because she wanted to be warm again, Suzanne flew up with me. On August 5, it was heavy wool sweaters, long-sleeved shirts, and slacks when we left Auckland. Sweaters were discarded and sleeves rolled up when we changed planes in Noumea. And we made a quick switch to shorts as soon as we reached the Hotel Rossi in Port Vila.

We had chosen to travel the week after the independence celebrations. Those who saw them said the celebrations were colorful and, for some, moving, as the British and French flags were replaced by the black, green, yellow, and red flag of Vanuatu. The name, I was told, means, "the land that always has been, is, and always will be." But this was not a vacation for us; I thought we would be unable to do anything toward recovering *Chidiock* during Independence Week, and hoped that with more time, the political situation would settle. In fact, the much-advertised rebellion had little effect upon Port Vila, except for the number of troops of various nationalities—British, French, Australian, Papua New Guinean—wandering about. And my concern that politics would achieve what the sea had not and cause me to lose *Chidiock* was soon put to rest.

When our airplane came in to land at Port Vila, I thought I could see the three green mountains of Emae Island to the north; but as with the replacement parts, the last miles were the hardest. For three days my attempts to borrow or charter a boat to go those forty miles were frustrated, and it was an increasingly depressed lone sailor who lay staring at the hotel-room ceiling each night.

There was a yacht in port, belonging to a man I will call The Owner, which I knew I could hire. I had known The Owner in other ports in

The Resurrection of Chidiock Tichborne

the past and didn't much like him, but when my last alternative was exhausted the following morning, I approached him and we made a deal—$300 for him to take us up to Emae Island and tow *Chidiock* back. I expected the experience to be unpleasant, and in a hundred petty ways it was, but I did not expect it to end almost in disaster. The worst consequence of being shipwrecked is that you are dependent on others. The Owner made it clear from the outset that he would run his own boat his own way. That is every sailor's right, and I have always before been careful to sail only with those I know and trust. Now I had no choice. But it was only a day sail up to Emae. A day to move *Chidiock* across the island to the anchorage. And a day sail back. What could go wrong?

The sail to Emae was fast and interesting because The Owner's boat was a trimaran, albeit of heavy displacement, and I had never before sailed on such a vessel. Reaching north we averaged just over seven knots, in smooth, upright sailing. It was amazing to look more than twenty feet across the cabin interior and still be seeing the same boat. How could that be us, way over there? No heeling. No fiddles on the tables. Enough deck space for a tennis court. Perhaps there is something to be said for such a craft, I thought. Going up.

Approaching Emae from the south I saw even less sign of its being inhabited than I had seen when drifting in from the east in May, and the impression that the island was deserted remained when we went ashore late that afternoon at the landing of an abandoned copra plantation and began walking along a lonely track through the jungle. In Port Vila, Fred Timakata, now the minister of home affairs in the new government, had said that the villagers had wanted to keep *Chidiock* and tried to refuse my "gift." He had implied that my ownership of her hung by the tenuous thread of the letter I had been given by the immigration services saying I would leave the islands on my yacht. The new government was assiduously fulfilling its promise to abide by agreements made under the colonial powers. But as we walked through the silent jungle on Emae, I still wondered if there would be a problem.

After fifteen minutes we came to the edge of the clearing where the main school is located. As always the children saw us first and came running, only to stop a few yards away and stare. I asked them where I could find Kalo Manaroto, the headmaster of the school and the man nominally in charge of *Chidiock*. After the requisite round of giggles, one of the boldest said, "Over there," and pointed to a building on the far side of the grounds.

It was Sunday, and most of the adults on the island had gathered for a feast after church. Word of our arrival had preceded us; as we approached the building, Kalo, accompanied by several men I recognized as village chiefs, came out with a great smile, and my immediate concern for *Chidiock* vanished. The people of Emae had treated me well before, and they did so again.

Because I wanted to see *Chidiock* before dark, we arranged to meet Kalo again in the morning, and then walked down to the beach, accompanied by an honor guard of children. And there, beneath a thatched shelter, sat the indomitable *Chidiock Tichborne*.

In another age, *Chidiock* would surely have become a legend on Emae Island, her story passing from generation to generation, embellished along the way, until she was firmly fixed in the distant myths of the tribe. Perhaps she still will, for she sat beneath her specially constructed shelter as though in a shrine overlooking the wild surf, and the abundance of drinking shells in her immediate vicinity gave proof that the villagers had already spent many evenings around her, talking and drinking kava.

Throughout the eleven weeks since I had last seen *Chidiock*, I had been troubled by the possibility that I had missed some fatal damage to her hull during my cursory examination of her the morning she came ashore. Now I climbed and crawled around, about, over, and partially under her. What had seemed too good to be true was nevertheless true: she had come unscathed through the surf without a scratch below the gunwale.

Just as in May the voyage had disintegrated further each day, now each day saw us further on the way to recovery. On Monday morning, with the help of Kalo and many other villagers, we lifted *Chidiock* onto one of the three half-ton pickup trucks that were the only vehicles on the island, and trundled her over the ridge to the anchorage. The tide was out, so I tied a line to a tree and another to a rock, and a few hours later, with a gentle nudge from Suzanne, *Chidiock* was afloat. It all sounds simple, for it was a simple act; but for me, and for Suzanne because she cared, this was a moment of great satisfaction.

The wind was blowing at twenty knots the next day, and The Owner wanted to wait; although I was impatient to get back I did not argue, and we moved *Chidiock* only from the shore to behind his boat.

Left with free time, Suzanne and I explored the abandoned plantation. The buildings were simple stick cabins rather than log cabins, and were void of furnishings, with one incongruous exception: A dark hut

The Resurrection of Chidiock Tichborne 27

long abandoned on an island isolated in the Pacific. A dirt floor littered with rat droppings, a broken outboard propeller, an empty tortoise shell. And, barely visible, nailed to the stick wall, a reproduction of a Picasso—*Woman with Mantilla, Red Background.*

The wind had not abated on Wednesday, but The Owner declared himself ready to go, although I sensed some indecision in his manner. Later he was to state that he had wanted to abandon us there because he was afraid of damaging his boat on the tow to Port Vila. We were to leave at dawn, but the anchor did not come up until almost 10:00 A.M. On the way to Emae we covered forty-nine miles by log; on the way back, twice that.

For the first several hours I rode in *Chidiock* because I did not know how much water she would take aboard and wanted to be ready to bail if necessary. The ride was exciting, with the rudderless *Chidiock* sheering from side to side as she was pulled at five knots through some fairly big waves; but she was so light she bobbed over them easily and never had enough water in her to enable the pump to draw. In late afternoon,

Moving *Chidiock Tichborne* to the truck for transportation across Emae Island.

I managed between waves to get back to the trimaran.

With our late start and the tri's propensity for making leeway, it became impossible for us to reach Port Vila before dark. At sunset I was on the helm, which was located in a pilothouse. I asked The Owner where the switch was for the compass light. "Don't have one," he said.

"It's burned out?" I asked.

"No. I've never had one."

"Then how do you steer a course at night?"

"Use a flashlight," and he handed me a monster powered by eight D cells, good for at least a half hour's blindness with each flash. The boat had refrigeration, a ham radio, and a built-in cassette player, among other amenities.

"You really don't have a compass light?"

"Nope."

After a long night of sailing on and off the coast in deteriorating weather, at dawn we were about where we had been at dusk, still fifteen miles from Port Vila and five miles north of the aptly if melodramatically named Devil's Point, known for a strong onshore current and locally rough seas.

The sky was leaden, the wind between twenty and twenty-five knots right on the nose—or, with a tri, noses. The tri labored through rather than over the waves, agonizingly slow, burying first one bow, then another, then another, so that great sheets of water poured across her deck. Big trimarans looked a little less attractive going to windward than when running free. Finally, on the first tack that could possibly enable us to shave past Devil's Point, The Owner headed in until it was obvious that he was going to close the land, and I could not refrain from asking, "Do you really think you can make it on this tack? It's a lee shore."

"Easily," he proclaimed. And perhaps he might have if two hundred yards offshore he had not backed the jib in the midst of a squall.

With her great windage the tri went into irons. Instead of bringing the jib across and going onto the other tack, which would have given us sea room and taken us out of danger, The Owner started the engine and tried to bring the bows back through the wind under power. When this failed he turned off and tried to jibe. The turn was too sharp. Two of the towlines were torn from *Chidiock*, and the boats smashed together. As could be expected, the boat that suffered the most from this collision was not the 20,000-pound tri. Fiberglass splintered from near *Chidiock*'s bow. Another gaping wound appeared amidships. I knew the one remaining towline would not hold, so I leapt down into

Chidiock and struggled to replace the bridle. By the time I had, The Owner had completed his jibe; it was impossible for me to get back on the tri; and both boats had drifted to the line of breakers on the reef.

With engine at full throttle and sails drawing, the trimaran fought for survival. Back in *Chidiock,* soaked to the skin, I was helpless. Two solid walls of surf pounded the reef and the rocky shore. If we went on the beach again, *Chidiock* was more likely to remain in one piece than I. I could only dive clear and hope she did not come over on top of me. From the tri, Suzanne stared back, horrified.

The Owner must be given some credit. Backing the jib again would have meant the end. There was only a narrow path to safety, neither heading too high nor falling off too far, and he steered it for a full mile. And if he almost put us on the reef, he did manage to keep us off. Getting off is what Suzanne and I did in record time when we reached Port Vila. While the anchor chain was still rattling down, we were back on land and had *Chidiock* tied to the dock at the Hotel Rossi.

Suzanne said, "I was sick with fear for you back there."

I said, "Remind me never again to go to sea on a boat with a refrigerator but no compass light."

On Monday, August 18, twelve weeks and one day after being wrecked on Emae Island, *Chidiock* took her place in the anchorage. She drifted under "full twig." This was a new rig I had devised, consisting of two tree limbs as masts and a third as a ridgepole, all guyed attractively with bright-green plastic clothesline. Its real purpose was to support the tent, but we incidentally provided entertainment for the breakfast patrons at the hotel. And that night we slept under our own roof, however makeshift.

After I patched *Chidiock*'s hull, there was very little to do but wait for the *Captain Kermadec* to come in. And then wait for the *Rodin* to come in.

Port Vila is a curious place with many attractive features, yet it lacks something, and people do not choose to linger there. Within only a few weeks *Chidiock* was the senior boat in the anchorage. I often found myself thinking that the red and yellow flowers on the hillsides were really very pretty, and the water was really very clean, for we could watch fish swimming near the coral ten feet below us, and the climate was really very pleasant for the tropics—so why didn't I like the place? I never did decide. Perhaps the reason was that I was stuck there. Perhaps I just like Fiji more.

It was a very quiet time.

Living under "full twig" in Port Vila, awaiting replacement parts.

I did manage to borrow and read a copy of Balzac's *Cousin Pons*, a novel that had been lost unread in both my capsizes in *Chidiock*, so I will never again have to hazard taking it to sea.

I bought a pair of shorts that proved the world is still safe for capitalism. They were made in China and had buttons on the fly. Buttons! Consider the time wasted while a billion Chinese button and unbutton. Consider the fortune to be made with the Chinese zipper concession.

We heard a new definition of a ketch rig, reportedly made by Radio Vanuatu's commentator at the parade of yachts during the independence celebration, "Here comes . . . a . . . er . . . well, it has one big-fellow mast up front and smaller one a little more behind."

And we waited for our ship to come in.

A day made for sailing. A steady ten-knot trade wind. Sunshine. Blue sea, shading from turquoise in the shallows to dark blue on the horizon. Tan sails fluttering as they are raised, then filling as the sheets are drawn home. Tan triangles arching up and out beyond my mind.

And one day they did.

The shipping office finally ran out of excuses on October 2, 1980, and the *Rodin* delivered more than a hundred containers to Port Vila. The man in charge of the wharf told me to come back "sometime next week." Instead, I came back the next day and with the help of one Customs official, two fork-lift trucks, and a half dozen grinning dock workers, we located and unloaded container number 730 345-0.

At 3:15 P.M. the next day, Saturday, October 4, after several hours of hammering, drilling, fastening, and tying, I rowed away from the Hotel Rossi dock and raised *Chidiock*'s sails.

We headed out toward the pass, came about and raced back through the anchored yachts, jibed, tacked, sailed in circles, sailed for the sheer joy of it.

The resurrection was complete. *Chidiock* lived.

Chidiock Tichborne resurrected, Port Vila.

2

A Gift of the Coral Sea

I reread the postcard.

> Dear Suzanne,
> I'll give this to someone to mail. Probably Charlie of *Patea*. Upon receipt you will know that I left Port Vila on Thursday, October 9, at 8:00 A.M. I will therefore arrive in Australia on October 27 at 11:42 A.M. Precisely.
>
> Love,
> Will

Then I rowed the card over to the other yacht and forgot about it.

I could have left that very afternoon, but all too often I go to sea like a man rushing to catch a plane. Always I have been glad to reach port, and always I have been glad to return to sea. But for this departure I felt no sense of urgency. The pitchpole in May had redefined time for me. Then, I had rushed to leave Suva only to find myself four days later drifting at a maximum of one knot in an inflatable dinghy. Now I was hardly being dilatory—the new masts, sails, and rudder necessary to make *Chidiock Tichborne* seaworthy again had reached Port Vila less than a week earlier—and spending the extra half day in port did not seem excessive, only unnatural.

I don't believe I waited because I was afraid, but my mood was decidedly somber. As I rowed ashore that evening for a final drink and dinner, I found myself dwelling on that word "final." I had spent a good many hours studying the alternate routes to Australia on the charts, routes that would take me island hopping south to Brisbane via Noumea, or north through the Solomons and New Guinea, before becoming disgusted with my caution and resolving upon the bold stroke. If I felt bogged down in the Pacific Ocean—and I did, having covered only 600 miles, and half of that while adrift, in what had stretched out to be a full year—the answer was not to pussyfoot around more islands, however pretty. I had been harbor-bound far too long. The proper action was to make the direct passage across the Coral Sea, the second-longest passage of the circumnavigation thus far, 1,500 miles west to Cairns, in northern Queensland. I felt better once I had made that decision, but was still, as I approached the ocean, more tense than ever before.

My tension manifested itself in many ways. Provisioning for what should be a two- or three-week passage, I found myself buying a few more cans of soup and then a few more cans of tuna and then a few more cans of fruit. And an extra tin of cabin crackers. And a full case of Coca-Cola. And another full case of plastic bottles of water. And a rigid water container, even though anything plastic is criminally expensive in Port Vila. Until at last, including freeze-dried food, *Chidiock* carried provisions to last two months. There was no danger of her being overloaded. *Chidiock* is a self-simplifying boat. In May she had thrown everything away and demonstrated how little is really needed to survive. Now, fully provisioned, she sat easily on her waterline.

I also had new airbags sent from Voyageur's; I tied all the water containers securely around the mast in the forward end of the cockpit; and *Chidiock* carried five buckets, two inside the aft locker and one tied in the stern well beneath the dinghy, where they should survive any eventuality short of being run down by a supertanker. But I did not block off the centerboard slot before leaving port, as I had once intended. Partially I left this undone because I believed I would still have been able to recover from the swamping in May if just one bucket had been left; partially it was because I saw potential problems with balance in self-steering, and damage in the event of another collision with a submerged object, if the board were fixed down; partially it was because I had a new plan to block off the slot with strips of closed-cell foam.

While adrift in May I had vowed, among other things, that if I ever again faced dying of thirst, my last sip would be of something better than Coca-Cola, so my last purchase in Port Vila was the best bottle of brandy in town.

At 8:00 A.M. on Thursday, October 9, the tarp came down and the anchor came up. People waved from the shore near the Hotel Rossi, and *Chidiock*'s bow turned toward the pass. The weather was lovely. The trade wind was blowing at eight knots, the sky was blue, the sun was warm, as *Chidiock* came alive beneath my hands, with the almost forgotten feel of the wind through her sheets, the sea through her tiller.

I steered out of the harbor and, just for the joy of sailing again, kept the helm all the way across Mele Bay. Off Devil's Point the waves peaked at eighteen inches. *Chidiock* seemed eager to reach the open sea.

We continued west until a few minutes before local noon, when I hove to in order to get a noon sight to check the plastic sextant I had bought to replace my World War II U.S. Navy model, lost in May. Never before had I realized just how much I had come to rely on that old sextant, how completely I trusted it. New mirrors every year or so. No index error. And land always appeared where it said land would appear, even after 12,000 miles in the Southern Ocean.

The plastic model impressed me in some ways. It was very well put together and in terms of current prices a good value. But although the noon sight proved to be accurate, I did not have confidence in the instrument. I was concerned that the plastic might be affected by changes in temperature, and I found the necessity of readjusting the index mirror before each observation more than a trifle onerous. One of the adjustment instructions was to sight on a straight vertical line, such as a flagpole. I wondered how many flagpoles I would find at sea. There was some consolation in the fact that Australia is a big target.

The wind was fair for continuing west, so it was with some reluctance that, after eating a croissant for lunch, I turned *Chidiock* north for Emae Island. I could not avoid thinking that if I later got into trouble one day out of Australia, I would hate myself, but *Chidiock* had been towed from Emae to Port Vila and I wanted to swing back across the track we followed while drifting to Emae in May, so as to make the circumnavigation continuous under what might be called our own power.

At 9:00 P.M. Emae's three peaks were silhouetted by starlight. We were a few miles east of the reef and close to the spot where four and a half months earlier I had cut the lines securing the dinghy to *Chidi-*

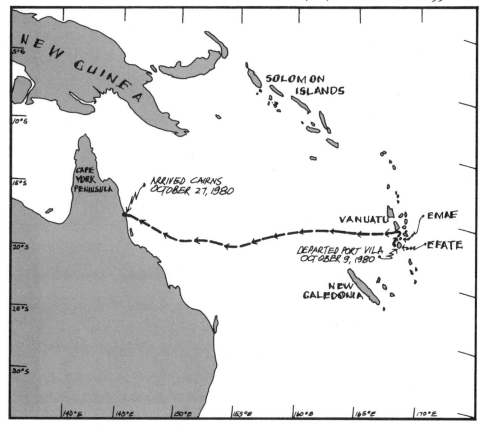

ock and started to row ashore. Then I had not known the island's name or even been certain of its location. Now I could see where I had rowed over the reef and where *Chidiock* had been found inside the lagoon. I could picture Fred Timakata's house on the hillside and where the various villages were and the faces of Kalo Manaroto and the chief of Sangava villege and the other Melanesians who were kind to me. But as always Emae Island remained mysterious. I knew the people were there, but from the sea at night there was no sign of them.

The wind was warm against my face, and in a few minutes we were clear of the north end of the reef. I let *Chidiock* run on for another mile, so that we would not be caught in Emae's wind shadow, before jibing to a course of 280° true. As the sails came across, the tension unexpectedly flowed from me. At last I felt we had come all the way back from the ordeal of May. I breathed deeply. *Chidiock*'s bow wave gurgled.

One cannot but wonder at the fundamental perversity of human nature that makes disaster so interesting and tranquillity so dull. The evidence of any newspaper is generally that good news is not news. Tolstoy began *Anna Karenina* by saying that "happy families are all alike; every unhappy family is unhappy in its own way." And in a book I had with me on the passage, *Legends of the Fall,* Jim Harrison wrote, ". . . for there is little to tell of happiness—happiness is only itself, placid, emotionally dormant, a state adopted with a light heart but nagging brain."

Yet even a circumnavigation in an open boat is not always hell and high water, and as we moved west from Emae Island, day after day the weather remained fine. When I had worried most, the sea lay down. Perhaps the greatest strength is found in mere persistence. Often I found myself thinking, If I had quit at Emae, I would never have known this. It had taken two years and thousands of sea miles, but at long last I was to have a fast, smooth, and relatively comfortable passage.

I set *Chidiock* up that first night on a port broad reach, and except for one night when we slid sideways down a wave and I took in for a few hours what proved to be an unnecessary reef, I did not touch a line for eight days and 1,000 miles of true trade-wind sailing.

The rhythms of sea life returned. Awakening with first light; breakfast of a vitamin pill, coffee, and cabin crackers—aboard *Chidiock,* cockpit crackers; a morning sight when the sun was 20° above the horizon; hours spent reading or thinking or just watching the waves from the shadow of the mizzen. The burning heat of midday, when I tried to catch the racing sun at its zenith of more than 80° with a succession of sights, in the midst of which the sextant often had to be readjusted, with a cloud as a substitute for the predictably scarce flagpoles. Lunch of cereal and powdered milk, augmented by a glass of lemon-barley drink. More reading when the shadow of the main reached me after 1:00 P.M. A late-afternoon sun sight. Dinner of freeze-dried food at sunset. (I was to arrive in Australia with all those extra cans still on board, and fully intend to continue to provision each passage as though for a shipwreck.) Then a small glass of brandy if I was feeling particularly at peace. And perhaps an hour or two of listening to Australian radio before going to sleep.

The miles passed effortlessly beneath the hull: a best day ever of 148, a best week's total of 861. And all so easy. Aboard a small sailboat there is no correlation between suffering and progress. Seldom did we take

A Gift of the Coral Sea   37

enough water aboard to enable the bilge pump to draw. And we had only five minutes of rain.

It was a passage made in harmony rather than conflict with the sea, a passage during which I had time to reflect upon other voyages made across those sparkling waters: Captain Bligh parallel to me three hundred miles north; Torres following orders and bravely daring the unknown when separated from his admiral; Bougainville almost exactly along my track. And I had time to consider the Battle of the Coral Sea. On my sixth day out I was little more than a hundred miles due south of 15°12′ south, 155°27′ east, where the U.S.S. *Lexington* sank. I tried to picture her on the bottom in 2,000 fathoms. It was difficult to imagine the Dauntlesses and the Zeros diving to the attack through these sunny skies. The sea bore no scars.

When I left Port Vila the wind had been south-southeast, so I had been able to swing north to steer well clear of the reefs off the north end of New Caledonia. Then the wind backed a point or two, our course changed from 280° to 260°, and in a week our latitude changed from 16° south to 19° south. At noon on October 17 my running fix put us just east of Marion Reef, the first of the detached reefs cluttering

The fastest passage, across the Coral Sea.

the Coral Sea several hundred miles off the Australian coast. Somehow I managed to summon the energy to do my first work in a week and jibed.

All afternoon I looked for the reef, although I knew that its maximum height is six feet, so even if my sights were accurate, I was unlikely to see it. The nagging doubt about the sextant had become ever more disconcerting. All of the observations had been consistent with one another and with my dead reckoning, but I should have been using the sextant to check my dead reckoning, not the other way around. It would not take much of an error to cause me to steer into the reef rather than away from it. A sight of surf, a bit of coral, anything, would have been most welcome; but it did not come, although the abundance of bird life showed that some land must be near.

I watched a frigate bird as he caught a huge flying fish and was then chased all over the sky by albatrosses. The fish was so big the bird seemed barely able to remain aloft. He flew like a truck going uphill. Twice he almost dropped his catch as the albatrosses darted at him. But finally he gained air space, flipped the fish up, and caught and swallowed it in one motion. I applauded.

Late in the afternoon another flying fish started from the water just off *Chidiock*'s beam. A huge brown-gray blur rose after it. The shapes merged in mid-air. A splash, and both were gone.

Even during the night, the birds continued to hunt overhead. The sky was clear and star-filled. I could not see the birds, and as I lay in *Chidiock*, it seemed as though the stars were cackling at me.

Two days later the trade wind finally died and my hopes of reaching Cairns in twelve days vanished as we made only eighty miles in the next seventy-two hours. Even that slowed pace was not unpleasant. We had gone so well the first 1,000 miles that a fast passage was still possible. I had good provisions and good books, and the sea was smoother than in most harbors. I spent a lot of time swimming to keep cool.

Finally the wind returned, backing to the northeast, and we dodged, presumably, around Abington, Malay, and Flinders reefs, none of which I saw.

The position at noon on October 23 put us thirty miles south of Cairns and sixty miles off the outer edge of the Great Barrier Reef. All day I sailed due west. On this part of the coast the reef lies only about thirty miles offshore and the land inland rises to more than 5,000 feet, but is often obscured by haze, according to the Admiralty pilot. I had planned my arrival for the full moon, and continued on until midnight, when I hove to. I saw nothing. No mountains. No coral. No surf. No navigation lights. No loom of lights from a city. It began to be eerie.

At 4:00 A.M., after a few hours' sleep, I turned *Chidiock* west again. Often visibility is best at dawn, and I wanted to be awake to search the horizon. I was. I did. Nothing.

Before a five-knot breeze *Chidiock* ambled on, and my doubts about our position increased with each successive hour, culminating in complete skepticism when a running fix at noon put us right on top of the reef. I peered hopefully over the side. Nothing. The wind died and we were becalmed.

With the sun's declination nearly that of our latitude, east–west position lines were easy to obtain. I took more sights, went over my calculations and the reduction tables time and time again. All of the sights came together. All put us well within the outer limit of the reef and only twenty miles east of two 5,200-foot mountains.

Chidiock drifted on until, at 2:00 P.M., I heard a low growl from behind us. I stood up and stared in the direction of the sound. The sea was a flat blue-white mirror of the sun, but after a while the growl was repeated and I caught a glimpse of a desultory wave a mile behind and to the south of us. So perhaps we were over the reef after all. I knew that the Great Barrier Reef is actually a great many small reefs, with countless passes between them, rather than the unbroken thousand-mile wall of coral I had imagined when I first began planning this passage, but this was ridiculous. How could I not see the greatest coral reef in the world? How could I not find an entire continent? Against all expert testimony, Australia seemed to be small, flat, and elusive. And then I heard a new growl from ahead and turned to see a low wave slop over.

For a while I considered letting *Chidiock* drift on. If my sights were accurate, and now it began to seem they might be, there was a way through the coral ahead. But my instincts said this was being too cavalier—I didn't know how cavalier I was soon to become—and it was wiser to stay clear and try to verify our position by the coastal navigation lights that should be visible after dark. So when a zephyr reached us from the east, I turned *Chidiock*'s bow and we ghosted away.

That evening the navigation lights graciously appeared where they were supposed to and I sailed slowly toward the one on Fitzroy Island, just off Cape Grafton, ten miles east of Cairns. I planned to stay awake all night, continuing in until I again sighted surf, and then sailing on and off until dawn.

It was a fine night, with *Chidiock* gliding along at a couple of knots beneath a full moon. Without warning at 11:00 P.M. a tired wave rose beneath us and I looked over the side and at last saw in the moonlight the Great Barrier Reef. It was six feet away. I prepared to come about, when a wild thought entered my mind: Why not just anchor? If a storm came up we could be in trouble; but the sea had been smooth for days, the coastal forecast was for calm conditions, there was not a cloud in the sky. By now we had sailed a hundred yards over the coral, and I had to do something soon, before the decision was made for me. I let *Chidiock* round up and lowered the anchor. Then I furled the sails and raised the centerboard and the rudder and sat down incredulously. Everything was very quiet. To the west I could see the light on Fitzroy, which I knew was only a mile from the mainland, but still I had not seen the land. Even now I could see no land except the coral beneath us. It was as though I had anchored in mid-ocean. This is very odd, I thought, and hardly a respectful way to treat the world's greatest reef. But it was *Chidiock*'s way, and at 1:00 A.M. we briefly went aground on the falling tide, enabling me to claim that we reached land on the fifteenth day out of Port Vila. *Chidiock* seemed to say, Compared with the reef at Emae Island, this place is nothing.

My hopes of reaching Cairns the following day were thwarted by light winds. Most of the morning we sailed west across the reef, sometimes in what is called Noggin Pass, sometimes deliberately along the rhumb line even when it was over coral. In Port Vila well-meaning Australian sailors had told me I would find it easier to avoid the reef by going south to Brisbane or Gladstone. They had not really understood *Chidiock*.

Sunset found me playing the last breath of breeze in an effort to reach the anchorage in the lee of Cape Grafton. I was too tired to row. Finally we rounded the point and found one other yacht at anchor in a shallow bay with an aboriginal mission along the shore. My intention to anchor off by myself changed when I noticed on the deck of the other yacht, *The White Horse of Kent*, one man and three nude nubile women. By now any fool would have known where he was, but I decided it couldn't do any harm to sail over and ask.

On Sunday there was no wind, and on Monday I rowed halfway to Cairns before a sea breeze filled in.

Monday afternoon, after finally convincing the officials I had come in from a foreign port, I telephoned Suzanne, who was staying with friends in Brisbane.

"What time did you arrive?" she asked.

"Eleven thirty-three."

"Wait a minute." And I listened to sounds of her rummaging through her purse. "Here it is," she said at last.

"What?"

"Your card. You were nine minutes early."

I was rather pleased. I had just completed the first crossing of the Pacific Ocean in an open boat. And I was back on schedule.

3

Cruising the Ghost Coast

Captain Cook fell asleep.

He was entitled to be tired on this night of June 11, 1770. The *Endeavour* had been groping along the east coast of the Australian continent, New Holland to him, since sighting land south of present-day Sydney on April 19. The captain had no way of knowing about the Great Barrier Reef, its southern end more than a hundred miles offshore at latitude 23° south. Now, in a few more minutes, at 16° south, he would find out.

Still it had been a slow, trying, dangerous sail, with boats out to feel the way ahead and a watch kept in the chains, heaving the lead, day and night, for the last thousand miles. Thus far all had gone well, except for Mr. Orton, Cook's clerk, who had fallen asleep one night so drunk that he did not awaken when someone cut all the clothes from his back, and not being satisfied with this, later returned to his cabin and cut off parts of both his ears. Even by modern Australian standards, that was drunk.

There had been two pianissimo notes of warning. Just before sunset Cook had his first glimpse of a coral shoal, and around 9:30 P.M. the soundings suddenly began to lessen. The captain was on deck, but when the soundings returned to 20 and 21 fathoms before 10:00, he believed it was safe to stand on. He gave his usual orders for sailing at night along an unknown coast and retired to his cabin, where he stripped to his underwear and tried to rest. I doubt that he slept well. He had too

Cruising the Ghost Coast 43

much responsibility; there were too many unknowns, among them the question of whether the strait to the west that Torres had reported a century and a half earlier really existed. If it didn't, they might have to remain along this interminable coast all the way to China.

The wind was gentle and the sun bright as *Chidiock Tichborne* and I sailed those same waters two hundred years later, on the morning of April 23, 1981, our second day out of Cairns, where we had waited out the wet season. I had a detailed chart and unlimited visibility, and I knew my position perfectly. The reef where the *Endeavour* had left her name and part of her bottom was only a mile to the east. *Chidiock* was being steered easily by the jib sheet, so I stood up, holding onto the mizzenmast, and stared across the sparkling water. There was not the least sign of coral. At night, the good captain had not had a chance.

A few minutes before 11:00, a cast of the lead from the *Endeavour* showed 17 fathoms. Before another cast could be made, the ship struck. By the time she hit the second time, Captain Cook was on deck in his drawers, but he was too late.

Captain Cook gave his orders with coolness and precision. Masts and yards were struck, boats put out to take soundings and set anchors, attempts made to winch the ship off. All to no avail. So they began to lighten ship. All night long, guns, ballast, casks, hoops, staves, oil, jars, decayed stores, everything that could possibly go overboard, did—twenty tons, thirty tons, finally almost fifty tons. Unfortunately they had gone aground at high tide, and the next high tide, at 11:00 A.M., was not enough by two full feet to lift them clear.

As that tide fell, the *Endeavour* began to take on more water. By noon two pumps were in operation; by midafternoon, three. The fourth was broken. But Captain Cook, ever the precise navigator, found time for a noon sight and noted a latitude of 15°45′ south.

As *Chidiock* gurgled north, I pictured the *Endeavour* lying there on her side. We had the same fine weather. All afternoon they pumped, not just the men, everyone: Mr. Banks, the ship's officers, even Captain Cook himself. There was no panic. They worked steadily to exhaustion. After all, they were on the far side of the moon. It would be years before anyone in England started to miss them.

Captain Cook's thoughts were grim. All possibilities seemed bad. It did not seem likely that they could get the *Endeavour* off, but even if they did, she would probably sink before they could reach the mainland. There were not enough ship's boats to carry all the crew. If somehow they were able to beach the *Endeavour*, perhaps they could

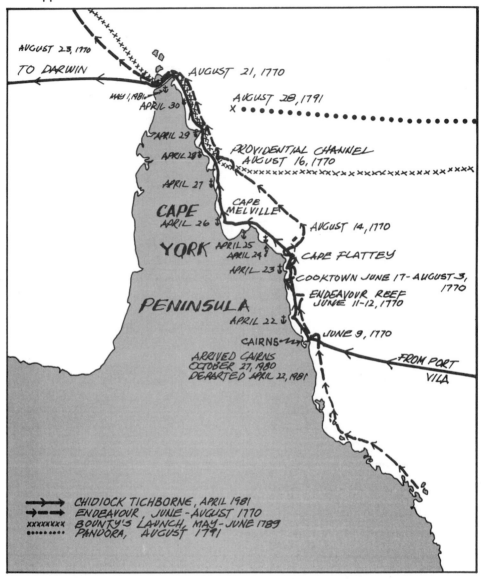

build a smaller ship from her timbers. But it seemed that even if they survived, Captain Cook's career would be at an end.

He did not have much hope for the next tide, but he had to prepare as though he did. As night fell and the tide changed, he detached a few men from the pumps to jettison more stores and to maintain tension on the tackles running to the anchors.

Shortly after 10:00, the captain decided to risk all and heave the ship off if humanly possible. All hands who could be spared from the pumps were turned to the capstan and windlass. Exhausted muscles bunched beneath sweat-streaked shoulders for one last effort. The hull groaned. Drops of water sprayed from the bar-taut anchor lines. And at 10:20, with a sharp crack, the *Endeavour* floated free.

The ship had 3 feet 9 inches of water in the hold. Captain Cook admitted to feeling fear for the first time. The man taking the depth of water in the well was relieved by another, who took the measurement in a slightly different spot. The difference was an immediate 18 inches. Until the cause was discovered, it seemed certain the *Endeavour* was going down fast.

I wonder what we would have known today of Captain Cook if the ship had sunk. Despite all his qualities of greatness, he was saved now, as he soon would be again a few hundred miles farther north, by chance. That final crack as the *Endeavour* slipped from the reef was made by a piece of coral breaking off, and the coral remained with her, plugging the worst of the hole in her hull.

Captain Cook scattered his emotions along that coast of green mountains 2,000 to 4,000 feet high. Cape Tribulation, named because it was where his troubles began, lay to the south of me. Abeam lay Weary Bay, where the *Endeavour* was slowly towed by one of the boats, while another searched the coast for a spot where the ship could be beached. They found it at the mouth of what is now the Endeavour River, twenty miles north, but they needed three days to get her there. And still out of sight to the north was Cape Flattery, which falsely flattered them into believing that the worst was over.

When I had raised anchor that morning at 4:00 A.M. I had planned to go into the old mining town of Cooktown, on the Endeavour River, but already I had changed my mind. At 11:00 A.M. the wind was too good to waste, and by noon it was too strong to risk crossing the bar. In my mind I watched Cook's men work the *Endeavour* in. They touched bottom twice, took a week to make the repairs, and then were trapped for more than a month by the southeasterlies before they could get back out. During that enforced respite, they became the first Europeans to see a kangaroo, and Captain Cook made a chart of the river that one could use today.

But although I wanted to think of Captain Cook, *Chidiock* was going like a bat out of Bullamakanka. The forecast at Cairns had been for twenty- to twenty-five-knot winds and rough seas. Just before we left, a powerboat had come into Cairns and created a new standard for anchoring on top of *Chidiock,* tied as she had been for five months fore and aft to a permanent mooring. When his dinghy hit *Chidiock* at low tide, the powerboat's owner casually remarked, "I think you're dragging into me," and when I raised sail, he said, "You're not going out in that?" I wasn't sure whether he meant *Chidiock* or the weather or both, and did not bother to ask.

The wind had not been bad, though, and we had made good progress that first day, and better the second even before the wind piped up to the forecast force and *Chidiock* began surfing at ten knots amidst miscellaneous bits of coral. Although I kept the jib tied to the tiller, I had to do most of the steering, and the result was a slight problem when I set a course for a distant headland I thought to be Cape Bedford and could not look under the jib again until the real Cape Bedford made an unexpected appearance directly ahead and, lamentably, somewhat to windward of us. There was no time to bother with foul-weather gear as I hardened up to a close reach to fight clear. I was somewhat bedraggled by the time I dropped anchor at sunset in Cape Bedford's comfortable lee.

The next morning I was awake and sailing before dawn in what was to become the established routine on this—for me—unique coastal passage. With dawn after 6:00 A.M. and sunset less than twelve hours later, an early start was imperative, and we were always underway less than ten minutes after I awakened. Anchoring in less than a fathom of water, I would sit up, extricate myself from the tarp, which seems capable still of devising new ways of trying to suffocate me, insert the rudder, unfurl the mizzen and jib, and raise the anchor, and we would be gliding across the dark, usually smooth water. Everything else could be attended to while underway. Inside the Great Barrier Reef there are just too many dangers, unless one sticks to the main shipping channel, which for *Chidiock* has its own disadvantages. I had planned our stops so that we would cover the 550 miles to Cape York in ten days, and en route we reached our intended stop every night but one, when we were becalmed.

A few people who had sailed this coast had not spoken well of it, but its isolation suited my mood exactly. Beyond Cairns there is nothing much except for the shipping in the main channel and the prawn boats, many of which were in the various anchorages as I entered. I was glad that the prawn fishermen and I were working different hours. I was on the day shift and they were on nights. We nodded as we passed—I on the way in to anchor, wash myself, and with an anxious glance for crocodiles, dive overboard to rinse off, while they were preparing their nets. At sunset, while I was heating my dinner, they would turn on their bright deck lights, up anchor, and chug away. At times they seemed to me like ponderous ballerinas performing an obscure dance, and I was always relieved when they were gone.

It had been years since I had made so long a coastal passage, and this one reinforced my belief that, while interesting, sailing beside land is more tiring than being offshore. The wind is less reliable; the waves are more confused; and currents are stronger, dangers more numerous, and demands on attention greater. Aboard *Chidiock*, my skin even suffered as much as it does at sea, because the weather was too hot for foul-weather gear, and while the seas were mostly low, the odd wave always managed to find its way aboard. But I was able to stand up part of each day while at anchor and usually even while sailing, so the circulation in my legs did not suffer.

On probably no other ocean-going vessel does simply standing up change your perspective more than it does aboard *Chidiock*, so I found many reasons to stand. The Admiralty pilot says of one cape that "from a distance it appears to be an island." This is not terribly useful when all capes appear to be islands if viewed from true sea level, as they are by one sitting in *Chidiock*, and that particular day, with land a mile away, I took a noon sight to determine which of several rather nondescript points was abeam.

More even than the solitude and isolation and generally fine sailing —for after the first two days we had only moderate winds except for a morning squall near Cape Direction and a few brief showers near Torres Strait—I enjoyed that coast because of its history. Captains Cook and Bligh and Edwards, and the unfolding of the *Bounty* mutiny, were all there. The coast, the sea, the season, the weather, all were as they had been. Only a little imagination was needed to bring the past to life. I even used a copy of Captain Bligh's chart for the last hundred miles.

As I sailed on, I was first rejoined by Captain Cook, who, upon extricating himself from the Endeavour River, followed the true sailor's longing for sea room and tried to get away from the coast and this maze of coral he called the Labyrinth. In this case it was the wrong decision made for the right reasons. I have made a few of those myself. For although he could not know it, there was no sea room for hundreds of miles in what was to become known as the Coral Sea. He did find his way through the main body of the reef beyond Lizard Island, only sixty miles north of Cooktown. The relief leaps from the page of his journal for Tuesday, August 14, 1770, when at last the *Endeavour* is beyond the breakers and for the first time in more than a thousand miles there is no bottom at 150 fathoms.

But no sooner had he safely escaped, as he thought and hoped, from the coral, than the land began to toy with him. For hundreds of miles the coast had been high, green, and tending north. Now the hills became lower and browner and fell away sharply to the northwest. The worried captain had no choice but to follow in this new direction, hugging the outside of the reef, which is a most unforgiving lee shore.

As I skirted Cape Melville on April 25, I saw the trick of geography that almost killed him. Beyond Cape Melville, which is so brown and boulder-strewn it reminds me of Baja California, the coast falls away to the south in a fifty-mile arc. From my boat I could see, fifteen miles ahead, the islands of the Flinders Group, and then, although I knew the coast was there, nothing.

Outside the reef, Captain Cook became more anxious with each succeeding mile. His job was to chart the coast, and he couldn't even see the bloody thing. He was also supposed to locate Torres's strait and determine conclusively whether New Guinea and New Holland were joined by land. Perhaps that void over there was the strait. The only way to find out was to go back through the coral, an irony that was not lost on the captain, as he recorded the happiness with which he re-encountered "those shoals which but two days ago our utmost wishes were crowned by getting clear of."

On Thursday, August 16, the lookout thought he saw the termination of the reef, and they sailed in. Only when the ship was too close for retreat could the men see that what they were approaching was just a narrow pass. The wind died, and they were becalmed. Inexorably the tide carried them toward the coral. Boats were set out, but although they were able to get the *Endeavour*'s bow around, they could not tow her off. Helplessly they drifted closer, just as I had during my last circumnavigation, in my engineless thirty-seven-foot cutter in the pass at Papeete.

No wind, a tide setting the boat onto a reef, no bottom for the anchor. I too had kept my bow pointed seaward toward a nonexistent wind. I too had kept watching the line of surf edge nearer. I too had known, as Captain Cook must have, that I alone was responsible for getting into the predicament. I too had hoped, as he must have, for something, anything, salvation. And I too was saved, as he was, by chance. If you go to sea, you had better know what you are doing, you had better be self-reliant, you had better be strong and persevering; but if you put yourself at risk long enough, you had also better have some luck.

At 7:00 P.M. on December 23, 1974, my cutter, *Egregious*, was where the *Endeavour* was at 4:00 P.M. on August 16, 1770. Let Captain Cook say it: ". . . between us and Destruction was only a dismal Valley the breadth of one wave." And then, when we were both considering what we would do after the inevitable wreck, a shadow of a whisper of a breath of breeze reached us both, and ever so gradually we edged our way clear—I to the open ocean and a minor disaster in the Roaring Forties, the good captain to a safe passage through the reef the next day and then a relatively uneventful sail to Cape York.

Again in Captain Cook's words, echoed by all aboard who ever wrote about his voyage: ". . . this is the narrowest Escape we ever had." To that point in our respective careers anyway.

We are accustomed to think of Captain Cook after his apotheosis into the Great Navigator, arguably the greatest. But we forget that on this first voyage he was not so secure. He did not come from the British Establishment. His father had been a farm laborer, and Cook had risen from the ranks through merit in an age when Family and Influence were all-powerful. If he failed to satisfy his masters on this his first important command, there were countless other men in the Royal Navy clamoring to make the next great voyage of exploration. So Captain Cook felt the need to justify himself in his log: "Was it not for the pleasure which naturally results to a Man from being the first discoverer, even was it nothing more than sands and Shoals, this service would be insupportable especially in far distant parts, like this, short of Provisions and almost every other necessary. The world will hardly admit of an excuse for a man leaving a Coast unexplored he has once discover'd, if dangers are his excuse he is then charged with *Timorousness* and want of Perseverance and at once pronounced the unfittest man in the world to be employ'd as a discoverer; if on the other hand he boldly encounters all the dangers and obstacles he meets and is unfortunate enough not to succeed he is then charged with *Temerity* and want of conduct."

In other words, no matter what a sailor does, some self-styled expert sitting comfortably ashore will say it was the wrong thing. Thank you, Captain Cook, from all of us who explore uncharted coasts of the human spirit.

The wind was blowing hard as I drove *Chidiock* toward Cape Direction. Providential Channel, where Cook re-entered the reef, still lay a few miles north, when through the rain I caught a glimpse of a tattered sail. Then the rain closed down. The waves were only three feet high, but uncomfortably steep and close together. It seemed that *Chidiock* was being set inside Cape Direction, and remembering Cape Bedford, I did not relish the possibility of having to harden up again to get clear. I concentrated on steering, so the call "Ahoy, *Chidiock Tichborne*" took me by surprise. I ducked under the loose foot of the main, and there, a few boat lengths to windward, was another open boat, a few feet longer than *Chidiock*, lug-sailed, deeper, and filled with men, so many I could not count them, sprawled all over one another. Their clothes were in shreds and they were obviously starving, but their faces were filled with joy. The figure at the tiller was recognizable, although a mere shadow of the well-fed ghost I had seen pacing the waves off Tofua Island almost two years earlier. "Young man," he called, "what took you so long?"

"Captain Bligh, I appreciate the 'young,' but I am in fact four years older than you as I see you today."

The nearness of land after the 2,600-mile sail from Tofua had tempered his usual choler. He even smiled as he replied. "Well, you are and you aren't. I may be only thirty-five, but that was my age back in 1789. I repeat, what have you been doing since we lost sight of one another in the Feejees?"

A gust caught the *Bounty*'s launch and drove her down on *Chidiock*, and for a moment we were both occupied with preventing a collision. By the time the gust had passed, *Chidiock* had pulled ahead, and I eased the mainsheet to enable the launch to come back within hailing distance. "She sails well," he called.

"But I am not so heavily laden as you," I said. "It would be interesting, though, to see how they sail just man for man."

The captain's spirit was incredible. Despite his ordeal his eyes gleamed. "Perhaps . . . no . . . it simply can't be done." He gestured toward the crew, all of whom were staring eagerly toward an island off a cape ahead. "History is what it is."

"They cannot see me?" I asked.

"No. Only I can. One of the many peculiarities of this ghost business. You were saying?"

"After leaving *Chidiock* in Suva for the rainy season, I set out again in May. Three days later we hit something that was floating in the sea.

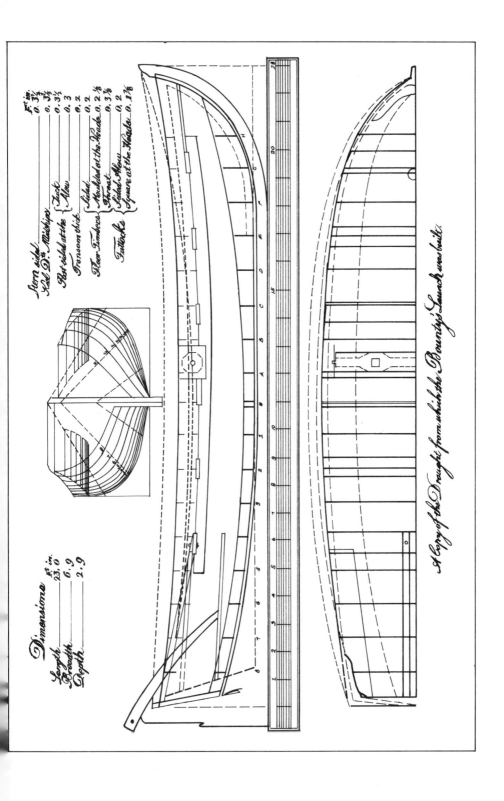

We were then halfway to Vanuatu, as people now call the islands where you tried to land but were driven off by the natives. I was shipwrecked farther down the chain. They gave me a somewhat better welcome than they did you."

The land was near, with gusts and cross seas curving around the high eastern side of the island, and for a while *Chidiock* again moved ahead. When we were in the lee, I hove to and reached for the Nikonos camera. The *Bounty*'s launch came on. "I'm going ashore here," said the captain, pointing at a narrow strip of sand.

I took the photograph.

"It will not come out," he said.

I shrugged. "Worth a try. It is said that there is a better anchorage beyond the point."

"I don't trust the natives on the mainland."

"But there is no one there."

"Not for you, but for me they are waving clubs and making threatening gestures." His voice became querulous. "You know I go to the island. Restoration Island I name it, both for the restoration of my ship's company to life and for the restoration of Charles II to the throne. It never did an officer harm to flatter the Crown, even if as individuals princes are more meretricious than meritorious. Do you sail in the morning?"

"Yes."

"Ah well. We will stay here for two days. The men need to regain their strength." A scowl crossed his face. "Though as soon as they do, they will become insolent and that fool Lamb will almost kill himself by gorging down nine raw birds. Scum hardly worth saving, but it is my duty."

I watched the much-maligned man head in to the island. The more I had studied him, the more I had become convinced that in all the great moments in his life—the *Bounty* mutiny, his service with Duncan at Camperdown and Nelson at Copenhagen, the Rum Rebellion when he was governor of New South Wales—he had not only been right but had also done his duty properly.

The launch was almost at the beach before I realized that we would probably not meet again. "Captain?" I called.

"What?" He was brusque now at the interruption.

"For two years I've been wondering, was that really marmalade I saw on your vest off Tofua?"

"Yes," he grunted and turned back to steer through the shore break.

I started to ask where he had obtained marmalade, but then even a ghost must want to get ashore after 2,600 miles in an open boat, and, reluctantly, I jibed *Chidiock* and sailed to join the prawn boats at Portland Roads. The mystery of the marmalade would remain unsolved.

I was right. I never did see Captain Bligh's ghost again, although the next night I anchored within sight of Sunday Island, his second anchorage, where he had handed a sword to William Purcell, the carpenter, and told him to either obey orders or fight. Purcell chose to obey. But I did observe from a distance the final scenes of the *Bounty* saga.

Two days north of Restoration Island, I looked seaward toward the reef where the egregious Captain Edwards wrecked the *Pandora*.

Immediately upon Bligh's return to England, the Admiralty dispatched Edwards in the twenty-four-gun frigate *Pandora* to track down the mutineers. The *Pandora* made for Tahiti via Cape Horn. At dawn on March 17, 1791, the ship passed just north of Pitcairn Island, where Fletcher Christian successfully sought oblivion; but the *Pandora* sailed on, and Edwards had to settle for those mutineers who had unwisely remained in Tahiti, along with the men who, although always loyal to Captain Bligh, had been prevented from joining him in the launch.

Edwards tossed them all, loyal crewmen and mutineers alike, into a small round deckhouse in the stern, which naturally became known as Pandora's Box. The Box could be entered only through a twenty-inch hole in the top. It was hot and foul, and the prisoners were kept constantly in leg irons. Edwards intended to return to England via Cook's Endeavour Strait. When Bligh learned of this, he predicted that Edwards was not seaman enough to make it. And again Captain Bligh was right, for on the night of August 28, 1791, after a three-day search for a pass through the coral, the *Pandora* went onto the reef.

Edwards can be forgiven for not being a Captain Cook or a Captain Bligh. He cannot be forgiven for permitting the ensuing panic, although apparently someone did forgive him, for he died in 1815 an admiral. The ship took on ten feet of water in twenty minutes, but she did not sink for several hours. Still, thirty-five men drowned, including four of the "mutineers," whom, despite their pleas, Edwards refused to release from Pandora's Box. That any of them survived was due only to Will Moulter, the boatswain's mate, who risked his life to unbolt the scuttle and toss down the key to their irons. Ever true to his nature, Edwards was by no means the last to leave the sinking ship.

In four boats, the survivors proceeded to Kupang, where they arrived on September 15. Two of Edwards's lieutenants, Hayward and Hallet, had had the pleasure of being midshipmen with Bligh, and thus found themselves reaching Kupang for the second time in a little over two years in an open boat. History does not seem to have recorded their comments, perhaps because in any age but ours their comments were unprintable.

And from the anchorage in the lee of Cape York, I could look north toward the channel Bligh surveyed when he returned to Torres Strait a year later, in September 1792, in command of the *Providence*. He had been commissioned to return to Tahiti to fulfill the *Bounty*'s original mission of transporting breadfruit to the West Indies, where it was to be used as cheap food for the slaves. The main shipping channel through the strait still passes through Bligh Entrance from the Pacific.

I smiled to myself as I sat aboard *Chidiock Tichborne* on my rest day at Cape York and recalled that this time Captain Bligh was successful. The breadfruit reached the West Indies, where, as expected, the trees flourished. The grateful planters even gave Bligh an expensive gift, but their gratitude was premature. The inconsiderate slaves hated the taste of breadfruit and starved rather than eat the loathsome stuff. If heroism and folly were not equally their own justification, one might even believe that it all had been in vain.

A white heron squawked as it flew over *Chidiock*, and brought me back to the present. Of all people, lone sailors should not examine heroism and folly too closely.

4

Sea Snakes and Shallow Seas

I've always wanted to meet the man who writes the Admiralty pilots. Surely he is a Dickensian character, wearing a frock coat, sitting on a high stool, scratching away with a quill amidst stacks of dusty tomes and papers. With his wry sense of humor, he must be one of the most entertaining companions imaginable. "Overfalls occur in Albany Pass," he once wrote; "therefore close attention must be paid to steering." And with wild shrieks of laughter, he doubtless fell off his stool and rolled on the floor, holding his sides. Advising one to pay attention to the helm in Albany Pass is about as necessary as telling a driver to stay awake when the car has just lost its brakes as it speeds down a mountainside.

I didn't have to sail through Albany Pass. I could have taken the easier shipping route through Adolphus Channel. But I wanted to see the site of Somerset, the first attempted settlement in the Torres Strait region, once intended to be the Singapore of Australia. And so I saw the site of Somerset. At very great length. Another man I would like to meet is the one who thought Somerset would become a great seaport. He must have had a sense of humor too.

Our last day's run along the east coast of Australia was to be short, only a little more than thirty miles from the marginal anchorage at Bushy Islet to Cape York. "Marginal" means that because of the swell coming around both sides of the cay and reuniting in *Chidiock Tichborne,* I had to wear foul-weather gear while cooking dinner. I had hopes when we set off the next morning of being behind Cape York for lunch.

As we approached Albany Pass at noon, my hopes remained undaunted. The pass between the mainland and Albany Island is only three miles long, and Cape York, although still hidden from view, is only another three or four miles farther on. If the tide had been with us, we would have been there in an hour. But a mile south of the entrance to the pass, without needing to consult the tide tables, I became well aware that the tide wasn't with us.

I prefer to approach land under reduced canvas. Usually, near headlands there are gusts capable of knocking *Chidiock* down, and visibility is much improved without the mainsail, so I lowered the main while we were still well clear of an off-lying rock. The southeast trade was blowing a steady twenty knots, more than enough to drive *Chidiock* comfortably under jib and mizzen.

The water flowed quickly past *Chidiock*'s hull. The sails strained. The boat felt alive. Ahead I could see the waves bunching up on the mainland side of the entrance to the pass. *Chidiock* sailed and sailed and sailed. She sang like a lark. She soared like an eagle. But although I tried to ignore it, keeping my eyes fixed determinedly on Fly Point, up ahead, ultimately I had to recognize that the rock remained abeam. I studied the seaweed drifting rapidly past. I studied *Chidiock*'s wake. They said we were easily doing five knots. But the rock remained abeam. I raised the main, and gradually we left the speeding rock behind.

I had read of Torres Strait: of how the Coral Sea to the east and the Arafura Sea to the west have separate tidal systems, with high tide in one often coinciding with low tide in the other; of how currents of up to eleven knots have been recorded, currents of seven knots are common, and overfalls occur where shallow fast-moving water encounters deep slower-moving water. But all this was more impressive when actually seen.

Skirting the worst of the overfalls by keeping to the Albany Island side of the entrance, and obediently paying close attention to steering, I entered Albany Pass at about the time I had expected to be enjoying lunch at Cape York. Somehow lunch was forgotten.

The pass is actually very pretty. Green hills rise a couple of hundred feet above the scalloped shores of the mainland and of Albany Island, facing each other across a quarter mile of water like pieces of a puzzle. The second cove on the mainland side is Somerset, a shallow indenta-

Sea Snakes and Shallow Seas 57

tion a hundred yards or so deep and two hundred yards across, completely exposed to the tidal currents. I had yet to see Singapore, but I did not anticipate any difficulty in mistaking it for Somerset, unless it too had only a single house ashore beneath a few palm trees. Across the pass on the Albany side was an enterprise that appeared more successful—a cultured-pearl farm—although why an oyster would want to study the arts is beyond me.

The wind continued to blow hard, and *Chidiock* continued to seem to sail fast; but the sailing was slippery, more sideways than forward. I felt as though we were on ice, skating from one side of the pass to the other before jibing for a quick slide back, gaining a few palm trees with each crossing.

The water was bumpy rather than rough, with a chop caused by the current from ahead and the wind dead behind. Jibing required close timing, for in the instant the main lost power as it swung across, the current would cause the rudder to stall or work in reverse. Twice we fell back onto the original broad reach and I had to tack rather than jibe in order to stay off the beach. Although I would have expected the current to be strongest in the middle of the channel, with possibly even a countercurrent near the shores, the opposite seemed to be true, and only by staying in the middle did we eventually make our weary way through the pass, at an average speed made good to leeward of less than one knot.

The current weakened as we cleared the north entrance to the pass about 5:00 P.M., but because we were now in the lee of the land I had for so long been admiring, so too did the wind. The sun was low over gleaming silver seas and the silhouettes of islands.

A narrow channel separates Cape York from York and Eborac islands. I had had about enough of channels for one day, but there was not enough time to sail around the islands before sunset and I wanted to get in. So, very nearly at low tide, with less than a fathom of water beneath us, *Chidiock* sailed one more channel. I am very fond of Australia, but it was a fine feeling when the last rock of Cape York was abeam and the continent lay south of us.

The next day was Saturday, and having sailed before dawn for ten successive mornings, I planned to remain indolently at anchor that day and then sail to Thursday Island on Sunday, go ashore to check for mail from Suzanne and buy a few fresh provisions on Monday morning, and set off for Darwin on Monday afternoon. But when I turned on the radio that night, the announcer wished us all a happy long Labor Day

Cape York, Australia.

weekend (Labor Day falls in May in that part of Australia), and I realized that the post office would be closed until Tuesday. I was not sailing to a tight schedule, but while one day's rest seemed a good idea, two seemed excessive, and I started to consider bypassing Thursday Island and sailing west on Sunday morning. By the time the post office opened, I could be halfway across the Gulf of Carpentaria.

Cape York was my introduction to the great tides of northern Australia. At high tide around noon on Saturday, *Chidiock* was a quarter mile offshore, but by the time I went ashore to stretch my legs a few hours later, the shore had graciously come to me, and I had to wade only a few yards to reach drying sand.

Cape York is splendid, with a line of mangroves beyond the high-tide mark, curious anthills six feet tall, spectacular views from the ridge of the peninsula, abundant bird life, and even a freshly painted sign identifying the place for those who are lost and might confuse it with the approach to the Sydney Harbour Bridge. It is my sad duty, however, to inform the Australian public that Cape York is in a disgraceful state of disrepair. The thing seems solid enough—good, hard, black rock—

but the sea and the rain are wearing it down. Loose stones and deep cracks are everywhere, and unless something is done soon, within the next ten thousand years or so, there will be three islands off the end of a diminished continent rather than two.

When through habit I awoke early Sunday morning, I was still undecided about Thursday Island. For a moment or two I lay there, staring up at the brightening sky, and then I got up and raised the anchor and set the sails. I told myself that I still hadn't made a decision, that I might anchor at one of the other islands; but really I knew better. The lure of the seemingly open sea ahead was too strong.

With the tide with us for a change, we shot through Cook's Endeavour Strait; its sand shoals had given the *Endeavour* some problems but posed none for *Chidiock,* and we were sailing across lagoon-smooth waters, clear of the Torres Strait Islands before noon. A great sense of peace enveloped me as the land receded; but it did not last. That the sea ahead was open was only an illusion that could not withstand the coming of the night.

Although I was not to see land, except briefly at Cape Wessel, until my next anchorage 600 miles west near Cape Don, the land was always near. For the entire distance to Darwin, *Chidiock* was in depths of less than thirty-three fathoms. Presumably because of this shallow water, combined with the strong currents, waves repeatedly built far beyond the height consistent with the moderate wind, often running eight to ten feet, with an odd, boxy shape that made for unpleasant sailing.

During that first afternoon, I had not noticed any other ships and felt alone, but as soon as the sun set, running lights were everywhere; and although we sailed away from the shipping channel as quickly as possible, we spent three of the next six nights wending our way thorugh galaxies of prawn boats.

Surrounded by prawn boats at night, we were surrounded by sea snakes during the day. I had seen a nice congenial sea snake wrapped around another boat's rudder in Suva a few years earlier, but I had never before seen one at sea. Now they were present every day, every hour. Big ones six feet long and as thick as a man's arm, sleeping in coils; small ones busily swimming to windward; some ignoring *Chidiock,* some watching intently as she sailed a snake arm's length away.

One of the most worrisome things about sea snakes is that they don't have running lights. Just as I knew that the prawn boats were around during the day even though I saw them only at night, so I knew that

the sea snakes were around at night although I saw them only during the day. This knowledge gave rise to a new worry. More than once my sleep has been disturbed by flying fish or small squid being washed aboard *Chidiock*, so why not by a sea snake? Reputedly sea snakes are very docile, but reputedly, too, they have the most potent venom on the planet, and who is to say that even the most agreeable of sea snakes might not in the confusion of finding himself an unwilling passenger on a small boat bite me by mistake? No matter how abject his apology, I would still be dead. Despite considerable deliberation, I have yet to devise a satisfactory sea-snake-aboard drill.

In addition to prawn boats and sea snakes, I also saw porpoise, turtles, leaping fish, flocks of birds, and a few manatees, "dugongs" to Australians. In all, between Cape York and Darwin, I saw more sea life and more shipping than I had seen on my entire first circumnavigation.

Averaging a hundred miles a day, we approached Cape Don, on the Coburg Peninsula, on Saturday morning. Although the landfall brought a feeling that the passage was over, Darwin was still ninety miles to the southwest across Van Diemen Gulf, and I went into a small bay north of the lighthouse to rest, intending to cross the gulf the next day. But once again the radio caused me to change my mind, for a strong-wind warning was issued during the evening news.

Chidiock was anchored in a few feet of water over coral, and I spent a hot, calm Sunday reading and snorkeling. The land ashore is a wildlife refuge and the bay seemed a good place for crocodiles, and later in Darwin I met people who said they had indeed seen crocodiles there, but the biggest creature I saw was a ten-inch angelfish hovering in *Chidiock*'s shadow.

I also wrote a poem there that I had owed Martha Saylor for two years.

> through the night
> on unseen wind
> and unseen waves
> I sail unseen
>
> sometimes
> in deserted coves
> I anchor
> unseen

soon
I will not be here
to be unseen
and the people ashore
will not be here
not to see me

All afternoon I waited in vain for the strong winds to make an appearance. That evening the radio repeated the warning, but when there was only a light breeze at 3:00 A.M., we left.

I had come to enjoy these predawn departures, and found this one no exception even though we bumped a coral head on the way out. The light from Cape Don winked comfortingly from abeam and then astern as *Chidiock* glided into the gulf under full sail. Until 4:00 A.M. the sea was peaceful and I was sleepy, and then came a puff that buried *Chidiock*'s lee rail. And then came a second puff, and within five minutes I was steering as the little yawl fought a forty-knot gale under jib and mizzen.

The rhumb line to the next possible anchorage, at Cape Hotham,

Becalmed off Australia.

fifty miles south of Cape Don, was a beam reach on which the seas threatened to swamp us. With Melville Island to leeward, I had no choice but to harden up and try to ease *Chidiock* over the breaking crests. Great lumps of water were coming aboard, but although I pumped with one hand while steering with the other, I was not able to clear the bilge.

Dawn revealed the ugliest sea I had ever sailed. The waves were only eight feet high, but rising from depths of less than seventeen fathoms, they were a foam-flecked bilious green and hideously malformed, and inside many of them as they toppled toward us were sea snakes. It was as though I were viewing the writhing snakes through thick glass, but I was too busy steering to feel more than momentary revulsion.

Dawn also brought sight of Melville Island four miles to leeward and confirmation that the bilge pump was broken. With *Chidiock* heeled so far over, water swirled high above the floorboards and I was able to scoop up some of it with the customized aluminum bailer welded for me by my friend Brian Voller in Cairns.

At 9:00 A.M. the wind began to decrease, and we were soon becalmed, with Cape Hotham in sight. The cape was typical of the Top End of Australia: a strip of blue sea, a strip of iron-red land, a strip of green vegetation. Drifting with the tide, we managed to get into its lee after nightfall.

That evening the radio again repeated the strong-wind warning, but we had only pleasant sailing the last forty miles to Darwin, although I nervously reefed every time the wind rose from fourteen knots to sixteen. The strong-wind warnings continued for three days after we were safely at anchor off the Darwin Sailing Club; but as far as I know, the only strong winds that occurred in the area were those we experienced for a few hours off Cape Don. Still, I could hardly complain that I hadn't been warned.

5

The Proper Storm

On a moonless night I found sixteen shades of darkness.

Six were in the sky: an over-all blackness of the heavens; a diffuse gray to the west, although the sun had set hours earlier; the pinpricks of the stars; a few scattered shadows that were clouds; the flow of the Milky Way; and sporadic flashes of lightning far to the north.

The sea revealed even less than the sky. It seemed to have turned in upon itself and to be studying its own depths for hidden memories. It breathed with deep, low respirations, in rhythm to a long, low swell from the south. The waves, only inches high and from the east, were a lighter gray than the swell, or—rather—than the back of the swell, for it was not visible until it had passed. The shadows of clouds, shadows of shadows, were impenetrably dark. And there were a few flashes of phosphorescence as *Chidiock Tichborne* ghosted forward.

On *Chidiock* could be found six more shades. The featureless triangle of the mainsail undulated above me. Around me was an indistinct cockpit. A solid black line marked the teak gunwale's absorption of all light. And there were the vaguely golden columns of the varnished masts; lumps of bags; and my own form, clad in foul-weather gear.

The foul-weather gear was worn in this instance not in anticipation of bad weather, but because everything was covered with evening dampness. For me, on even the best of nights, foul-weather gear serves as pajamas.

I wondered about the impressionist tenet that all shadows have color.

In all that I saw, only a few stars, the masts, and the foul-weather gear revealed even subdued color, hidden as though beneath a thousand years of soot. Yet perhaps more color was there.

When I had exhausted these permutations of darkness, my mind moved outward. Darwin lay a week behind; Bali, I hoped, less than a week ahead, although after several fifty-mile days I was not making any predictions. Sometime since leaving Darwin, *Chidiock* and I had completed 10,000 miles. I was not certain just when. I am a sailor, not a bookkeeper. We might be at 10,300 or we might be at 10,600. It did not matter. Yet 10,000 miles was something of a milestone, and this particular passage was the final phase of the transition that had been coming about since Cairns. The trade winds and the open Pacific had given way to seas crowded with shipping and dominated by land. Although I did not intend to, I could sail practically all the way to Gibraltar in sight of land. The thought was appalling, and I realized that perhaps only the Pacific and the Southern Ocean are truly open. Something deep inside me already missed the Pacific, even as something else was drawn on by the exotic names appearing on the new charts: Sumbawa, Lombok, Bali, Java.

Darwin had been a good stop, surprisingly so. I suppose the impression of Darwin I had before arriving there had been based on a photograph of the muddy commercial basin. Actually, the anchorage off the Darwin Sailing Club outside of town was clean, with a good landing on a sand beach. A kind of frontier spirit exists in the Northern Territory, as it does in far-northern Queensland, and people were very friendly, if given to gloating over their weather during the dry season. Such gloating is fully justified. In almost six weeks, we had ten drops of rain and exceptionally low humidity for the tropics. What I recalled most about Darwin, though, was the wildlife. In a city of more than 50,000 people, nature has not been subdued. Two-foot-long lizards, called goannas, walk among the tables on the grounds of the Sailing Club. One of these gave me pause when it refused a scrap of a meat pie I had been eating. Hawks soar overhead everywhere. Manatees browse through the anchorage. And the occasional crocodile chases someone up the boat-launching ramp. The last such incident occurred just before my arrival, but we did see a five-foot-long croc swimming lazily along off the beach one morning. I did not subsequently swim ashore from *Chidiock*.

This new beginning, this departure from the familiar world of Australia en route to the unknown of the East, caused me to recall my

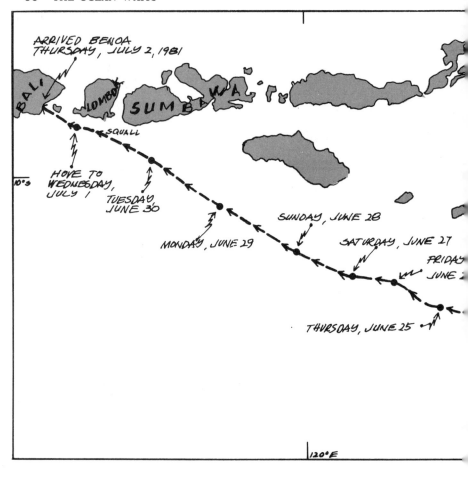

departure from San Diego more than two years earlier and to consider what had changed in 10,000 miles. Two things stood out. Now I knew the voyage was possible. The departure from San Diego had been a leap into the unknown, if a calculated one in a tried hull. Viewed objectively after 10,000 miles, the odds on our successfully completing the circumnavigation seemed to me about the same as those for any other boat, although weighted somewhat differently. We might be overwhelmed a bit earlier than some vessels if caught by a freak storm, but we would better survive the more likely crises, such as going onto a reef.

The other major difference was that when I had left San Diego I did not know if I would see Suzanne again, while now I knew that she would be in Bali on July 3. There is for me great contentment in being

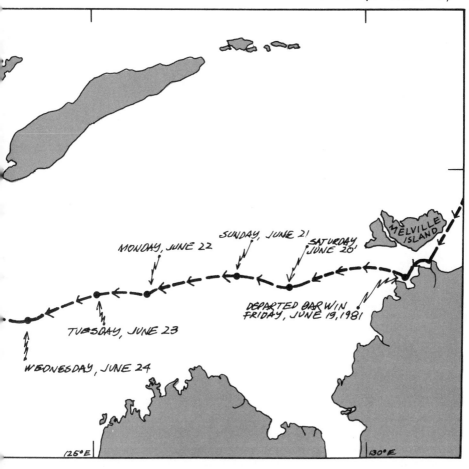

able to enjoy solitude at sea and still to share harbor life. Jokingly we had described Suzanne's function on the voyage as that of Recreation Director; it was in truth much more than that. Life on *Chidiock* was often a struggle to impose purpose in a medium of chaotic change, although it might not seem so on this smooth night, and my feelings for Suzanne were one of the few constants in that chaos. She had shared the limitations of an open boat as a home, reduced her worldly goods to a single duffel bag, learned to cook good meals on a camp stove, and endured a succession of potentially final farewells. I think it was Winston Churchill who said that his wife was the sheet anchor of his life. That is what Suzanne had become for me.

Other things too had changed in 10,000 miles, but they were only details. I had worked out a standard sea diet based on freeze-dried food. I knew how *Chidiock* would act when hove to in fifty knots of wind. I was carrying water in rigid containers, despite stowage problems, because collapsible ones had proven unable to withstand life in an open boat. And both *Chidiock* and I had a few new scars and showed our ages, although we hoped not excessively so.

As *Chidiock* slouched along, I thought, Well, if we aren't going very fast, we aren't paying a very high price in wear and tear on boat or crew either. In fact, except for a few mold spores developing in the freshwater supply, we don't really have any problems, which is not bad for a passage, particularly one that began, despite my superstitious friends, on a Friday.

For eleven days and 800 miles *Chidiock* eased her way westward. We did not in that time ship a single wave. In boredom I took many more sights than usual and knew our position with rare precision. I even stopped winding myself into the tarp at night.

Light winds were to be expected during this time of year, yet I had known passages that began quietly and ended noisily, and was not altogether surprised when on the eleventh day, thick clouds rushed down upon us and rain began to fall. The island of Sumbawa was not far off, but its volcanic peaks, ranging to over 12,000 feet, were hidden by the storm. That night there were not sixteen shades of darkness; there was only one: absolute blackness outside of me matched by absolute blackness within. At 11:00 P.M., instead of rushing blindly on, steering by feel down waves I never saw, I hove to.

We did not resume sailing until 9:00 A.M. the next day, after I had managed to grab three quick sights of a sun indistinct through clouds and over a ragged horizon of eight-foot waves. Usually I would not attempt to use the sextant aboard *Chidiock* in such conditions, and I was annoyed that when sights had not been essential, a few days earlier, they had come easily, but now that I needed them, they did not. Two of the position lines were a mile apart and the third was just eight miles farther east, which I considered acceptable. I concluded that the east end of Lombok was due north of us. Bali was sixty miles west, too far to reach before sunset. I could only hope to get close enough to enter port the following day.

In midmorning a promontory on Lombok became distinct for a few minutes before being lost in another squall. At sea visibility was improving, with most of the clouds passing harmlessly overhead on their way to loose torrents on the high islands.

For several hours Lombok played hide-and-seek with us, but by 2:00

P.M. I could see enough of the coast to recognize that we were now off the west cape and sailing into a trap. Bali, although still not in view, lay only thirty miles away. In the first ten miles were the swift currents of Lombok Strait, running at up to eight knots. The next ten were bordered by the island of Nusa Penida. And then the last ten led to Benoa Harbor, on Bali, safety for a vessel once inside but until then a lee shore. It was a box, blocked to the north and west by land, and as effectively to the east by winds of thirty to forty knots. We could still safely escape by reaching off to the southwest, but to do so would be to risk being blown past Bali during the night.

The little yawl dashed on while I considered the unappealing alternatives. When 1,700-foot-high Nusa Penida came into sight at 3:00 P.M., I turned *Chidiock* into the wind and hove to under mizzen alone.

We were backing down directly onto the island, which I estimated to be about eight miles distant. Even at just one knot we would be on it during the night, and if this night was to be as black as the previous one had been, we could not afford to get too close. For the moment, though, we were safe, and it seemed odd to be hove to during daylight.

I sat in the cockpit for a while, trying to judge our rate of drift. In an hour, Nusa Penida definitely drew closer, but not as rapidly as I had feared. So on the assumption that somehow we would reach Benoa safely, I took this opportunity to wash myself and to shave.

As sunset neared I managed to heat a package of freeze-dried beef stew, but I could not succeed in brewing a decent cup of tea. The view to windward was not promising. Heavy clouds showed no sign of clearing. The view to leeward was not promising. Individual trees on Nusa Penida were distinct. I stared broodingly to the southwest. That way was open. We could reach off now. Sooner or later this storm would end and we would wind up somewhere. I imagined Suzanne's reaction if after being in Bali for several days, she received a telegram from me in Java. Thoughts, calculations, plans, worries, fears, balanced one another, and I finally did nothing. We would be all right until at least 10:00 P.M. In the meantime I could try to sleep.

A few minutes after I had covered myself with the tarp, three waves hit us. The first caught *Chidiock* abeam and threw her sideways in a great blast of spray; the second seemed to take her from below and toss her into the air, like a juggler; and the third came from ahead, lifting the bow until the little yawl seemed in danger of performing her first backwards somersault. I pulled the tarp away and began pumping the bilge.

Although we were west of the strongest currents through Lombok

Strait, we were obviously in the midst of a battle between strong wind and strong current. These were the conditions we had found several weeks earlier near Cape York, here greatly magnified. Ten-foot waves leapt up all around us, fell, smashed into one another, rebounded, re-formed, and broke again.

I was more angry than frightened. Of all the miserable places to have to heave to, I thought. The jagged waves cast long shadows in the fading light. The air temperature was tropical, but I felt cold, as though *Chidiock* were being tossed about among frozen mountain peaks. The way to the southwest seemed ever more inviting, but I did nothing except sit and wait; and when after fifteen minutes no other waves had repeated the assault of the first three, I lay back, pulled the slimy tarp over my head, and again tried to sleep.

Unexpectedly, sleep came. There was no reason for me to be especially tired. Until the day before, I had been as comfortable aboard *Chidiock* as I would have been in harbor, yet I found myself dreaming. A sea snake was in *Chidiock* and I kept trying to hit him with an oar, but I was able to move only in slow motion and the snake kept slithering away. In the dream *Chidiock Tichborne* became a long marble corridor, down which I endlessly pursued the snake. After forty-five minutes of this restful pastime, I awoke. Night was complete. Nusa Penida had disappeared. But from the west came a faint loom of light, the first sign of Bali.

I returned to sleep, but throughout the night I awoke at intervals of thirty to forty-five minutes. The result was a wide range of dreams, but at least the sea snake did not reappear.

When I had decided to hold our position and await developments, I had hoped that the sky might clear or the wind decrease or the seas diminish or *Chidiock*'s angle of drift change so that we would miss Nusa Penida. Any one of these would have been enough, and the third or fourth time I awoke, I realized that just as *Chidiock* is a self-simplifying boat, so this night, which had threatened to become an ordeal, had turned into a self-solving problem. Half the sky was clear, and in the starlight, Nusa Penida lay safely north of us. The wind had dropped below twenty knots, the seas to around five feet. I permitted myself a smile. Sometimes it really does happen. You lie down and cover your head and it all goes away. My awakening at short intervals continued, but it was unnecessary, for conditions only continued to improve. Not long after midnight, I could make out the revolving beacon at Benoa Harbor.

The next morning was sunny and warm, with such light wind for a while that I began to be concerned that we might yet be carried south of Bali by the currents.

By 10:00 A.M. we were only two miles offshore and I caught a glimpse of patches of white in the distance, which I thought at first were waves breaking against a cliff. Only as we drew closer could I see that they were really sails and that the sea was full of them, inverted triangles of multicolored cloth on *gujung*s, the local one-man fishing craft, which darted about like swift water spiders.

On the chart Benoa appears easy to find; it is the first opening in the coast north of the south end of Bali. But soon I began to wonder. A new set of clouds had spread rapidly over the sky; the wind had increased to fifteen knots; and the storm appeared to be preparing for act 2 by washing sea, land, and sky, and repainting everything a uniform gun-metal gray.

The fishing boats, which had been south of me, began speeding home. As the first of them neared, I could see the fishermen, wearing long-sleeved shirts and long pants and conical bamboo hats. Hand lines trailed from reels in the sterns of their small trimarans. The vessels' narrow center hulls and bamboo outriggers were well maintained and decorated with colorful designs.

The *gujung*s easily outstripped *Chidiock,* then making six knots, and

A hitchhiker on the way to Bali.

the first twenty or so confused me by continuing beyond a break in the palm trees that I had thought led to Benoa.

Boat after boat streamed past, with another fleet running before a black line squall to the west, and all of them sailed determinedly north.

I let *Chidiock* close with the coast until we were only a few hundred yards beyond what was definitely the first opening in the shore. It gave no other sign of being a harbor; I could see no ships inside, and the waves on the reef seemed to be breaking solidly.

Another group of *gujungs* approached. I backed the jib and let *Chidiock* forereach across their course. Clutching the mizzenmast, I stood and pointed toward the shore. "Benoa?" I yelled above the rising wind.

The nearest fisherman pointed with an oval loaf of bread he had been eating from one hand while steering with the other. From my perspective I could not tell whether he was pointing in or up the coast. "Benoa?" I repeated. But he had already turned away and the reply came from a second fisherman, who, as he whizzed by, gestured for me to follow. By now I could see that several of the boats were almost to the surf, and I retrimmed the jib and trailed after them.

With the boats of the fishing fleet showing the way as they passed us on both sides, finding the channel was not difficult; it involved a starboard broad reach followed by a jibe to a port broad reach. The surf had looked solid because the reef from the north overlaps the reef from the south.

Rain was falling heavily on the land and behind us at sea. The *gujungs* were bright jewels against dark velvet. Some of the fishermen smiled, some made shy hand motions that might have been meant in greeting, some stared at me curiously, and most ignored me. Finally one called in English, "Where you from?" Thinking that California was too far, I settled for "Darwin." He looked surprised, then grinned and gave me a thumbs up.

By the time I was off Benoa fishing village, the first of the *gujungs* had already been pulled above the high-tide mark on the beach. Larger native sailing craft lay at anchor inside the harbor. An intricate Hindu statue stood beneath palm trees. Flute music came from somewhere. Sailing in amidst the fishing fleet had made this perhaps our most beautiful entry into a port yet. We had reached the East.

6

The Battle of Bali

We sat waiting on the steps of the temple. The sun was very hot, and others sat beneath palm trees or beside the houses along a track leading away from the village. From time to time we had to move aside for women going up or down the steps or for girls selling cold drinks or clothing, which they carried tied in bundles on their heads.

Everyone waited patiently, although even in the shade sweat ran. For the first hour most of the people in the crowd were tourists. I found myself watching a beautiful, tall, blond girl in a purple sari with metallic threads that flashed in the sunlight when she moved, and a German who kept making adjustments to a movie camera on a tripod. After a while, though, the crowd began to swell with villagers.

Just before noon a man climbed the stone steps of the temple and began beating out a slow rhythm on a gong.

When I had been in Bali for a week, I wrote to a friend, "So far Bali is winning, but we are regrouping for a counterattack." I still don't know who won.

The clichés are that Bali is beautiful, colorful, inexpensive; that there are impressive mountains and fine beaches; that the Balinese are happy, easygoing, religious, friendly, artistic. And the clichés, except for one about bare-breasted Balinese maidens, are true. To deal with the most critical matter first: there are lots of bare breasts and bare other things on the beaches in Bali, but they are all attached to Westerners. The few bare-breasted Balinese women we saw were ancient and withered. Balinese women under age eighty cover not just their breasts but everything else as well, with conical hats, long-sleeved and high-collared shirts, and ankle-length sarongs. What the clichés ignore is that Bali is also noisy, dirty, crowded, poor, and overrun with motorcycles, *bemos* (small trucks, with camper shells and benches in the back, that—like *les trucks* in Tahiti—serve as public transportation), and petty officials.

The Balinese experience, if you are living on a boat at least, is schizoid and stressful. Eventually Suzanne and I even began to have some of the symptoms of stress: fatigue, weight loss, low tolerance for frustration, quick anger. Yet I must not sound too negative. In the fashion of a true schizoid experience, Bali left some very good as well as very bad memories. The contrasts were the only constant. They began upon my arrival and continued until I left. They occurred countless times every day, causing me to expend a great deal of energy in endlessly readjusting to the good and the bad. Perhaps this continuous strain is one reason why few yachts linger long in Bali, despite its undeniable charm, with most not remaining the full forty-five days the Indonesian government generously gives visitors to explore all 13,000 islands in the archipelago. Those forty-five days are not per island, but for the whole country, which means roughly 300 islands per day. After some deliberation, I concluded that this required just too much raising and lowering of the anchor, and decided to remain in one place.

My entry into Benoa Harbor had been perfect—sailing fast before a line squall, being led through the pass by a fleet of fishermen in *gujungs*. Once inside the harbor, *Chidiock* and I fought our way to the yacht anchorage against tidal currents strong enough to heel over the large buoys marking the main channel.

After anchoring near a half dozen other yachts, in what was at that moment ten feet of water, I inflated the dinghy and rowed ashore, where I found a barnacle-encrusted dinghy-destroying stone wharf and, eventually, the Harbor Master's office. There I was presented with a document that required the signatures of officials in seven offices before I could be granted entry. Seven offices. This was for me a new world record, one which I fervently hope will never be challenged. Seven! One office, the Harbor Master's, even had to be visited twice, once at the beginning of my odyssey through Indonesian bureaucracyland and again at the end; and one, Immigration, was located ten miles away in Denpasar. Seven! A few more and they could become a fast-food chain. Harbor Master. Customs. Immigration. Port Police. Port Administra-

The Battle of Bali

tion. Health. And the Navy, which doubtlessly wanted to be aware of my movements to prevent a sneak attack from *Chidiock*.

In fairness I must say that all of the officials, except those in Customs and Immigration, were courteous. Their main function seemed to be to write a few particulars—my name, boat name, last port, etc.—in pencil in old account books. I especially liked the man in the Navy office, which was housed in a tiny wooden shack stuck behind oil-storage tanks. Assignment to Benoa Harbor is not, I expect, a step toward quick promotion. The poor man was effusively, almost pathetically, glad to see me, another human being, anyone at long last, as though he had been marooned, as I suppose he had been. And he seemed sad when I left and he had to return to sitting in his immaculate uniform, hands folded, staring at the wall, dreaming of what? A moment of valor in flaming battle? Retirement? A new motor scooter?

Customs and Immigration were different from the rest, and from each other, but each proved that Parkinson's Law has not yet come to Indonesia. This is not because there are too few officials, but because there are too many. It is simply impossible, even for a bureaucratic genius, to stretch the available work to fill the time allotted for its performance. For example, while waiting in the Immigration office one day for a clerk to deign to honor me with his attention—the Denpasar Immigration office was by far the rudest it had ever been my misfortune to deal with—I counted eighteen officials sitting at various desks around the room. Of these, only two were even pretending to work, and they were of course doing nothing more productive than moving pieces of paper around. The other sixteen were doing nothing at all. And they weren't even doing it with style.

In Customs the officials were just as idle—five men woke up when I entered the office, and then they all stood around and watched with great interest as I signed my name to a few forms; but at least they were entertaining.

I was surprised when three of them said they were going to accompany me to inspect my yacht. My suggestion that this force was unnecessarily large for so small a vessel was ignored, and we proceed to the wharf, where we boarded their launch, which was of course larger than *Chidiock*. The fatigue I normally experience at the end of a passage vanished as I anticipated possible developments.

During my two-hour sojourn ashore, the tide had gone out. At high tide Benoa Harbor is a mile wide. At spring low tide, it is fifty yards wide. As was obvious when the launch swung around the raft of fishing trawlers, this was a spring low. *Chidiock* was swinging with the wind, so she was not yet aground, but mud and eelgrass were visible just off her stern.

"What your boat?" asked one of the officials as the launch roared up to the anchorage.

I pointed at *Chidiock,* but he had already dismissed the tiny yawl from his mind and was looking at the other yachts.

"What boat?"

I pointed again. This time his eyes followed my arm, then opened wide. "That?"

"That. The water around her will be very shallow." I held my hands ten inches apart. But he was not to be deterred from his duty. Fortunately, the launch was not going very fast when we went aground.

I never did know who was in charge. In truth no one was as the three men peered over the side, rolled their eyes, looked alarmed, shouted at one another, flung their arms about, tried to push off with oars, dropped things overboard, stood around, looked increasingly worried as the tide drained away, shouted some more, and generally did a good imitation of the Keystone Kops.

I offered some token assistance, but felt that my responsibility had ended with my ignored warning. I didn't really care what happened to the launch. In a few more minutes, I would be able to walk home.

But I did learn who was the lowest-ranking of the three officials, for it must have been he who finally took off his shoes and socks, rolled up the legs of his uniform, and reluctantly slid into the filthy water to try to push the launch off. After several more minutes of slapstick, he succeeded, thus ending the Great Indonesian Customs Inspection of *Chidiock Tichborne.*

As soon as the gong stopped, men burst from the compound and ran to a bamboo tower. The tower was ten feet tall and was covered with white and gold paper and with streamers of every color. It was tapered and was capped by a gold canopy over a narrow pallet. With a grunt, the men lifted the tower and carried it around to the entrance of the temple.

Women filed silently down the steps and began shuffling along the road. Over their heads, they held a long train of white cloth. From a distance they looked like the legs of a giant centipede.

A bamboo ladder was positioned against the tower and the body, itself wrapped in white cloth, was brought out of the temple. This was a heavy bundle, and the men strained as they handed it up the ladder.

One man remained on one side of the tower and tied the body to the pallet with bamboo lashings, while another placed offerings of clothing and food and cups and ornaments in the tower. Two live birds were tied to the corner of the canopy.

When everything was in place, curtains were drawn around the pallet until only the end of the bundle could be seen.

I must trust *Chidiock Tichborne* to forgive me for disclosing that she is not perfect. Two of her limitations became apparent in Bali: she is difficult to live on in a polluted harbor that has no shore facilities, and she is not a good hospital ship.

The main problem was water.

We had been in harbors before in which we could not swim or wash ourselves. Indeed, probably a majority of our longer stops had been spent at harbors of this sort: Cairns, Suva, Pago-Pago, Papeete. And we had been in ports where there were no shore facilities, such as Neiafu, Tonga. But Benoa was the first place where we were faced with both problems simultaneously.

This side of death, most problems have solutions, and there were solutions in Bali, but nowhere else have Suzanne and I spent more time and effort on the mere fundamentals of life.

Drinking water was available ashore in Benoa at a couple of taps, but it had to be paid for. In July 1981 the going rate was eighteen cents to fill a five-gallon jerry can. The water didn't look bad, but it tasted slimy. Some sailors drank it untreated without apparent ill effect. We put chlorine bleach in ours, and our subsequent illness was not caused by the water.

One might assume that if water was available for drinking, it could also be ferried out to the boat for other purposes. But this assumption does not take into account tides and water pressure. At best, the water came from the taps at a trickle. Often there was no water pressure at all, and we had to leave a container to be filled by the owners of the taps. And we couldn't transport large water containers from the shore when the tide was low.

Washing clothes and cooking ceased to be problems when we arranged to have our laundry done inexpensively by a woman ashore, and when we learned that in Bali it is cheaper to eat out than on the boat.

One of the very best things about Bali is the food. Usually dinner cost less than four dollars for both of us. Fortunately we enjoy spices,

Drying out in Benoa Harbor, Bali.

for the national dishes—*nasi goreng* (fried rice) and *mei goreng* (fried noodles)—are hot; but every kind of food is available, from Chinese and Indian and Indonesian to tacos and pizza and hamburgers. There is even a Kentucky Fried Chicken outlet. We took a bucket of the Colonel's finest back to *Chidiock* one day, just for a change from *soto ayam* (Indonesian chicken soup), squid in wine sauce, *satay* (meat with peanut sauce, barbecued on bamboo skewers), and turtle steaks.

But keeping ourselves clean was an ongoing struggle. For the first two weeks, enough rain fell almost every night to fill the dinghy for a bath the next morning, but then the weather turned fine and we had to resort to bathing in the surf. After being looked at rather peculiarly as we carried our bottles of shampoo into the waves off crowded Kuta Beach, we found a more deserted beach south of Benoa fishing village.

We have always tried not to look like boat bums, and have been pleased when people have said, "You certainly don't look as though you've just stepped off an eighteen-foot boat." I regret that in Bali we usually did look as though we lived on an eighteen-foot boat. Or under one.

Chidiock's capability as a hospital ship was tested because of Su-

Suzanne using our private bathtub, Bali.

zanne's birthday. Usually we ate in inexpensive restaurants at Kuta Beach, but to celebrate on July 6, we went to high-priced Sanur Beach and had lunch at the most expensive hotel on Bali. As a direct result of this extravagance we contracted severe cases of Bali Belly. For three days we had fever in addition to the other usual symptoms. Running a fever while lying beneath *Chidiock's* dark-green tarp on a stifling hot day in the tropics is an all-too-vivid preview of hell.

I have not decided what morals to draw from this. Perhaps to repent. Perhaps to avoid expensive restaurants.

The procession was a parade.

The men sweated and strained as they carried the tower through the village, but they were happy, not solemn.

Traffic piled up behind us, but when the drivers saw the reason for the delay, they did not lean on their horns.

People came from the shanty shops to join us, crossing the drainage ditch beside the road on planks of wood, as though crossing a moat.

At the crossroads in the middle of the village, the tower was turned in a circle three times. The crowd cheered at the completion of each revolution and each time the tower was successfully tilted to clear over-

head power lines. Once, the tower leaned over so far it seemed certain to fall, but men rushed from the crowd to help and the body did not touch the earth.

Our way, even after we left the narrow paved road for an even narrower path beside a rice paddy, was always bordered by walls: walls hundreds of years old, hidden beneath thick layers of dirt and green-black mold; ruined walls, carved with crumbling gods; new walls of cinder block or of brick; walls so high we could not see over them; walls so low they were mere suggestions of ownership; well-cared-for walls, covered with fresh paint; forgotten walls, reclaimed by the jungle.

I had not realized before that Bali is so much a place of walls, but after that day, I saw them everywhere. On so small and so crowded an island, walls are a necessity.

Kuta Beach is a zoo in which the animals walk around and view one another. The Balinese shyly or slyly watch the tourists; the tourists watch the Balinese and the other tourists.

The Balinese find Westerners very funny, if often shocking. Although they are too polite to show it, most of them are embarrassed by how little we wear on the beach; but those who are not embarrassed are quite willing to leer. If travelers find themselves judging a country on the basis of its shop clerks, then shop clerks may judge a country on the basis of its travelers. The Balinese shop clerks are likely to view the Westerner as a big, meaty Australian, unwashed, unshaven, riding a rented motorbike, stoned out of his mind on magic mushrooms, wearing a sarong, and with a Sony Walkman in his ear. Or the Balinese see the Westerner as a potbellied, middle-aged, sunburned, American or German fool, so rich he pays five times more than an article or service is worth.

Neither I nor Suzanne is by nature a bargainer, but bargaining is a way of life in Bali. Nothing has a fixed price, even when it seems to. And everything is renegotiable every day. In some ways this became irritating after a while. We would go ashore in the morning and want to charter a *bemo* to take us the five miles to Kuta Beach, and the very same man who had taken us the day before for 1,000 rupiahs—about $1.30—would start off by asking for 2,000. Or we would want to catch one of the launches that serve as ferries to Benoa fishing village, and if we unfortunately arrived at the landing at the same time as a group of tourists, we would have to wait until the tourists had made their own deal, at 500 rupiahs a person for a ride that normally cost 150 or 200.

The Battle of Bali   81

As a visitor I expect to be overcharged, but not by several hundred percent.

Sometimes, as in the shops selling wood carvings in the village of Mas, asking prices are so far from the going prices as to be self-defeating. This is always true in places where the prices are initially given in American dollars. Our greatest bargaining coup came on a carving that was priced at $95. Since we had no intention of spending anywhere near that amount, I told Suzanne it wasn't even worth bothering about, but after a prolonged campaign, she walked away with the statue for $26.

A common language is not necessary for such negotiations. However, a surprising number of Balinese do know at least some English, which they have learned in school or through a regular program of the Australian Broadcasting Corporation's overseas service, or from tourists. The children, five to ten years old, who sell cold drinks at Kuta Beach, earning about a dollar for lugging an ice chest around all afternoon after being in school all morning, are particularly eager to improve their English.

But there are places, Poste Restante at the Central Post Office is one, where some knowledge of Indonesian is essential. The Indonesian post office has only two speeds—fast and lost. Unfortunately the Indonesian language book Suzanne had bought in Darwin did not prove too helpful. It did enable us to utter such useful sentences as "The sheep dog was running about the paddock"; "Our cannon will be seen by the enemy"; and the ever popular "He has already been murdered." But it failed to help us ask how to get to the bus station or if there were packages for us at the post office or where to buy kerosene. Even after we found the right place, kerosene was a problem because the man kept trying to sell us hashish instead.

There are many beautiful young Balinese, but no beautiful old ones. More even than the inhabitants of other tropical lands, the Balinese age quickly and badly. In the countryside, this can be attributed to a poor diet, consisting almost entirely of rice, hard work, and inadequate medical care; but even in the towns few people over age thirty are physically attractive.

As a people, the Balinese care deeply for their religion and their arts. An island of Hindus in a Muslim nation—one can tell the people are Hindus merely by looking at the sleek cows and the starving dogs—Bali has 20,000 temples, ranging from the Mother Temple on the slopes of

One of the 20,000 Hindu temples, Bali.

Mount Agung to small temples perched on offshore rocks isolated at high tide. Offerings of flowers, food, and incense are found everywhere: at the edge of the surf, on the dashboards of *bemos,* on statues of gods on bridges, in front of shops and homes, even on bureaucrats' desks. Usually the gods in public places are covered with sarongs. I never saw anyone actually wrapping one around a statue, but the sarong is usually clean and unwrinkled.

Much of the art now produced in Bali is directed at tourists, but the Balinese were painters and carvers and dancers long before any tourists were present. One day we heard from friends on another yacht that there would be dances near Benoa fishing village. The site was an obscure temple in a clearing just off the beach, and the scene reminded me of a country fair. The music, played on drums and on an instrument resembling a xylophone, with a bell-like sound, began at 3:00 P.M., with each village performing one of the traditional dances, which combine the lessons of a morality play with the broad humor of burlesque. There was no admission charge. We were the only non-Balinese present, and we all left in the early evening. The people were dancing for themselves, and they continued, we were told, until 3:00 A.M.

Reading a copy of *Time* magazine one afternoon on a beach in Bali, I realized how little I had come to care—indeed, how little most of the world cared—about the great issues concerning my fellow countrymen.

I could imagine asking an old man picking weeds from among the young shoots in a flooded rice field if he worried about a mid-life crisis. Or what he, who earned $400 in a good year, thought about the epidemic of cocaine use in Hollywood, where one woman admitted to spending $1,000,000 on cocaine in ten years. And I could imagine asking his wife, carrying loads of gravel on her head for a road-construction project, and prohibited from entering the temples when she was menstruating, if she was in favor of the Equal Rights Amendment.

At such a time America seemed not so much decadent as merely frivolous.

Thousands jammed the cremation grounds. The heat and smell became stifling as we jostled and swayed against one another. Bamboo towers rose like islands from the sea of people. Some were shaped like animals; some, like mythological beasts; some, like flesh-consuming gods. Three held bodies.

The body we had followed was placed inside a giant white paper cow, along with the offerings of food and clothing, but not the live birds. The squawking birds were tossed like a bridal bouquet into the clamoring hands of the men who had carried the tower through the village.

It seemed to take much longer to transfer the offerings from the tower than it had taken to place them there. The crowd sagged as people began to faint. Finally the back of the cow was lowered.

A cloud of smoke drifted down on us. Then there was smoke everywhere and flames shot up into the sky as all the towers were lit.

The white cow crumbled in a wave of sparks. Beside me a small boy sat on his father's shoulders. His eyes were huge, as though he was seeing himself, someday, there in the flames.

One of the most difficult things to find in Bali was silence.

At dawn the view from Benoa Harbor was beautiful: a foreground of golden-pink water; a middle distance of land, which as the sun rose

Hindu cremation, Bali.

became the yellow, acid green of young rice; and in the distance the pure cone of Mount Agung, floating serenely above the clouds. But all this beauty was accompanied by the constant day-and-night throb of the generator at the trawler dock.

We would lie on Kuta Beach, looking out at the surf and at Bali Strait. We could not see—but we had visited—the temples almost a thousand years old, on the rock off the point to the north and on the cliff to the south. The smudge of land in the purple light of the horizon was Java. But every few seconds a Balinese came by: "You want massage." "You want cold drink." "You want carvings." "You want batik." "You want rings." "You want paintings." We knew that these were poor people trying to eke out a living, but we grew tired of saying *tidak, terima kasih*, which is more effective than English. Apparently the peddlers think that people who learn to say no thank you in Indonesian mean it.

The noise on the roads was terrible. The capital, Denpasar, which we visited only when we had to, must have the worst traffic in the world for a city of 100,000. *Bemos,* motorcycles, horse carts, bicycles, buses, trucks, cars, all race six or seven abreast down two-lane streets, passing on either side, horns blaring constantly. A pedestrian is not safe anywhere, not even on the rare sidewalk.

So it was not surprising that one of the places we came to like best in Bali and one in which we began to spend almost half our time, alternating days there with days spent in the fray, was tranquil Benoa fishing village.

As we walked along its beaches on our first visit, something seemed strange. We stood still for several moments before we realized that for the first time in Bali we were alone and for the first time there was no man-made noise. Nothing but the wind in the trees and the surf on the reef. It was exquisite.

The village is just a mile across the harbor, but one cannot row over there, because of the tides. We usually took a ferry, for about twenty-five cents. Presumably it can also be reached by land, for it sits on the end of a peninsula down which runs a rough road; however, its three dirt streets are almost always empty of vehicles. There is no electricity or running water.

We went over initially to eat at a restaurant we had been told about, one of two or three there, all specializing in turtle. Often we would see turtles penned up, being fattened for market. We usually ate at the Sunrise Restaurant, run by three young brothers. The Sunrise is noth-

At anchor off Benoa fishing village, Bali.

ing more than a shack with four tables set in the sand beneath a tin roof, but it has a beautiful view of the reef and the food is good.

After bathing farther down the beach, we would walk back for an early dinner, because the ferries do not operate after dusk. We would eat turtle—turtle steaks, turtle *satay,* sweet and sour turtle, turtle soup —until we began to fear we might grow shells, and watch the *gujung*s sail back from the day's fishing.

From Madē Gerip, who lives in the village and runs Bali Yacht Services, some of the fishermen had learned that I was on "the little boat." For some reason they were less amazed that I had crossed oceans than that I had "no machine"—that is, no engine. Yet they themselves had no machines.

The sight of their colorful sails speeding in toward the pass always made us happy. At high tide some of the more daring sailed directly across the reef, but we were told that in the past year three of them

Taking the catch to market from a *gujung*, Bali.

had been killed when they misjudged the waves there. Luffing the sails, the fishermen would run the boats gently onto the beach, and within five minutes everything would be broken down and stowed away: masts lowered, outer hulls untied, boats carried above the high-tide mark, the day's catch of tuna carried away by the women.

I studied the *gujung*s. Of about the same length as *Chidiock*, they had much else in common with her: shallow draft, easily removable rudder, absence of engine and deck. I did not ever see a *gujung* that was not well cared for, and most were painted with far more elaboration than was functionally necessary. In Bali, even when people are poor they find ways to make things look attractive. Many of the *gujung*s had eyes painted on the bow, and some even had smiles.

I was told that until recently, sons usually took up the work of their fathers in Bali, but now many of the sons of fishermen are going off to work in Denpasar. I do not blame them for wanting more money, but there is no doubt in my poor sailor's mind which life I would choose if I were Balinese.

Ashes. Filled the sky. Covered the ground. Caught in our hair and eyes. We breathed shallowly behind our hands.

The smoke had dispersed the crowd. Low flames licked at the frames of charred towers.

As we made our way from the grounds, the smoke thickened, then swirled and thinned to reveal a monstrous face, a mask somehow untouched by the fire, striped red and black and white, its great mouth turned upward in a hideous grin.

I wondered if it was a vision of death. Or a symbol of life renewed beyond the ashes. Or just a final, appropriately ambivalent image for Bali.

7

Dire Straits

The sunrise was an apology—a bright-orange world of color, glowing from beyond the volcanoes of Lombok in the east, turning Bali's mountains from black and gray to gold and green, revealing a glassy sea filled with drifting *gujung*s. A half mile inside of us drifted the large native sloop at which the freighter had sounded her horn an hour earlier. It was as though the elements were saying, See how fine the world is. Doesn't this make up for yesterday? But the elements were wrong. Nothing could have made up for yesterday.

There are three possible routes from Bali to Singapore. You can sail around the south end of the island, continue west below Java to Sunda Strait, and then work your way up the west side of the Java Sea. This route is the longest, but offers the least exposure to adverse currents and the greatest likelihood of fair winds. You can sail around the south end of the island and then head north through Bali Strait, which separates Bali from Java. This route is the most direct. But I had spent many days gazing out at Bali Strait from Kuta Beach and knew that the winds on that side of the island are usually light and fluky. Or you can simply turn to port upon leaving Benoa Harbor, sail forty miles on course 065° to clear Cape Ibus, Bali's easternmost point, then change to 320° to cross the Bali Sea. On the chart this route looks easiest, particularly if you ignore the symbols that indicate strong currents and overfalls in Lombok Strait. I respected Lombok Strait, but I had faced strong currents before, and sailing forty miles there seemed preferable to going two or three hundred miles out of my way. The owner of a forty-five-

Departure from Bali.

foot ketch anchored near us in Benoa, an American sailor who had, he said, been sailing Southeast Asia for a dozen years, offered the unsolicited advice that I should take the long route around Java. He flatly stated that *Chidiock Tichborne* could not make it through Lombok Strait. He was nearly right.

After the tedious procedure of clearing on Friday with the seven different sets of officials, I had *Chidiock* underway Saturday morning, August 8, 1981, by 8:30, and we had a pleasant sail across the harbor, tacking against a light southeast wind. I waved good-bye to Suzanne, who was standing on the point of land near Benoa village, and we made our way out the pass at slack water, reaching the ocean just after 9:00.

The weather was fine, as it had been every day in Bali for the past three weeks. The wind was building and gave promise of reaching the normal twelve to fourteen knots by noon. Visibility was good, and I could see the pyramid-shaped hill that stands less than ten miles from Cape Ibus.

For three hours all went well. The constant current setting through the strait from the north did create bigger and, more critically, steeper waves than were warranted by the wind, but these were only about five or six feet high, half the size and much less dangerous than those I had encountered during the storm on my arrival five weeks earlier.

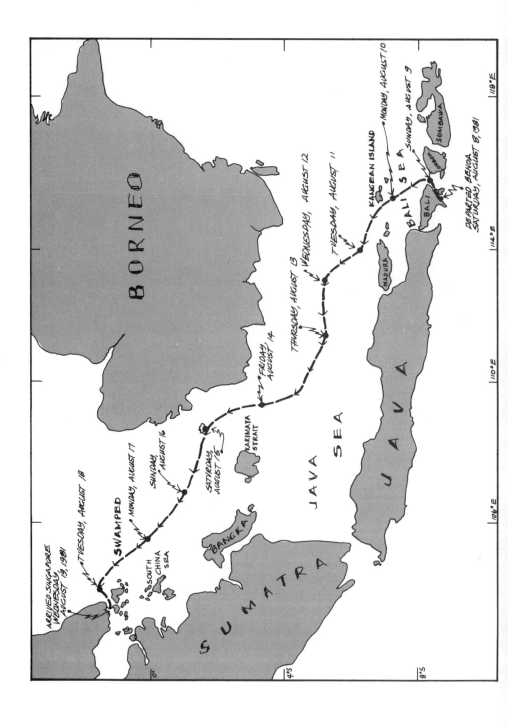

Someone had said there was sometimes a countercurrent on the Bali side of the strait. That is the trouble with local knowledge, particularly when, as in this case, it does not come from local people. "Someone." "Sometimes." Someone else had said that the currents through the straits ran at eight knots, and someone else had said, twelve. Unfortunately I was never able to test the countercurrent theory, for we were quickly forced away from Bali, and I soon began to wonder, as I had on our arrival, if we would clear the neighboring island of Nusa Penida, although this time on the opposite side.

By noon the white cliffs of Nusa Penida were too close and I had let *Chidiock* fall off the wind to a very broad reach, because I could see that, however incongruously, nearer the island the wind died while the waves increased.

So far we had covered almost fifteen miles, although not all in the desired direction. With a speed made good of four knots, the forty miles on course 065° would require ten hours. Sunset comes early in Bali, but we could be through the strait just after dark, and I had planned the passage to take advantage of the moon, which was approaching fullness. We should have some light until midnight. Satisfied with our progress, I reached down for the plastic bag containing lunch and ran afoul of a marketing expert.

Chidiock was being thrown about too much to self-steer, so I had to keep a hand on the tiller. For that first lunch I had bought two crusty French rolls and a package of sliced cheese. I ripped the package open with my teeth and started to put the cheese on the bread, but discovered that each slice of cheese was wrapped in its own individual piece of paper. Doubtless this packaging appeals to housewives ashore, but it gave me problems. The tropical heat had glued the paper to the cheese. My reputation as a great chef is not so secure that it can survive a failure to make a sandwich. Steering with my elbow, I attacked the problem with both hands.

The first piece of paper finally came free and immediately flew up to plaster itself to my eyeglasses. For the next few minutes *Chidiock*'s course resembled that of an Irishman on Saint Patrick's Day. I did briefly consider how I could ever explain if disaster should overtake us just then: "Well, you see, I was attacked by a piece of cheese."

I ducked the next piece of paper, which proceeded to decorate the mainsail. The next could not remain aloft long enough to do any damage because it took along half the cheese, and sank.

I have no idea how many slices of cheese were in that small package. I began to feel like a magician who keeps pulling scarves from a tiny box. When I had pulled out several hundred slices, and *Chidiock* and I and the surrounding ocean were a fathom deep in tattered bits of paper and even more tattered bits of cheese, an infinitesimal amount of which had by chance come to rest on one French roll, I admitted defeat and threw the remainder away. Vestiges of the Great Cheese Massacre remained until Singapore. I ate the second French roll plain.

By 2:00 P.M. we were well into Badung Strait, the western arm of Lombok Strait. Then the wind died. The lighthouse on Nusa Penida was abeam. It was still abeam at sunset, a situation which, while disappointing, was better than the one a few hours later.

Like some nocturnal animal the flat sea came to life with the fading of the light. Without preamble a patch of water a few hundred yards away suddenly leapt into a frenzy of two-foot-high waves. A few minutes later another patch to seaward erupted into similar waves, which rapidly spread around us and collided with the first area of disturbance. Instantly *Chidiock* was out of control. As the moon went behind a cloud, the yawl drifted rapidly backwards and then began to spin, slowly at first, then faster, no matter what I did with the tiller. A friend I spoke to later in Singapore was aboard a Swan 65 anchored that evening at Nusa Penida. He said that they had seen me turn toward the shore and had thought I was trying to come in to wait out the calm at anchor. When, a few minutes later, they caught a glimpse of me in the moonlight, *Chidiock* seemed to be pointing southwest, back toward Benoa, and they did not know what to think. And then the moon went behind another cloud and they did not see any more of us at all.

For twenty minutes *Chidiock* performed her insane dance. I never saw a funnel-like depression into which I feared we might be sucked, and we did not ever spin so rapidly that I became dizzy, but I do not know how to describe the sea's motion except as that of a whirlpool formed where conflicting currents met or were deflected by some underwater obstacle.

The chaotic face of the ocean showed no appreciable change when, as abruptly as she had begun, *Chidiock* stopped spinning. Small waves continued to leap about noisily, and there was still no response to the helm; but I quickly decided I preferred the dullness of remaining on one heading, even though I now had to crane my neck to check for shipping where previously a view all around had been effortlessly presented to me twice a minute.

The remainder of the night was a confusion of snatches of sleep; of drifting backwards, forward, sideways; of the lights on Nusa Penida fading, while those on Bali brightened; of my making preparations to row as the murmur of surf on the Bali reef became a roar; of—at last —that lovely sunrise, which revealed us to be five miles south and west of our position at sunset, although I have no idea how many miles we traveled to get there.

For the next few hours the wind was not sufficient even for the *gujung*s. I wondered what time the fishermen had started their work, whether the wind would ever return and—when, at 9:00 A.M., I calculated that we had made good less than twenty miles in our first twenty-four hours at sea—wether I should not reconsider the advantages of the alternate route south of Java, although while we were becalmed any such consideration was purely theoretical. I could not recall a slower start to any passage. Singapore lay roughly a thousand miles abeam. Abeam. We had not even reached the pyramid-shaped hill that had seemed so near from Benoa. At this rate we might reach Singapore in October.

At noon the wind returned, and by sunset we were off Cape Ibus. So bald a statement of what was subjectively so momentous a change. No one in the world that morning had wanted anything more than I had wanted wind, and no one in the world was more pleased that afternoon than I was when the wind returned and *Chidiock* began sailing purposefully.

Sunset was perhaps even more spectacular than the dawn. Although the slopes of the mountains near Cape Ibus fall steeply into the sea, they are a deep green, and many of them have been terraced, in what must have been heroic labor, to grow rice.

From a few miles offshore, I could see past those first mountains to the pure cone of Mount Agung, 10,000 feet high, which divided the sunset. Above it the sky was an intense blue. To the north, blood red. To the south, subtle shadings of pastel rose and peach.

I had never before sailed into the lee of a two-mile-high mountain and was concerned about its wind shadow and downdrafts. If San Diego's Point Loma, only a few hundred feet high, often creates a ten-knot increase in wind, what would Mount Agung cause? But as we drew under the protection of the land, the choppy seas became smooth, the wind increased only to twenty-five knots, and we experienced no great gusts. Under reefed sails *Chidiock* romped north. She seemed to be almost as glad as I to leave Lombok Strait behind.

Between Bali and Singapore one sails through an entire inventory of seas and straits: Badung Strait to Lombok Strait proper to the Bali Sea to Kangean Strait to the Java Sea to Karimata Strait to the South China Sea to Singapore Strait. Almost every day sees a new name on the chart.

The wind held, and after taking a day and a half for the first forty miles, we covered over a hundred miles on each of nine successive days.

On the first of those splendid days we crossed the Bali Sea. In order to get *Chidiock* to self-steer, I had to head higher than I wanted; and late Monday afternoon found Kangean Island in sight to the northeast, while directly ahead was a strait that was marked on the chart with those sinister wavy lines symbolic of strong currents. We could jibe and run west to another strait, forty miles away, but to do so would mean skirting a series of unlit reefs at night. Clutching the mizzenmast, I stood and studied the sea. The waves did not appear psychotic, but then, how much warning had they given on Saturday night? I decided that we could make it through, and we did—uneventfully, except for the odd behavior of a ten-foot-long shark.

I have seen few sharks at sea and none who acted as this one did. We were almost upon him before I saw his dorsal fin, but he made no effort to move from our path. As *Chidiock* slid by, he bent himself into a U, as though trying to bite his own tail, and lay motionless in the water. When we had passed, he straightened out, swam twenty yards ahead, then stopped to form another U and lay motionless until we had passed again. He leapfrogged us in this peculiar manner four or five times before he disappeared.

The Java Sea was filled with haze and small craft. Rumors of pirates that I had heard ashore were matched by reports on the radio news broadcasts while I was at sea of pirates preying on the Vietnamese boat people. I have always contended that any pirate who happened upon *Chidiock* would probably offer me assistance, but you never know when you may meet a pirate in need of a good dinghy and I was somewhat suspicious when a couple of fishing craft changed course to look us over. Presumably they were only curious, like the shark, for they too soon disappeared.

The haze was a source of greater concern. Every morning the sun climbed dripping from the sea, like some engorged red spider crawling slowly up a wall, and during most of the day, it was surrounded by a halo. So was the moon, at night. High clouds blew rapidly about. In other seas I would have concluded that a storm was impending. But when the wind remained moderate, I finally accepted these conditions as being normal for the area.

In the Java Sea after shaving off the mustache.

One night, though, *Chidiock* felt out of trim. I could not figure out quite why, but somehow she was not properly balanced. So in the morning I shaved off the mustache I had been wearing since my first attempt at Cape Horn in 1974. *Chidiock* immediately began to sail better, thus providing additional proof that to reduce windage aloft always pays.

After making our way west for two days in the Java Sea, we jibed to the north for Karimata Strait, between Borneo and Billiton Island, and I solved another problem, one that had been plaguing me since the first days of the voyage.

The beginning of this solution had come when the bilge pump broke while I was crossing Van Diemen Gulf in May. The original bilge pump had been installed in the aft end of the centerboard trunk. The installation was very neat, but the intake hose was fixed horizontally and a few gallons of water were always left sloshing about the bilge. As long as I lived on the windward side of the cockpit, this did not matter, but if we had to change course and I found myself to leeward, I had to either make what was under sea conditions a major move, untying and shifting bags and oars and water containers, or live with those few gallons splashing up over the floorboards and soaking me with every wave.

In Darwin I installed a new bilge pump, on top of the centerboard trunk. This installation was not nearly so neat as the original, but it had several advantages: it provided easy access to the pump for repairs or for clearing a blockage; the discharge hose could be led overboard, since it was not fixed, as the old one had been, to discharge into the centerboard trunk, which on *Chidiock* is all too frequently submerged; and, best of all, it enabled me to suck up practically all of the water in the bilge by moving the flexible intake hose around like a vacuum cleaner. The importance of this change cannot be overstated. It was the single greatest advance so far toward making *Chidiock* a more satisfactory home while at sea. And it took me only two and a half years to find it.

Our landfall at 3,376-foot-high Karimata Island came on the morning of August 15. We were under the lee of Borneo, although the island itself remained hidden in the mist.

Shipping, mostly large cargo vessels and tankers, was visible most of the day; at noon two patrol boats roared angrily through the strait, heading north.

Beyond Karimata Strait we were sailing in the South China Sea. We were also soon sailing in the Northern Hemisphere, for we crossed the equator on Monday, August 17, 1981. This seemed incredible. We had been in the Southern Hemisphere since early December 1978, and now, unless the Red Sea proved impassable, we would remain in north-

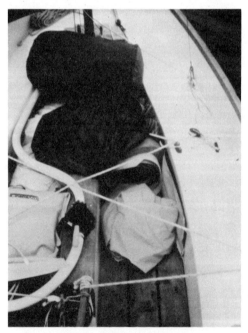

Cockpit, showing new bilge pump and sheet-to-tiller self-steering.

ern latitudes for the remainder of the circumnavigation. We had sailed slightly less than half the course, but psychologically this recrossing of the equator meant that the voyage was half over.

The only difference between late winter in the Java Sea and late summer in the South China Sea was a dramatic increase in shipping, and I managed only brief naps during our last night at sea, as running lights moved all around us. The wind finally weakened in the early morning hours, and dawn did not bring the sight of land that I had expected.

At 7:30 A.M. the sky cleared and I managed to get a sun sight. Depending upon our latitude, the resulting position line put us between seven and sixteen miles off the Indonesian islands south of Singapore. Trying to decide whether to head due west until we made a landfall or to continue northwest toward where I thought we would find the mouth of Singapore Strait, I studied the chart for several minutes. When I finally made up my mind to continue northwest, I put the chart back into its Voyageur navigation bag. Just as I did so, a gust of wind staggered us. I turned. The sky astern, clear enough ten minutes earlier to permit a good sun sight, was pitch black. I leapt for the main halyard, but I was too late.

The squall, of a type that is locally called a Sumatra, caused winds of forty-five knots in Singapore, and flattened the fully canvased *Chidiock Tichborne*. Fighting to maintain my balance, sickened by the sight of the ocean flooding over the gunwale, I clawed down the flogging mainsail. It was not enough. *Chidiock* still lay on her side and water continued to pour in as I fumbled for the submerged jib-furling line. When I had first bought *Chidiock*, I had thought furling gear ridiculous on so small a sail, but I was very grateful now not to have to move my weight forward to drop the jib. As the sail rolled up, *Chidiock* regained her feet.

Waves and stinging rain splashed aboard, but the worst of the damage had already been done. Only a few inches of freeboard were left and the cockpit was full to above the centerboard slot. All of the despair and depression I had felt during our last swamping, a year and 5,000 miles earlier, again swept over me. As I sloshed my way aft, I could only think that this was to have been our last day offshore this year, and now suddenly it might instead be the last day of the voyage.

But if we were badly swamped, we were much better off than we had been after the accident near Vanuatu in 1980. Here there was little danger of my being killed. I could easily reach land in the inflatable dinghy if necessary. I had airbags, with which I might try to raise *Chidiock* higher in the water. The bilge pump discharged overboard. And, most importantly, this time I had a way to bail. Actually I had several ways: I could use the five buckets and also the bailer welded for me by Brian Voller. A couple of sheets of yellow Ensolite floated away from my bedding, but everything else remained secured to the boat. Untying Brian's bailer, I began.

I have described bailing so often that I cannot imagine I will ever have anything new to add. Initially, it always seems a hopeless race against the incoming sea, but it is a race I have usually won and I did this time too. Obviously I will never know with certainty, but our recovery from this swamping strengthened my belief that if I had had even a single bucket left, I could have recovered off Vanuatu as well.

In a half hour the water was below the floorboards and *Chidiock* was again able to sail, but the squall was still hard upon us, with fierce rain that beat the sea into a white froth and winds of thirty-five knots. Having no idea how long it would last, I began to be concerned that we might be driven north of Singapore. I looked around. This squall was no worse than the one that had hit us in Van Diemen Gulf. It was not even as bad, for here no waves full of sea snakes were breaking over us. If we had sailed then, we could sail now. I eased the mizzen, which had remained up, and unfurled the jib, and we began to smash our way west, steering less by the sails than by how much of the ocean we scooped up with the lee gunwale.

An hour later my concern proved to have been justified. The squall passed, leaving *Chidiock* becalmed beneath a sunny sky. Low hills on the horizon were too far away to reveal detail, but a majestic parade of shipping identified them for me. Coming down from Bangkok, coming up from Sunda Strait, coming in from Hong Kong and Manila and Yokohama and Los Angeles and Seattle, and going out toward all those ports and more, the great ships moved on the highways of the sea. They converged on a tower a few miles southwest of us. My pulse raced as I realized what that meant. The hills ahead were Malaysian. During the squall, in zero visibility, *Chidiock Tichborne* had been driven helplessly across one of the busiest sea routes in the world.

After the shipwreck in Vanuatu people said I had been unlucky. If so, my luck had just evened out.

8

In the Middle

Forty. The Big Four-Oh. And I was clearly in the middle. In the middle of my life—at the very least—and in the middle of a solo circumnavigation.

Several acquaintances asked if turning forty bothered me. The question came as a surprise, for I had been looking forward to that birthday. For three generations, no man in my family had reached forty, which may be one of the reasons why I long ago came to terms with my own mortality; and I found it particularly satisfying that I, who had taken the greatest risks, had achieved that age.

I suppose that for some people forty is traumatic, but to me it was not. In my view, life is divided into three parts. Youth is longing. Maturity is being. Old age is remembering. In these terms I knew the exact date I had become mature, which is a polite way of saying middle-aged. It was Saturday, November 2, 1974, the day I set sail on my first attempt at Cape Horn, the day I stopped longing and started being. Perhaps I would begin to feel old when I found others who lived more radically.

A fortieth birthday is a time of inventory. I took mine that afternoon of November 11, 1981, in the beach house my grandmother had lent us in San Diego, after we had flown to California for a visit while I waited for the northeast monsoon to reach the Indian Ocean. Ashore, that house was the most appropriate place I could be, for much of my life had revolved around it. I had spent my summer vacations there during high school in the late 1950s, sitting by the sea, smoldering with voyages. I had lived there for a few months with my first wife after we graduated from college in 1963. Suzanne and I had stayed there after I completed my circumnavigation in 1976. I had begun the open-boat voyage less than a mile away in 1978.

So I asked myself, What do you have to show for forty years? And with surgical ruthlessness I drew up the answer: Two voyages—one solo circumnavigation completed, one half completed. Three books—one published, one soon to be published, and one half completed. Three paintings—two of them self-portraits which were done twenty years ago, when I thought painting might be my medium, and which still said what I wanted them to. Twenty-eight poems. Experience of the world and the sea. One small, fine boat. My having loved and been loved by five women. Pride. Scars. Cape Horn. A surprising number of friends for a solitary man. Suzanne.

I came to an abrupt halt and thought for a long time about the things the list lacked. Some of them, such as a home, I missed.

Inevitably the next question was, Is it enough? And without needing to think, I accepted the reply that came: Yes.

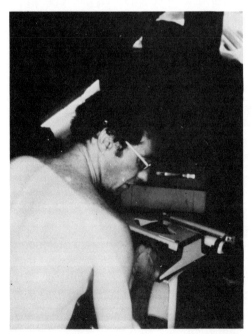

At work.

In the Middle   103

From the middle of life, then, and from the middle of my voyage, I saw the other parts of the experience of the sea, which is more than just wind and waves. The end came first.

Macao is the East as Singapore is not. Consisting of two offshore islands and the tip of a peninsula on the Pearl River estuary, a total of six square miles of land occupied by a quarter million Chinese, Macao is still a possession of Portugal, although obviously with the approval of China, which supplies, among other things, its drinking water. Macao is a place of curiosity, beauty, charm, history, and the sea.

Not long after dawn one morning, as junks were ghosting through the mist, we rode a cab from the old Bella Vista Hotel to the barrier gate between Macao and the endless brown hills of China. Then we walked back, through narrow, twisting, crowded streets, past firecracker factories and temples, through Portuguese forts dating from the sixteenth century. We saw the stone table where the first treaty was signed between the United States and China more than a hundred years ago, the painting of the Laughing Buddha, statues of the eighteen wise men of China, one of whom is Marco Polo, a collection of Chinese art housed in what were originally the local offices of the British East India Company, and a hill from which a goddess had ascended to heaven.

There was a wonderful contrast between the noisiness of the alleyways, filled with people selling everything from clothing to dried fish whose heads were covered for some reason with paper hats, and the serenity just a step away inside a temple or garden. My need for space and solitude is perhaps extreme, but it is a need that many, if not all, men share, a need that the Chinese have understood and filled ingeniously for centuries.

It was all fascinating, and Macao and Hong Kong, forty miles away, which we visited on our trip back to California, are the best reasons I have yet seen for sailing to the Orient; but we were really just tourists until we found the Anglican church.

This was a greater achievement than it sounds, for we were on our third attempt with our second map to find a way through the warren of alleyways surrounding the church. I had almost decided that I should have brought my sextant and a compass when we came to a high stone wall. According to our maps the church was just on the other side of the wall, and according to our instructions, we would have to knock on a door for admittance. The problem was that there was no doorway in sight. Working on the premise that there must be a way through or around every wall, we turned left and started walking.

When we finally found it, the doorway was open, framing a small, white, steepled church. No one was about. We stopped for a few moments at the chapel, and then walked back to what is known as the Old Protestant Cemetery.

I had come to believe, particularly after witnessing the Hindu cremation ceremony in Bali, that other peoples handle death better than Westerners do, but perhaps I had mistaken the trite blandness of some American funerals for the essence of a tradition. A hundred years ago, Westerners in Macao did things better.

Although a few missionaries and merchants, and a few wives and children, are buried in the Old Protestant Cemetery, it is in essence a sailors' cemetery, a young sailors' cemetery, for few survived the trials of the sea and the diseases of the land, including war, to reach forty.

The character of the cemetery comes not just from the dates on the tombstones but from the succession of people who have maintained the graves and kept the memories alive for more than a century, and from the openly expressed sentiments on the tombstones. None of these are elaborate, not even the one for Lord Churchill, forebear of Winston, who died in Macao in 1840 while serving as captain of H.M.S. *Druid*.

Wives were "deeply mourned" and "sorely missed." Men died "after a lingering and painful illness" or "fell from the rigging" or were killed while "storming the heights of Canton." Children were "lamented for a lifetime."

I was not looking for something to write about, but instinctively I felt, as I had with the *gujung* fishermen of Bali, a kinship with these men, whose white tombstones were surrounded by neatly trimmed grass in a tiny cemetery far from their homelands. This is one end to the experience of the sea. Another is found in the depths of the sea itself. They seemed to speak to me with a single voice, and that voice said, "Live passionately. Now."

Before we turned and walked back through the portal to the crowded city, I copied the inscriptions from the tombstones of two of my fellow sailors:

>   Sacred
>   To The Memory
>   of
>   George H. Dungan
>   Who Departed This Life
>   May 9th, 1857
>   aged 29 years
>
>   The Fort is reached
>   The Sails are furled
>   Life's voyage now is over
>   By faith's bright chart
>   He has reached that world
>   Where storms are felt no more
>
>   This stone was erected by his
>   Old and esteemed friends
>
>   Sacred to the Memory
>   of
>   Fred Duddel
>   Who Departed this life
>   November 1, 1857
>   Aged 38 years
>
>   "Poor Wand'rers of a Stormy Day
>   From Wave to Wave We're Driven
>   And Fancy's Flash and Reason's Ray
>   Served But to Light the Troubled Way
>   There's Nothing Calm But Heaven"

They created a line that day, a pure curve, sweeping down, running forward, then thrusting up proudly into the sky. And the formation of that curve was the defining act of man, the creation through skill, intelligence, and desire, of order from chaos.

For years I have given much of my life to boats, but they have all been made of fiberglass. I like fiberglass, which has no soul but many virtues. Yet my imagination has never been captured by that type of construction as it was when I visited, in a lot near the railroad tracks in San Diego, Howard Wormsley and John Freiburg's misnamed Coaster Boat Works—misnamed in that the vessel being built, out of wood, was hardly a coaster.

Partially I was awed by the scope of the project, a sixty-five-foot-long gaff schooner, displacing 100,000 pounds. A total of 12,000 feet, more than two miles, of planking was being milled. The 30,000-pound keel was the biggest ever cast by Keelco in Los Angeles. Epoxy glue came not in finger-sized tubes, but in fifty-gallon drums, one each of hardener and of resin, costing $1,400 wholesale. Even more I was struck by the creation of something out of nothing, or to be precise, out of a stack of lumber that looked nothing like a boat.

Using a modified WEST system, Howard and John were building up the deadwood when I first went by. It was then about ten inches tall. The core of the transom had already been laminated and was leaning against the back fence, with fourteen station frames. I smiled with admiration for the audacity of men and for the complex ties that link seemingly unrelated parts of life.

At the very moment I stood watching a hunk of mahogany being clamped in place, those ties reached out to my own boat, *Chidiock Tichborne,* half a world away on a mooring in Singapore, to the Protestant Cemetery in Macao, to Russ Kneeland, the American businessman, living in Mexico, for whom the schooner was being built, and to the cold, wild waves of Cape Horn, where he hoped to sail her.

I had never met Mr. Kneeland, but I felt an affinity for him—how could I not, when someone told me, "He is like you, obsessed and driven"?—and I believed I understood his motives, although I would not have acted on them in the way he had done. I prefer small boats to big ones and reliance on self to reliance on ship's timbers. In any event, the schooner would cost more money than I have made in my entire life.

Big ships do have their own mystique. Suzanne and I had gone day-sailing on a seventy-footer in Singapore, and as the sun went down, we needed only a small leap of the imagination to transport ourselves back to a clipper ship in what is erroneously called the Golden Age of Sail. I leave it to some academician to provide the statistics, but I believe that there are more good sailors making more good passages alive today than ever before. No one else seems to have said it, so I will: the Golden Age of Sail is now.

Why spend a lot of money on a special boat? Why use your skills to build one? Why sail a voyage?

The Spanish have a proverb, A man should plant a tree, write a poem, and have a son.

It is all the same: an affirmation of self, the creation of something that would not have existed if you yourself had not lived. Mallory's famous response to those asking why he wanted to climb Everest—"Because it is there"—is precisely wrong. I have no patience with those who remark that the cliché "Lord, thy ocean is so great and my ship so small" applies more to me than to anyone ever before. It is nonsense. The sea is not capable of greatness; man is. I sail not because the sea is, but because I am. And I expect that is why Russ Kneeland was waiting two years for his special boat to be built, even though he could have bought something off the rack and sailed for the Horn the next day.

Two weeks after that first visit, Suzanne and I went back to Coaster to witness the delivery of the keel.

The deadwood was now more than ten feet tall at the stern and extended out in a long tongue designed to fit over the keel. Having been built up from pieces of wood weighing less than eighty pounds each, the deadwood now weighed, at Howard and John's estimate, about 5,000 pounds. A separate piece that had been laminated for the stem weighed about 800 pounds. A template had been made and holes drilled in the deadwood for the keel bolts. The day's exercise was to put the pieces together. It sounded simple, but I suppose we all wondered if it would be.

The crane arrived on time, at 11:00 A.M. Working close to overhead power lines, the crane operator was an artist; he lifted the deadwood delicately to the side of the yard. Howard checked the level of the railroad ties on which the keel was to rest, and then we all sat around and waited.

The keel arrived somewhat late from its journey down the freeway on the back of a flatbed truck. Two other keels were on the truck, one of them for a forty-two-foot IOR machine, but they looked like toys next to the schooner's massive chunk of burnished lead. Flat on top, bottom, and back, with the forward edge angled like a bow, the keel was as long as *Chidiock Tichborne* and weighed more than thirty-five times as much.

Lifting eyes were threaded into the keel and attached to a lifting bar to spread the strain. Lead, being a soft metal, could bend if lifted incorrectly. As the crane cable came taut, we all came taut. Because of the overhead power lines and the size of the keel, very little maneuvering space was left for the crane, which would have to lift the keel up several feet to clear a fence, carry it laterally for twenty feet, and place it as precisely as possible on lines drawn on the railroad ties. No moments until the final move to launch the schooner would be more critical or more dangerous. Howard and John knew what they were doing; the crane operator knew what he was doing; the men who had cast the keel knew what they were doing. And it all went without a hitch.

My favorite part came when the keel was safely positioned and the boatyard hangers-on got to help apply bedding compound. Gallons of the thick gray gunk were dumped on the top of the keel, which had been cleaned with acetone, and we were all given rubber gloves and putty knives to spread it around. I realized then that an unacknowledged reason for building boats is to provide grown men and women with an excuse to mess around in muck.

I had wondered why the twelve pairs of bolts cast into the keel were of different lengths, the longest forward, the shortest aft. As the deadwood was lowered, the reason became evident. Only one pair of holes had to be aligned with one pair of bolts at a time. Halfway down, the deadwood caught, but a few blows with a sledge hammer moved it on. And when the giant washers and nuts were tightened with an equally massive wrench, the pieces fit together perfectly.

Then the crane lifted the stem into place. The line had been created. From disparate segments of wood and metal had been born the basic flowing line of a ship, a ship that one day might be tested by cold waves five thousand miles to the south.

I was sorry that I would not be able to see the schooner grow. I think I would have learned a lot. But it is not enough to be a spectator to life. One must be a performer as well; and soon it would be time for me to sail again.

9

Another Start

"Your next port?" asked the clerk who was completing my clearance papers in the Port Authority of Singapore office.

I looked over his shoulder at the huge world map on the wall. I knew where I was going—to Suez as quickly as possible. The last words Suzanne had called to me as I passed through the gate at Los Angeles International Airport on December 27, 1981, were "See you in Cairo," and the last she had whispered to me a moment earlier were "I hate the separations." But Suez was depressingly far away, more than 5,000 miles. I planned to stop somewhere in the Indian Ocean, but could not decide where: the free port of Sabang, off Sumatra? Galle, in the south of Sri Lanka? Male, in the Maldives?

The clerk was becoming impatient. "Djibouti," I blurted, although I had no intention of going that far. I would let the weather decide. Surely no one was going to complain when I entered some closer port in an open boat.

He raised his eyebrows. "Djibouti?"

"Yes."

"You are the first yacht to clear for that place. How do you spell it?"

I told him, not because I am a good speller, quite the contrary, but because I had bothered to learn. It was proof that the voyage was turning toward home that I had also checked the spelling of "Mediterranean" and "Caribbean," and that to rejoin me in Egypt, Suzanne would fly not west, but east. So, "Djibouti" I said, innocently unaware how terribly my world would change in the coming weeks, how much completely unexpected would happen, and how it would turn out that I would never see the place.

At 8:00 the following morning, Tuesday, January 5, 1982, as the sun was painting the clouds lavender and gold, I cast off the line to the mooring at Ong Say Kuan's, where *Chidiock* had been resting for four months, and we began to drift with the tide down Johore Strait. It was less a departure than an extraction. My destination was west, but a causeway blocks the strait in that direction and we would have to sail first ten miles east, then ten miles south. With the breath of wind, we would be lucky to be clear of Singapore Island by nightfall.

About thirty other yachts drowsed at moorings in the glassy water. Palm trees and heavy vegetation lined the shore, on which lay a half dozen scum-covered wrecked hulls that filled and emptied with every tide. Earlier, at dawn, the cry of the muezzin could have been heard

Dinghy dock at Ong Say Kuan's, Singapore.

from the nearby mosque, but now there was only the crowing of roosters from the jungle. Ong Say Kuan himself is a nice enough man of about fifty, who putters around the sheds ashore like a coolie until he has to go into the city. Then he puts on immaculately tailored slacks and a silk shirt, climbs into his new Mercedes, and drives off. But the bureaucrats of Singapore would be hard pressed to find a more inconvenient place for transient yachts. As always, when I looked at the jungle, which is actually an abandoned rubber plantation, I found it difficult to believe that a city of 2,500,000 lay only a few miles behind it.

When Singapore wants to do something right, it does it very well, as shown by the contrast between arriving in the usual tourist manner and arriving by yacht. Singapore is a city with its hand out—not to beg, but to make a deal. Singapore's life is as a port and its only true attraction is duty-free shopping. As a tourist, you land at the brand-new $400 million Changi Airport. You walk through a lovely terminal filled with waterfalls and fountains. Fifteen or twenty immigration officials are on hand, so lines are short. Your baggage arrives so

Hauling out on palm tree, Singapore.

promptly you hardly have time to change your money. Customs smiles you onward. Inexpensive taxis await to carry you along freeways toward the high-rise hotels and the shops of Orchard Road, which offer everything from inexpensive bargains and wonderful food to Rolex watches and French designer clothes. Singapore wants you to stay a couple of days, spend money in luxury and comfort, then get back on a plane and be gone.

When you arrive by yacht, regulations require you to thread your way through some of the heaviest shipping traffic in the world. Doing this is difficult enough under power and truly hazardous under sail; Singapore, founded to served sail-driven shipping, has long forgotten the sailing vessel. Then you must tie up to Finger Pier, inappropriate for anything smaller than an ocean-going freighter. You must present yourself at several different offices, some of them blocks away from the waterfront. And when you finally have your entry papers and visa—good for two weeks only unless you and each of your passengers can produce more than $2,000 U.S.—you must move your boat all the way around the island to the moorings far up Johore Strait. I can think of no other place that presents equal problems to the visiting sailor. Even if you arrived at Finger Pier at the crack of dawn, which is most unlikely, you would still be hard pressed to be settled at the mooring area by nightfall. And it is not that alternatives are lacking. Changi Yacht Club has fine new facilities, which could easily handle cruising boats if the authorities wished it. The authorities do not so wish, and Changi turns the coldest possible shoulder to visitors.

Singapore is a good place for reprovisioning and the best in thousands of miles for obtaining spares. If what you need isn't available locally, it can be sent quickly from anywhere in the world. The problem, once you are at the mooring area, is getting back into town. The bus service is good and cheap, but to reach the nearest bus stop requires a walk of more than a mile, the first half of it on a muddy track through the jungle, utilized also by the odd cobra. This track is so bad that many local cab drivers refuse to venture onto it; several, who had lived in Singapore for their entire lives, said to me in wonder, "I never knew this was here."

Once at the bus stop, you are faced with a ride of up to an hour and a half, depending on traffic, to the heart of the city. Thus going to the Central Post Office is like commuting into downtown Los Angeles at rush hour; the round trip takes about three hours.

I think this time spent in hot buses was one of the reasons why we felt the heat more in Singapore than we had elsewhere. The daily temperature was about 90°, not unusual for the tropics, but the heat-trapping concrete of the city, the exhaust fumes, our wearing more clothes than usual—long pants for me, dresses for Suzanne—the absence of a sea breeze (for Singapore is landlocked), and the lack of a convenient place to swim, all combined to make 90° in Singapore intolerable, particularly during the long walk home from the bus stop in late afternoon with a full backpack.

The wind was very light as we set out on the morning of January 5, but the tide carried *Chidiock* away from the other yachts at a couple of knots. It was like being on a river. Johore Strait is about a half mile wide near Ong Say Kuan's, much to the delight of the smugglers who blast across on moonless nights at more than forty knots, running electronic equipment from Singapore to Malaysia and sometimes tin from Malaysia to Singapore. The first time one of them roared through the mooring area, I thought a jet fighter had

Sailing on Johore Strait, Singapore.

mistaken *Chidiock* for an aircraft carrier and was coming in for a landing.

In the evening and at dawn the strait is often pretty, for at these times one can see only the mirror surface of the water, not what is floating beneath it. Sembawang Hospital, a mile west of Ong Say Kuan's, dumps several thousand gallons of raw sewage into the strait each day, causing anyone who goes into the water to run a high risk of catching a painful and tenacious infection known as Singapore Ear.

The land on either side of the strait is low. Heavy industry, steel mills, shipyards, are scattered along the banks. As we drifted through the still-cool morning, I recalled that these waters have their history. We were on the course that had been followed by the *Prince of Wales* and the *Repulse* as they steamed out in December 1941 to their destruction and that of the British Empire. I was one month old when they went down. And a few miles behind us was the point

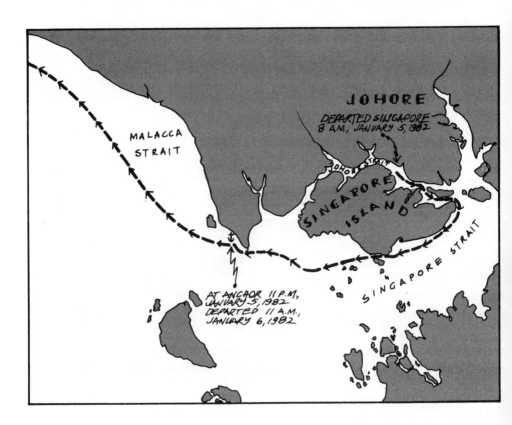

Another Start 115

where the Japanese had crossed the strait to capture Singapore, after the inept attempt of the British engineers to destroy the causeway during their retreat. The engineers set off the charges at high tide; after the demolition, only five feet of water covered the causeway at low tide, and even the Japanese could walk across. An Englishman, Noel Coward—not I—said of Singapore before the war, "It is a first rate place for second rate people." A few miles ahead of us was the site of Changi Prison, where thousands of Commonwealth soldiers, betrayed by self-serving politicians and incompetent generals, had died.

Maneuvered by several tugs, a great hull came up the strait, heading toward Sembawang Shipyard, and I turned our bow to drift closer to the Singapore side. Unladen, the 200,000-ton tanker cast a great shadow; it was a wall of steel obliterating the sun.

A bit of wind ruffled the brown water and for a few moments *Chidiock*'s bow wave played a merry tune, but too soon we were again just drifting. I wondered if we would make it around Changi Point before the tide changed at noon. With more than 5,000 miles to go before I could see Suzanne, I was drifting slowly in the opposite direction.

I studied the sky. The morning clouds were breaking up. If the weather followed the usual pattern, we would have some wind in an hour or so, and probably a thunderstorm, with too much wind, in midafternoon. The Sumatra that capsized us in August on the South China Sea side of Singapore Strait had demonstrated how quickly the weather can change over land-dominated water; and several times while at Ong Say Kuan's, I had seen clear skies replaced by violent thunderstorms within minutes. The day looked as though it was going to be pleasant, but around Singapore one could never tell.

True to form some wind did reach us in an hour, and the little yawl began sailing faster than the tide. Just before noon, when we were off the modern clubhouse of the unfriendly Changi Yacht Club, the wind suddenly shifted 180 degrees and increased to more than twenty knots. Slipping into my foul-weather parka, I played the mainsheet, and with *Chidiock*'s lee rail scooping up brown foam, we beat the last mile, dodging a steady stream of tugs towing barges of sand to one of Singapore's many land-fill projects.

Once around the point I was happy enough with the east wind as I eased sheets and we sped across the shallows off the airport. Steering *Chidiock* with my knee, I ate a typical Singapore lunch—Kentucky

Fried Chicken. If Colonel Sanders could find his way to Bali, he certainly couldn't miss Singapore, where Western food and clothes and cars are very much in vogue. McDonald's, A & W root beer, and Swenson's ice cream all do a thriving business; and one of my favorite ads on Radio Singapore describes Hang Ten clothes as being "as exciting as a Malibu sunrise." Mystique is obviously everything, for anyone who has been there knows that Malibu is a nothing beach by world standards, just the best of the bad lot around Los Angeles, and that since it faces west, its sunrises are hardly noteworthy. Still, Singaporeans keep hearing of Malibu on records and television shows, and presumably the ad works.

By 1:00 P.M. we were able at last to turn so that the compass lubber line was at the western half of the card as we sailed along the south side of the island. In the distance stood the towers, up to fifty stories high, of the central business district; stretching toward them were countless high-rise apartment buildings. Perhaps no other city in the world has been as self-renewing as Singapore. More than two-thirds of its residents have been relocated during the past decade.

The longest passage, departure from Singapore, January 5, 1982.

Singapore is proud of its economic success, but the price has been regimentation of, to me, an unacceptably high degree. Singapore is, in fact, the world's largest Skinner box, led by one of the world's strong leaders, Cambridge-educated Lee Kuan Yew, a man who has cut across history and whose will I admire, if not the city he has shaped to that will.

The Singapore government is nominally democratic; but one party, the conservative, business-oriented People's Action Party, wins all the seats. The government tells the people what it wants them to do and then provides consistent rewards for compliance and consistent punishments for transgression. For example, there is an antilitter campaign. Litter bins located every few yards make it easy not to litter, and a $500 fine makes it painful to do so. As a result, Singapore is the cleanest big city in Asia.

There are also campaigns against long hair for men, for birth control, against smoking, for the use of public transportation, for team spirit, for high productivity at work, against spitting in public, and for courtesy. My favorite campaign poster, however, is one intended to promote the use of Mandarin Chinese. It says, "Speak more Mandarin. Less Dialects." It says just that. In English.

Some of the campaigns are, even by government admission, somewhat less than successful. Lee Kuan Yew said during a radio interview, "The Singaporean is a calculating creature. He will be courteous when he sees that courtesy means profit." A visitor's typical experience is that the Singaporean has yet to see this.

Chidiock began wending her way among the hundreds of ships anchored in the roads of one of the world's four busiest ports. The ships are so numerous that they constitute a separate floating city. *Chidiock* first entered the anchorage used only by the smaller freighters, which carry cargo that is off-loaded into the lighters plying the Singapore River. Because the ships, although comparatively small, were all more than large enough to blanket *Chidiock*, I kept as close as possible to the shore.

Dark clouds were gathering over the city's skyscrapers, and by the time we were off the container facility and into the narrow strait between Singapore and Sentosa islands, heavy rain was falling inland. Many men called or waved to me from the ships tied to the wharfs. One ship, *Sphinx 4*, home port Alexandria, flew the Egyptian flag. I wondered what the men would think if they knew that I was sailing for their homeland.

Singapore River.

Playing the gusts as the wind swirled off buildings and ships, we sped across smooth water between the islands. As we went under the cable car that connects Singapore with Sentosa, I remembered the day a couple of months earlier when Suzanne and I had ridden across to visit the Sentosa War Museum.

The museum is known for its wax figures depicting the surrender of the British to the Japanese in February 1942 and the surrender of the Japanese to the Allies at the war's end in 1945, but I was struck by an ad that proves that human nature is unchanging and that avaricious merchants will be avaricious merchants in any circumstances. It was printed in the lower-right-hand corner of the front page of the *Malay Mail* for February 19, 1942, which is displayed in the museum. The paper is headed "New Order Special Fall of Singapore Edition." The ad is as follows:

> Banzai!   Banzai!
>
>
>
> **VICTORY**
> **FOR JAPAN!**
>
> Fall of Singapore
>
> **HURRY TO**
> Gian Singh's
> **FOR RISING SUN FLAGS!**
>
>
>
> 20, Java Street   Kuala Lumpur

    The fall of Singapore was of course one of the decisive events in recent world history, destroying the myth of white European invincibility. But the attempt by the Japanese to present themselves as freeing their brother Asians from European domination for altruistic reasons failed. The Singaporeans and Malaysians I talked with felt, as had the Balinese, that the Japanese were worse overlords than the Europeans had been. Today, Singapore newspapers carry cartoons, like those in American publications, showing the Japanese coming back to buy what they could not hold by force.

    Tugs, lighters, ships moving into the strait or away from the docks, ferries, tourist launches, were in motion all around us. Then the rain hit, and we were seemingly alone. I leapt forward and let go the main halyard. To be capsized here would be disastrous. By the time I had the sail furled, I was so wet that donning foul-weather gear was pointless.

    Instead of increasing, the wind dropped away. I had noted the compass course to clear the end of Sentosa, but it was not the nearness to land that troubled me. Through hissing rain, I could hear ships and smaller craft moving, but I could see nothing beyond our bow. Peering through rain-streaked glasses, I sought a glimpse of anything. The sails hung limp, heavy with water. Even if I raised the main, we would have no maneuverability. We were sitting ducks. As I fumbled for the oarlocks, the rain stopped and visibility returned.

Sentosa Island was behind us, and the heaviest traffic was a few hundred yards north. Ahead lay scattered reefs and the anchorage for the big ships, the supertankers bringing oil to the refineries on the west side of the city. Dozens sat there. Some wind returned, and I reset the main and headed toward them.

When night fell we were in the midst of those great ships. As their cabin lights came on, we sailed silently between them, seeking clear air. Smells of cooking, sounds of music, drifted down. The anchored ships posed no danger to us, nor did the pirates who had been plying Philip Channel, a few miles to the south. More than a half dozen times during the few months I had been in Singapore, those pirates had come under the cover of darkness in small, fast powerboats from the maze of islands on the Indonesian side of the strait to board and rob ocean-going ships; but I was convinced that *Chidiock* was too small a fish for them to bother with, even if by ill chance they saw us. Still, the awareness that real pirates were near did not leave me.

By flashlight I studied the chart. We were in thirteen fathoms of water. The idea of anchoring there, *Chidiock* among the behemoths, had some whimsical appeal until I considered the consequences if the tankers started to swing with a change in wind or current. Five miles ahead lay a low hill, barely discernible in the blue-gray dusk. This was Piai Point, the southwest corner of Malaysia. If we could reach it, I could drop an anchor and rest without fear of being run down. Everything depended on the tide.

Since leaving Ong Say Kuan's eleven hours earlier, we had drifted and sailed almost forty miles, but we were only a few miles closer to Suez than we had been that morning. Well, I thought, letting my mind reach back across the Pacific, Suzanne, it is a start.

10

Pirates of Malacca?

The throbbing diesel awoke me just as they turned the searchlight on. Befuddled with sleep, I sat up. The brilliant light blinded me as the other boat circled *Chidiock Tichborne*. What the hell is going on? I wondered as I tried to clear my head. I glanced at my watch—4:00 A.M. The wind was steady at twenty knots. The preceding day, our first inside Malacca Strait, the wind had died and left us drifting on the edge of the shipping channel until sunset. Then it had increased to force 5 and we had sailed close-hauled toward the shore through an unpleasant three-foot chop. At midnight, concerned about approaching land too closely, I had anchored in ten fathoms a few miles south of the flashing light on Point Gabang to get a few hours' rest. Perhaps I had been wrong about pirates leaving *Chidiock* alone, I thought, as the mysterious boat swung around us twice more. There was nothing I could do now but wait. Malaysian voices rose above the wind and spattering rain. The light steadied about twenty yards off and began to draw slowly nearer.

As my vision adapted, now that the light was not directly in my face, I saw that those aboard the other craft were only fishermen hauling up a net; but they were coming much too close. A taut line slapped against *Chidiock*'s gunwale. Our bow was being pulled under. The raked bow of the forty-foot fishing boat rose high on a wave, then slammed down, just missing *Chidiock*'s bumpkin. "Get back! Get back!" I screamed, pushing against the rough planks of the fishing boat, not trying to fend her off as much as to use her immovable weight to push *Chidiock*'s stern away. A boy appeared on the deck of the other boat. "Get back!" I repeated.

"No English," he shouted down.

I waved my hands. The bow dropped until he was momentarily at eye level with me. "Back. Back." I gestured with my hands. He turned and called aft, someone eased the float line on the net, and they drifted a few yards downwind.

I scrambled forward. As I had feared, our anchor line was caught in their net. I was fairly certain we were over a mile offshore, and I had not seen their small unlit marker buoys when I set the anchor in darkness. Now more than a hundred feet of line, fourteen feet of chain, and a fifteen-pound CQR anchor were entwined in the fishermen's net. There was no way I could save everything, but perhaps I could retrieve the anchor.

The searchlight swung, blinding me again. Shading my eyes with one hand, I called, "My anchor is caught in your net," even though I knew the words would not be understood.

The wind and waves were so rough that just hauling up the anchor would have been a chore; with the added strain from the other boat's swinging on the net, the task was nearly hopeless. The first twenty feet of line came easily, but then the net snarled tight around the rode; I had to lean over the bow and untangle it, pull in a few feet, untangle, pull.

My hands were bleeding by the time the chain finally came to the surface. There was no way it would pass through the net, so I grabbed the metal, gasping with pain as salt water ate into my torn fingers. The fishing boat started to come closer; perhaps the men wanted to see what I was taking from their net. Not turning toward them, I yelled, "Wait. Wait." There was the anchor; I caught it and swung it aboard *Chidiock*.

With the anchor and chain and most of the line retrieved, I moved aft to find a knife and to prepare to get underway. The fishermen watched as I inserted the rudder and set the mizzen and jib. The sails throbbed in the wind. The heavy reinforced clew of the jib just missed my head as I crouched over the rode. Hoping the line would pull back through the net, I cut it just above the chain, but the line jammed. I slashed with the knife again, and suddenly *Chidiock* was drifting fast downwind. In my haste to reach the tiller, I almost jabbed the knife into my thigh.

Pirates of Malacca? 123

In a moment we were under control and drawing away from the other craft. I did not feel that I had been negligent, but then the incident had certainly not been the fishermen's fault. I was glad I had not damaged their net. Presumably they were poorer than I, even if their boat was bigger.

The compass was not in place and I was disoriented until the Point Gabang light appeared off to starboard. Trimming the sheets, I steered toward it. After dawn I would sort things out.

For four days we paralleled the Malaysian coast, sailing a narrow path between the picket line of ships to the west and the low land to the east, anchoring whenever the wind died, as it did several times a day, making good thirty-five or forty miles each twenty-four hours. My badly swollen fingers, with clear serum oozing from beneath crusty scabs, were not helped by the repeated handling of the anchor, but the swift current in Malacca Strait keeps the water cleaner than it is around Singapore and no infection set in.

The erratic wind continued to blow from off the land until we were past the town of Malacca. What is interesting about Malacca is what is not there. Once the greatest seaport for thousands of miles, Malacca is now a sleepy town void of major shipping.

On Sunday morning, January 10, the wind shifted to the south, and by early afternoon we were off the islands around Port Klang, two hundred miles north of Singapore. Beyond Port Klang the Malaysian coast falls away to the north, so I was happy enough to leave the land and reach off to the northwest before this unexpected southerly. At about 4:00 P.M. the last sliver of Malaysia disappeared from view. I noted in my log that this land was probably the last I would see for a while. The forecast proved to be among my less accurate ones. Land was in sight during five of the next seven days.

I would have been quite pleased had the southerly lasted all the way to Suez, but I knew that somewhere ahead we should find the northeast monsoon, which, once we were clear of Sumatra, would enable us to reach across the Bay of Bengal to Sri Lanka. I had not yet decided whether to stop at Sabang.

My much-admired southerly deserted us just after sunset. The water was too deep for anchoring, so I had no choice but to drift and hope we did not lose too much. The currents in Malacca Strait had been changing with the tides, but seemed to set more strongly to the south than to the north, flowing, I estimated, at up to three knots.

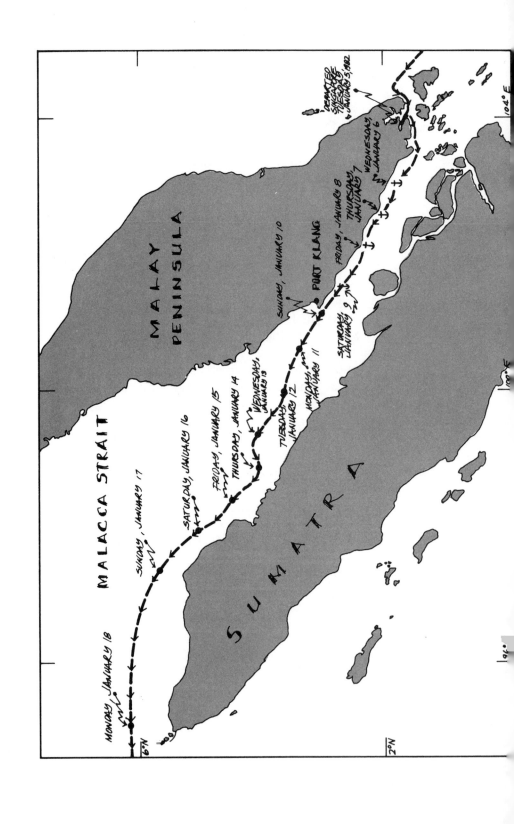

After a few hours, a light breeze filled in from the northwest, heading us, but any breeze was better than none, so I trimmed *Chidiock* to sail due west.

I did not get much rest that night, nor for many nights to come. We were east of the main shipping route, but the lights of countless small fishing boats cut the darkness around us, and once we sailed into a huge mess of driftwood and came to a dead stop. No damage was done, but freeing *Chidiock* from the mess took almost an hour.

At noon the next day I used the sextant for the first sights on this passage. Navigation thus far had been merely a matter of comparing the coast with the chart.

Working up to local noon, I took a couple of shots before routinely checking the instrument at 0° altitude. Shock rushed through me when I looked through the eyepiece and found the horizon lines far apart. I brought them together and stared at the micrometer in disbelief. There was an error of 39 minutes of arc. How could this be when the sextant had worked perfectly the last time I used it? But then I recalled that I had cleaned it after the swamping that last day in the South China Sea, and had had no way to check it around Singapore. I berated myself for not having done so while at anchor along the coast. I don't like to adjust sextants at sea, but the experience I had gained with the plastic model while crossing the Coral Sea had taught me how, and I soon apparently had the error removed. Still, I was disturbed. You should be able to trust your compass and sextant; now I would have to be even more skeptical than usual about observations until I could verify them against a known position.

A sailor I had met in Singapore had written from Sri Lanka that Malacca Strait was a nightmare, and as I went night after night with only snatches of sleep, the passage did take on some of the characteristics of a nightmare for me. The human machinery breaks down from lack of sleep faster than from deprivation of anything else, including food or water. For four days and nights we ghosted and drifted across Malacca Strait, constantly headed by the wind when there was any. We made about forty miles a day, but these were twenty-four-hour days, for we could not anchor and often just drifted north on one tide and helplessly back south on the change. When we were caught for two nights in the shipping channel, I kept the oars ready for instant use. Oddly, I became angry at the ships for moving too slowly. Probably they were steaming at better than ten knots, but because visibility was good I would often see a ship that was more than an hour away, and then I could not sleep until she was close enough for me to be certain she would pass safely.

One night an island was in view to the north at sunset. We were slowly sailing toward it on starboard tack. In the middle of the night, I tacked *Chidiock* and we headed west. At dawn I opened my eyes and saw an island dead ahead. My reaction was a repeat of what was by now the theme of this passage: What the hell is going on? With increasing daylight, I realized that it was not the same island. This one belonged to Indonesia and, according to the chart, was used as a prison.

For the rest of that day and part of the next, we sat in proximity to that island. The pause gave me the opportunity to take a good series of sun sights and I became confident that the sextant was accurate to within at least five miles.

When not taking sights, I spent some time on maintenance—resplicing the anchor rode, going over the side to scrub *Chidiock*'s bottom, and finally, with copious amounts of WD-40, freeing the zipper of my foul-weather pants, which had frozen tight during the idle months in Singapore. No longer would I have to lower them completely for every call of nature, a most welcome improvement aboard an open boat.

Malacca Strait was full of debris. In addition to trees, logs, planks, and weeds, there was a lot of stuff thrown from ships or washed from the shores—bits of plastic, articles of clothing (I saw one red rubber sandal one day and what looked to be its mate twenty miles away the next), and several fluorescent light bulbs.

Sunset on Thursday, the fifth since we had left the Malaysian side of the strait, set the sea on fire and gave me my first view of the mountains of Sumatra. That night a loom of lights to the southwest marked the city of Medan. I welcomed these signs of our minimal progress, until dawn disclosed that we had unwittingly sailed into a trap, from which we were not to escape for three days.

Although land was not visible, except in glimpses, until Saturday afternoon, we were too close to Sumatra. The nights were clear and calm until an hour or so before dawn, when the moisture-laden clouds built up against the coast. Friday and Saturday mornings saw us drenched by heavy rains. Gusts of wind came from all directions. *Chidiock* would dash along at five knots for five minutes, then she would sit sullenly in the downpour, then the wind would fill in behind us for five minutes, then it would head us for ten.

I had used only a few gallons of water thus far and my remaining supply was more than adequate to last until Sri Lanka, so I did not try to catch any; but out of curiosity I took the top off my daily two-liter water bottle during Friday's squall. It was overflowing almost instantly, so I got water for one extra day. There was so much fresh water that I was pumping it steadily overboard with the bilge pump. A few weeks later I would be wishing I had saved more.

By late morning each day the rain ended, and the equatorial sun soon dried everything out, including me. Despite *Chidiock*'s intermittent bursts of speed, we usually came out of the rain about where we had gone in. This was just another variation, more dangerous and more uncomfortable than ghosting and drifting, on going nowhere.

Saturday morning found me very tired and depressed. Our daily runs for the six days since we had last anchored added up to 224 miles, assuring us of our slowest week ever at sea no matter what the seventh day's run might be. At noon we were beating slowly past a village named Keudepeureulak—the village was considerably smaller than its name—when I had another encounter with fishermen.

A number of open sampans, twenty to thirty feet long and powered by big outboard motors, had been moving about near us. Now three of them started back to the village. They changed course to pass close to *Chidiock*. Each boat held two or three teen-age boys. As they neared, something about them reminded me of a motorcycle gang.

I waved and smiled. The boats began running circles around the slowly sailing *Chidiock*. One of the boys called out in Indonesian and made a gesture of smoking a cigarette. I nodded my head negatively and said, "I don't smoke." Another boy made a sign of drinking. I pretended to misunderstand and pointed at one of my water containers. While my attention was thus distracted, the third boat sneaked up from astern and attempted to loop a line over one of *Chidiock*'s stern cleats. Immediately I tossed the line back into the water. There was a moment of tension. False smiles disappeared. The boats moved a little way off and the crews conferred. *Chidiock* continued to sail. Gradually the fishing boats fell behind us. Angry glances darted our way. Engines roared into life. I prepared for another onslaught, knowing that if they were really determined to board us there was little I could do, but when I glanced back, the boys were laughing and calling to one another and heading for the shore.

Naturally, I gave this incident some thought. No harm had been done, but then who but a fool would bother with an open boat? I wondered what would have happened if I had been aboard a normal-sized cruising boat with Suzanne. In late 1981 and early 1982, while professional pirates were attacking shipping around Singapore, yachts were attacked in the Gulf of Thailand and on the west coast of the Malaysian peninsula near the Thai-Malaysian border. Boats were robbed, men stabbed, women raped. I am not repeating mere rumors. These incidents were reported by the Singapore Broadcasting Corporation and in the *Straits Times*.

I have always said that I do not believe in carrying weapons aboard a yacht. I am not certain that I intend ever again to sail in the vicinity of Singapore or Malaysia, and I do not wish to overstate the problem, but I have changed my mind. If I ever do sail there in a conventional boat, I will have guns on board.

Sunday morning brought us at last to the northeast corner of Sumatra and to the northeast monsoon. A final run of 70 miles brought the week's total to 294, a record of futility that I hoped would never be broken, but that lasted less than two months.

At our vast speed of a solid three knots, Sabang was a day away, and I started a letter to Suzanne, to be mailed from there.

> Sunday, January 17
> Off Sumatra
> Dear Suzanne,
>   I'm writing this in the back of my navigation notebook, hoping it will not get too wet before I reach port.
>   Only three weeks today since we were last together, yet it seems forever. Unfortunately I am still off Sumatra, and I am at the end of my slowest week ever at sea. You can imagine what joy it is to have 5,000 miles ahead of you and be making thirty miles a day, with shipping all around all the time. Hopefully things will improve. I'm trying to get offshore today beyond the shipping and beyond the coastal weather.
>   I'm in good health so far. Except for a deluge each dawn, drifting is dry if frustrating. The wind right now is from the northeast. May it be the monsoon at last.
>   Other than reading—I've finished *Noble House* and *Horn of Africa* and am now on *Fire from Heaven*, about Alexander the Great—and swimming over the side, I've naturally thought of you and us a great deal. Before I go on with those thoughts, you probably would like to know that I've chopped my hair off short and that two fish are swimming beneath *C.T.* They are about two feet long, green-blue in color. They've

been with us for several days. I see the phosphorescence as they dart out to catch somebody to eat at night. They both look rather startled and annoyed when I drop in unexpectedly for a swim.

I am very tired, though. Physically tired, but more mentally tired, tired of everything almost, certainly tired of the sea and this terrible slow passage. You have said that I choose to sail the voyage, but what it really seems to have become is that I choose not to quit, which is not quite the same thing. There is not much joy when I consider the poor sailing we have had so far and the thousands of miles still to go before I can see you again.

I have realized that the two times I have been happiest during the past few years have been not at sea but at the beach house at Cook's Beach, New Zealand, and in the cabin in Julian, California. Perhaps we were happy in those places because of the calm contrast to the storm and stress of the voyage, but I think it was more than that. I believe you feel the same way too. I only know that I would rather be sitting around a potbellied stove or walking along a deserted beach with you—not a potbellied you—than doing anything else right now. And we will just have to start making some plans and saving some money so we can do so someday.

While I've been writing this, Sumatra has at long, long last disappeared from view. I hope this wind lasts. It's 9:00 A.M. here. I've been awake since 4:00, when the rain started. It's sunny now, so I'm drying out.

I am fourteen times zones ahead of you. As I write, it is 7:00 P.M. Saturday in San Diego. I wonder what you are doing and try to picture you at this very moment. I love and miss you incredibly. And I hope to hell this wind holds.

Will

That wind truly was the beginning of the northeast monsoon, and it did hold. Our next day's run was 126 miles, and Monday noon found us ten miles north of Sabang, sailing fast to the west. After the famine, there was no way I was going to waste such wind and go into port. Sabang was forgotten. So was the letter, which was never mailed. By the time I found it and gave it to Suzanne, it was too late.

A few hours later I saw the last land before entering the Bay of

Bengal, a circular rock labeled appropriately on my chart, "Rondo." I wrote in the log:

the last island off Sumatra

islands passed
are women unloved

11

The Longest Passage: A Specimen Day

FEBRUARY 1, 1982

1:10, 2:35, 4:05 A.M.   At intervals of an hour or so, I awoke, propped myself up on an elbow, ducked my head under the jib sheet, and looked around. *Chidiock Tichborne* was sailing smoothly and dryly at four knots. I noted with satisfaction that no running lights were in view. We had again moved north of the main shipping route across the Indian Ocean. After a minute or two, I lay back, and I was soon asleep again.

6:15 A.M.   Blurrily, I woke up for good. The sun was just above the horizon, coating the sea with a thin white light, and the sky was cloudless. In a few hours the heat would be fierce.

The good night's sleep only partially made up for the four preceding rough nights. I had not really slept well since we were on the other side of Sri Lanka.

I rearranged the flotation cushions. "Discard when waterlogged," their labels said. They had been new less than a month earlier, but cushions, like a lot of things, live fast on an open boat. By all reasonable standards they were already waterlogged, but they were still less hard than the floorboards and so had escaped consignment to the deep. I summoned the energy to strip off my foul-weather gear. Although not a single wave had come aboard during the night, the gear and my skin were wet. For a few moments, while the wind evaporated the moisture, I was pleasantly cool.

Until after 7:00 I just sat there, watching the low waves, listening to *Chidiock* reach along.

7:25 A.M. Like a sluggish lizard whose blood has finally been sufficiently warmed by the sun, I moved, first leaning forward over the jib sheet to give the bilge pump a few strokes. As expected, it drew only air.

I pushed myself up until I was sitting beside the mizzenmast, to which was tied the orange plastic one-liter measuring cup I use for certain calls of nature. Too-dark urine provided confirmation of my fatigue.

Every action seemed difficult. Repeatedly I lapsed into immobility, just sitting, gazing out to sea. Something was wrong. I hadn't been at sea all that long—what was it? twenty-six days? twenty-seven?—and conditions hadn't been all that rough. Perhaps the problem was diet. I was not hungry, but I would have to force myself to eat more. My experience of storms at the end of a passage had perhaps made me too conservative. Certainly I had to keep a reasonable reserve, but there was no point in saving sea rations to eat in port. I needed to regain strength, and I would have to start doing some exercises.

My hands had been running over my legs, seeking salt-water boils, infection. Suzanne had commented in the past that picking at my skin had become an unattractive nervous habit I continued even in port. She was right. All I could say was that I had reason to be nervous. I leaned forward and groped in the bin beneath the starboard seat for the plastic medical kit, so that I could paint a couple of places on my legs and forearms with iodine.

8:03 A.M. I was a few minutes late in taking my morning observation of the sun because as I started to open the stern locker to get the sextant, I was distracted by the sight of a ship coming up from the southwest. At first I saw just an irregularity on the horizon, and because I had thought I was well away from shipping I kept staring until I was certain that it was a ship. She irritated me. What was she doing in my part of the ocean?

Usually I catch the sun at 20° above the horizon. When one is into a passage, it is easy to know what time the sun will reach this point. But that morning the sun's altitude was 21°57′ when I got around to taking my sight. It really did not matter. In the tropics the sun's bearing

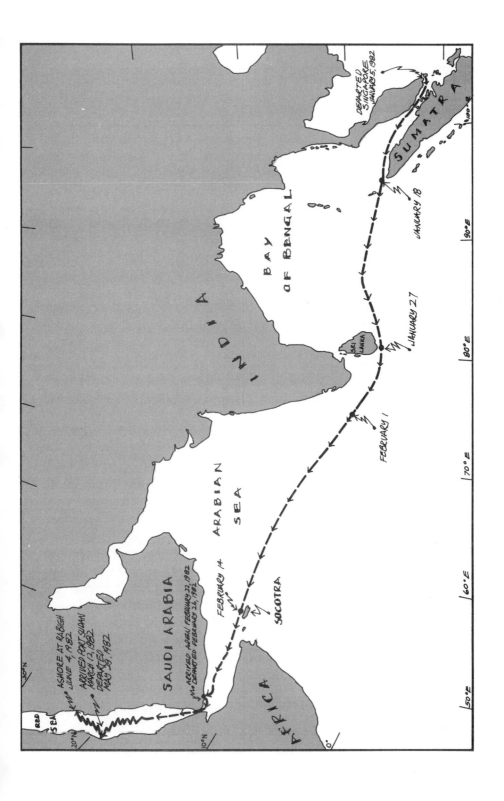

does not change very rapidly in the early morning or late afternoon. The position line put us farther west than expected; I attributed the discrepancy to an unpredictable current. Where would navigators be without currents to provide excuses for errors in reckoning?

For five days and 400 miles, since dipping below 6° north near Sri Lanka, we had been struggling to get back above 7° north to clear the Maldives. The morning line put the nearest two Maldive atolls within ten miles of us. I was still cautious about the accuracy of the sextant after adjusting it at sea in Malacca Strait, but even allowing a reasonable margin for error, today should bring us either to land or safely past it.

8:34 A.M. Sitting back down on the floorboards, I made breakfast. The food bag lay beside me on the aft port side of the cockpit well.

I unzipped it and began the tedious but necessary task of untying plastic bags. At each end of the duffel bag, separated by packages of freeze-dried food and cans and jars that needed no special protection, were perishable supplies, such as crackers, rice, dry cereal, sugar, granola bars, and dried fruit. These were stored in triple plastic bags, so to get the six crackers that accompanied a vitamin pill for breakfast, I had to untie and then retie three bags. I seemed to spend a good proportion of my time untying and retying bags. Today I would keep count.

I allowed myself only one cup of instant coffee. As usual I did not heat the water, but drank the coffee at air temperature. And as usual, I wondered why it tasted like bacon.

When I had left San Diego to return to Singapore, my grandmother had given me a bottle of what she described as "special" vitamin pills. To me vitamins are vitamins, and I had not bothered to look at them until I was at sea. Presumably she had thought them to be special because they were big enough to choke an elephant. Swallowing one each morning and evening provided me with much of the bulk in my diet.

I also noted at breakfast that no one had yet brought to the attention of the public one of the important details in provisioning for a small-boat passage: because of the way small boats bounce around, a sailor must buy thick jams rather than slippery jellies, which slide off crackers before they can be eaten. Sticky smears on my legs and *Chidiock's* floorboards testified that in Singapore a jar of blueberry preserves had deceived me.

The Longest Passage: A Specimen Day   135

9:40 A.M.   After using the head bucket—and untying and retying two bags to get toilet paper—I took my clothes off, except for my hat. I put some 5 percent PABA sun-screen lotion on my face and forced myself to do some exercises. Even on a day of such smooth sailing, exercising is not easy, but I managed fifty knee bends, balancing myself with one hand on the tiller, and two hundred and fifty counts of running in place while sitting. These, along with some stretching motions, used up all my energy for a while, and once again I sat looking at the sea.

There was no sight of the Maldives. I wondered how far north we were. With a longitude of about 73° east, local noon would not be until 12:23. I found myself thinking that if we had stopped in Sri Lanka we probably would have left port today.

The northeast monsoon had blown steadily all the way across the Bay of Bengal. Day after day beyond Sumatra we had had fine, comfortable sailing, with runs of between 105 and 130 miles. The depression I had developed during the miserable progress in Malacca Strait was diminished by each five degrees of longitude we swiftly passed. But I tried to think of this passage in terms not of distance but of time. In a larger boat, I had once done more than 18,000 miles nonstop, but in an open boat, 5,000 miles, no matter how I divided it, was simply too far to contemplate, particularly since the hardest sailing, a beat several hundred miles up the Red Sea, would come at the very end; so I told myself when I left Singapore,' "Don't think of the distance. Think that if you

Chidiock at sea.

just keep going for three months, including whatever time you spend in port, you'll be in Suez or close enough for Suzanne to rejoin you." Where the byword on my first circumnavigation had been "Cape Horn by Christmas," on this one it became "Suzanne by the end of March."

I leaned over and took the chart from my Voyageur navigation bag. A week earlier I had been 200 miles due east of the port of Galle, at the south end of Sri Lanka, happily looking forward to being ashore, eating fresh food, getting some exercise, and, I hoped speaking to Suzanne by telephone. In Singapore I had allowed three weeks to cover the distance to Galle. That Monday it appeared that despite the slow early going, we would actually get there in twenty-two days. But on Tuesday a wind blew that changed my life.

Having sailed the Indian Ocean once does not make me an expert, but I assume that the northeast monsoon blows harder where it is diverted by the Indian subcontinent. It certainly blew harder for us as we approached land.

At noon on Tuesday, January 26, we were thirty miles off the Sri Lanka coast, sailing fast under reefed main and jib. The waves were not big, but they were rough. We were doing what I have come to call one-hand-on-the-gunwale sailing. Without hanging on I would have been thrown around like a rag doll. One moment I was deciding how close I wanted to come to the coast that night, so that we could enter Galle before sunset on Wednesday; the next, a wild idea had me in the forward part of the cockpit, checking the water containers tied to the mast. I had left Singapore with about twenty-three gallons of water, in five containers. Thirteen gallons, in three containers, was left. Even without rationing that was enough for a month. And without much sacrifice I could cut back on my consumption a little, drink one cup of coffee in the morning instead of two, put less water on my cereal at noon. I had plenty of food. Why go into Sri Lanka at all? The interlude would be nice, but the only thing I would really miss would be talking to Suzanne; I wasn't even certain that would be possible, and even if it was, it wouldn't last more than a few minutes.

My mind opened and became excited by the leap into the unknown. The passage from Singapore to Djibouti along our course would be more than 4,000 miles. No one had ever sailed an open boat that far without going ashore. India and Sri Lanka had always been among the places I most wanted to see, but I could hardly do justice to Sri Lanka in a brief visit and I knew I would not enjoy playing tourist without Suzanne. If I swung farther south, I might avoid the wind shadow of

The Longest Passage: A Specimen Day   137

the island and have continued good sailing. Suzanne would have to go for several more weeks without knowing if I was still alive, but she would assume that I had been unable to call and that mail was slow. Communication from former French colonies seems to be generally good. With luck, the day on which I could telephone her from Africa would be not much later than the one on which a letter from Asia would have reached California. And the great unthinkable distance of Singapore to Suez would have been vanquished.

Once considered, the idea carried me inevitably along. All the frustration of Malacca Strait, all the desperate longing to get ashore, were swept away. Four thousand miles nonstop in an open boat. I needed the new challenge. And, for a day, I was happy.

Before sunset on Tuesday, we recrossed the shipping route, and that night the loom of a light to the north marked Dondra Head, the southernmost point of Sri Lanka. We had our best day's run of the passage during those twenty-four hours, covering more than 140 miles by Wednesday noon. But no sooner were we past Galle than the wind died. Wednesday night we were becalmed. Thursday I had to steer by hand as we slid down sharp waves under jib and mizzen. Friday we were becalmed. Saturday there was again too much wind. Sunday we were becalmed. There wasn't a decent day's run in the lot, and I found myself brooding, as I contemplated the steadily diminishing supply of water, that if I had known this was going to happen I would have stopped at Galle. I would have stopped if the wind had changed a single day, even a few hours, earlier. Futile thoughts. It was too late now.

11:00 A.M.   The wind was backing to the north and weakening, and as our course of 290° became a close reach, I changed from sheet-to-tiller self-steering to simply tying the tiller a few degrees to windward.

Frequent clumps of seaweed and floating reef plants indicated that land was near. I climbed up beside the mizzen. A mile ahead of us the ocean was peculiarly disturbed. Speculation that it might indicate a reef ended when the disturbance rushed toward us. I barely had time to climb down from my precarious perch before *Chidiock* was attacked by four-foot waves created by a tidal current sweeping around the Maldives. We hobbyhorsed to a standstill. A wave broke completely over the bow and soaked everything in the cockpit, including the foam bedding pads that had almost dried in the sun.

For an hour I could do nothing but brace myself in the corner of the cockpit and hang on with both hands. The seas were like those in

138   THE OCEAN WAITS

a Japanese print, with sharp, jagged fingers reaching out from each crest. As midday approached, I became increasingly anxious that I would miss a noon sight.

12:45 P.M.   There are myths about waves rolling endlessly on around the ocean, but my experience is that even in the Southern Ocean, waves are usually transient and local. Off the Horn, I had force 12 winds and twenty-foot waves one day and was becalmed on glassy seas about a hundred miles farther east less than two days later.

These waves off the Maldives certainly died as suddenly as they appeared. Ten minutes before local noon, *Chidiock* sailed into smooth water, enabling me to get a good observation of the sun. The resulting reading of latitude 7°20′ north put us well clear of the nearest atoll. The ocean ahead was open all the way to the island of Socotra, off the horn of Africa. Singapore lay 2,000 miles behind us; Djibouti a bit over 2,000 ahead.

I put the chart away and opened the food bag for a lunch of Quaker Natural Cereal, bought in Singapore, with four tablespoons of powdered milk, the last of a can bought in Cairns, Australia, almost a year earlier, and a handful of dried fruit. As I tossed the empty milk can overboard and retied the bags of cereal and fruit, I reminisced about how long and far some foods last. The record aboard *Chidiock Tichborne* was set by a tin of Fiji Crackers, bought in Port Vila in October 1980 and finished in the South China Sea in August 1981. Fiji Crackers are my favorite to take on passages, but they are, I expect, something of an acquired taste, being heavy and hard to chew. Gnawing a Fiji Cracker is a good way to pass a slow morning. Even when fresh, they clank together like wall tiles. But I can honestly say that the very last Fiji Cracker from that tin was every bit as good as the very first.

1:45 P.M.   The worst part of the day. The sun was so high, there would be no shade until after 2:00. It was much too hot to read. Too hot to think. I lay dazed in the cockpit, a wet shirt draped over my head, waiting for the shadow of the mainsail to grow.

2:30 P.M.   I imposed discipline on myself and artificial patterns on the voyage by rationing certain limited supplies—some by distance, some by time.

To break the long afternoons, I carried cans of soft drinks, but the firm rule was that the day's can not be opened until after 2:30. Often I found myself checking my watch every few minutes from about 1:30

The Longest Passage: A Specimen Day 139

on, like some office worker anxious for a coffee break. Now that I had extended this passage far beyond the distance planned for in Singapore, the cans would last only if I limited myself to one every other day. So on alternate days, as long as we maintained reasonable progress, I had a cup of water flavored with Tang. Today was a Tang day and very hot, and the drink, anticipated for so long, was gone in a minute.

Among the other rationed items were batteries for my radio receiver; no matter how weak the signal, these were changed at intervals of not less than ten degrees of longitude. The next change would come after 70° east.

A five-gallon water container had to last fifteen degrees of longitude, no matter how many days it took to cover that distance. The next change would be after 60° east.

But I changed clothes every seven days regardless of the distance covered. Fresh clothes were important less because they were clean than because they were dry, however briefly they stayed that way.

Instinctively I ducked as a tiny squid shot up out of the water and splatted against my shoulder. I scraped it from my skin, threw it back, and resumed reading *The Good Earth*.

4:15 P.M.   I put down my book.

So often at sea I find myself wishing that the wind would change—that it would be stronger, be weaker, move a point in one direction or the other. But this wind was perfect. We were making five knots smoothly on the desired course. As far as I was concerned, this wind could last forever.

When you make more than one circumnavigation, you must meet yourself somewhere. I looked south. Six years earlier I had been down there at this time of year, capsizing twice in a survival storm in the Roaring Forties, staggering onward, although I did not know it, toward Auckland and Suzanne. It was nighttime now in California. I thought of Suzanne asleep in the beach house in San Diego. I was still sailing toward her, but this time I knew it. I missed her terribly and had never loved her more.

5:28 P.M.   My world was divided into four horizontal bands: *Chidiock*'s white hull; a blue strip of sea; the rust-colored mainsail; another blue strip, of sky.

The sun was nearing the western horizon. To prepare for the night, I liberally coated the dead skin on my buttocks, and the patches on my right knee, right wrist, and right elbow, with Desitin; I donned my shorts, T-shirt, and foul-weather gear; and I switched from my sunglasses to the regular pair.

Sitting on the side seat, I opened the locker and removed the stove, a pan, the teakettle, a flashlight, and the radio bag. Dinner would be freeze-dried sausage patties mixed with Minute Rice, tea, and a can of fruit cocktail. Reaching the sausage required opening one bag; reaching the rice, three; reaching the tea and matches, three more.

Usually the hardest part of cooking aboard *Chidiock* was getting the stove lit, but this was a rare one-match night, and soon the water had boiled and the rice and sausage patties were ready.

I ate from the pan as the sun set into a gentle rosy haze. Washing the pot and fork was just a matter of leaning over the gunwale. Then I sat back, sipping my cup of tea, and watched night come on. In pleasant conditions, this is my favorite time of day. In rough conditions, dawn is my favorite.

As the darkness grew I became more aware of sounds: the hissing and gurgling of *Chidiock* speeding through the water, a click and groan from the rudder, a soft thump as a wave caught us abeam, a squeak from the mizzen. Nothing threatening, just regular, gentle passage sounds. *Chidiock Tichborne* was getting the job done.

When the tea was gone, I took the radio from its four bags. These should be the last bags of the day. I checked the tally. Including the times I had opened the navigation bag, the grand total was twenty-six bag openings.

I was too late for my favorite program, the BBC's "Sports Roundup." My stay in Australia had enabled me at last to understand cricket scores, and the BBC had even told me a few days earlier that San Francisco had won the Super Bowl. I played with the dial, switching from the BBC to an English-language station in Sri Lanka to various stations playing Indian music to Radio Australia, until I finally settled on a country-music program from England.

9:00 P.M.   I lay on the foam pads, the tarp tucked beneath my chin like a blanket, and stared up at the half moon directly overhead.

After a while I took off my glasses and wedged them beneath the food bag.

9:30 P.M.   I dreamed that I was ashore in a hotel somewhere on one of the Greek islands. The hotel was high on a hill overlooking a dark-blue sea. Suzanne was sitting on the balcony. A breeze ruffled her hair.

The Longest Passage: A Specimen Day 141

Two cold drinks were on the table beside her. I had just taken a long, hot shower to wash away the dirt of months at sea. I dried myself with a white towel. I started to walk toward her, but somehow I could not cross the room. I would be walking, then back drying myself. Walking. Drying.

9:55, 10:30, 11:40 P.M.   At intervals of about an hour, I awoke. *Chidiock* continued to sail well. No running lights were in sight.

12

The Longest Passage: Landfall

At my first sight of the Arabian peninsula, I turned around and sailed away. This was one of the smartest moves I ever made. I should have kept on going. I sailed away not because the distant sand dune was so unappealing, but because that one glimpse was all I needed to verify our position. Our destination, Aden, lay eighty miles to the southwest.

All across the Indian Ocean I had conducted an irrelevant debate with myself about whether to go to Aden or to Djibouti. Aden was more conveniently located and reportedly less expensive. However, South Yemen, of which Aden is the capital, had a radical Communist government that had at times treated Western yachts badly; and I had been told in Singapore by someone who had a friend who had a friend that in the previous year yachts had been permitted to remain in Aden for only twenty-four hours. This was critical to me. After seven weeks at sea, I needed more than a single day in port.

The debate was irrelevant because the wind made the decision for me, blowing mostly from the southeast in the Gulf of Aden rather than from the northeast, as predicted by the pilot chart. This wind was carrying us directly to Aden. We had passed Sabang. We had passed Galle. But 4,000 miles was enough. I had only three gallons of water left. I could not sail past the front door of another port without going in. And I felt confident that once in, although neither *Chidiock Tichborne* nor I was physically in bad shape, I could convince the authorities not to kick us out.

The Longest Passage: Landfall 143

The immediate problem was the one made too familiar in Malacca Strait: walking the tightrope between the shore and a parade of shipping. However, here we had wind; the shore was dry and stark rather than lush and wet; and all the ships were tankers heading to or from the Persian Gulf.

Once *Chidiock* had settled on a port broad reach, I took a sun sight. I had hoped I could plot it on the larger-scale chart of the southern Red Sea, but the line fell beyond the margin, and I had to go back to the small-scale chart of the entire Indian Ocean. I was sick of that chart. One of the modest pleasures in making a long passage is changing to a new chart, but I had been stuck with N.O. 721, "Indian Ocean, Northern Part," for weeks, for lifetimes, forever it seemed. I recalled feeling this way, during my first circumnavigation, about the chart showing the South Atlantic from Cape Horn to the Cape of Good Hope. What was surprising now was that while my overwhelming impression was of slow sailing, our daily average was eighty-three miles, respectable for a boat as small as *Chidiock*.

As I studied the chart, I saw that our noon positions across the western Indian Ocean were spaced at regular intervals, with one exception, until we were near Socotra. The exception was a sixty-mile day that resulted when a front passed over us with thirty-knot winds. One might think that stronger winds would mean greater boat speed, and so they might during a race, but on a long passage aboard *Chidiock*, strong winds usually slow us down. That particular front almost slowed us down permanently. The waves were six to eight feet high and breaking. White water was everywhere. I was steering, working hard to keep the little yawl from broaching as she surfed down a steep wave, when less than a boat length ahead I saw foam covering what appeared to be a rock just below the ocean's surface. Knowing we were a thousand miles offshore, I still forced *Chidiock* into a wild jibe. The starboard rail dipped into the sea as I scrambled to shift my weight to port. Another wave threw us farther sideways before I could regain control. I stared down into the huge eye of a pale-brown, almost white whale, about the size of *Chidiock*. She was only a few feet away, heading in the opposite direction. For an instant we hung there, suspended on a wave and in time, staring at one another. To me the whale looked startled, then annoyed, as though she was thinking about me what I usually think about a ship: What is this thing doing in my ocean? Then her massive head dropped, her flukes rose, *Chidiock* surfed on, and she was gone. I do not know how I looked to the whale.

The remaining days in the Indian Ocean had been marked by only the smallest of incidents: getting Radio Qatar for the first time, and learning that halfway up the Persian Gulf the temperature was only 50°; opening my last five-gallon water container. I had a three-gallon container in reserve and was using water only at the expected rate, but I felt a profound uneasiness at opening that last big container.

The weather had been mostly good. Great continents of cloud raced over us, usually without any dramatic increase in wind and always without rain. I ate more, did more exercises, generally felt stronger physically than I had earlier, and continued to read books about China, in which my interest had been aroused during our brief visit by air in late 1981. Since leaving Singapore I had read *The Good Earth, Noble House, Manchu, The Crippled Tree,* and *Man's Fate.* But, although I was not certain of the causes, something was wrong with me mentally. Many people have thought so for a long time and will be pleased to learn that I now agreed with them. You make a voyage like this inside yourself. For me, being alone had become like being in a too familiar room. Perhaps I was just bored with my own company after spending two of the last eight years at sea alone. Perhaps there was a shortage of something essential in my diet, a shortage that had not become critical on briefer passages. Or perhaps I was not getting enough to eat, or enough real exercise. Or perhaps I was feeling the cumulative stress of knowing constantly that at any instant an open boat can slip across the edge to disaster, and the cumulative frustration of waiting out countless calms when I had so far to go. Probably a combination of all of these was affecting me. The symptoms were not clearly defined. I was extremely tense, even when there was no immediate reason to be. I felt edgy, uneasy, somehow just plain wrong, as I have never felt at sea before.

These vague symptoms turned into open rage a few days past the island of Socotra. I had been warned to stay well away from Socotra, which belongs to South Yemen and is suspected of being used as a Russian submarine base; but after seeing no land since the last island off Sumatra, I was not sorry to sight Socotra about twenty miles southwest of us at dawn on February 14. I did not know it at the time, but a valentine from Suzanne showing two camels in love was waiting for me a thousand miles to the west in Djibouti.

I had tried to prepare myself for a period of fluky winds as we made the transition from the Indian Ocean, where the winds had been fluky enough; but I was not prepared for the currents, which ran contrary to the pilot charts.

The Longest Passage: Landfall

Having sailed over 18,000 miles aboard *Chidiock*, I had become adept at judging our boat speed; so when, on the morning of February 17, after sailing at what I believed to be five knots since the preceding noon, I took a sun sight and came up with a running fix that gave us a run of only fifty miles, I was somewhat distraught. Repeated observations proved that my calculations were correct. Suddenly I exploded. I screamed at the indifferent heavens. I pounded my fist on *Chidiock*'s gunwale. I took the dividers and stabbed them into the *Nautical Almanac* in the best tradition of executing the messenger when you do not like the message. After a while, I calmed down to what had become my usual tenseness. And when our progress was equally poor the following two days, I did not react so violently.

One night *Chidiock* and I had what was our worst experience yet with pollution at sea. In early evening the running lights of a ship became visible a few miles ahead of us. They remained stationary and I began to wonder if we were going to run into her or if we should offer her assistance. I fantasized a great tanker sitting dead in the water. Tiny *Chidiock Tichborne* sails up and gently bumps into her amidships. For a moment nothing happens. Then the tanker slowly rolls over and sinks. *Chidiock* sails on. Clearly, I had been at sea too long.

So, for the safety of the tanker, I changed course; but by the time we neared her position, she had resumed steaming for the Persian Gulf. I don't know if she had been working on her engines or cleaning her tanks, but a few minutes later I smelled oil. At first I thought my small plastic container of kerosene was leaking. It was not. The smell became overpowering. I shined the flashlight on the sea. We were sailing through a great oil slick, which coated *Chidiock*'s topsides and took us two ghastly hours to cross.

Halfway up the Gulf of Aden we had another encounter with ships. These tried to rescue me, which was very nice except that I did not want to be rescued and they almost capsized us in the process. I suppose their thinking was, If he doesn't need rescuing now, he damn well will when we're through with him.

At 11:00 A.M. I was minding my own business, reading and sunning myself, when I heard engines behind me. I glanced back and found *Chidiock* had become part of an armada. Five warships were almost upon us. My first thought was that they were Russian, although this did seem a somewhat excessive force to send after *Chidiock* just because we had looked at Socotra from a distance. As the ships came abeam, I was relieved to see "Navy" painted on the side of one of them. Since I could not see the flag, I did not know what navy was meant, but although I am not fluent in Russian, I thought it unlikely that the Russian word for "navy" is "navy." Perhaps they were not hostile.

In majesty we sailed in company for all of a minute, but the rest of our little fleet was moving faster than *Chidiock*. When the warships were a mile ahead, a helicopter rose form the deck of the largest ship and swung in a long arc back to us.

Her first pass was made at a reasonable distance. I waved at the two men in the helicopter, who seemed to be staring down at me as the whale in the Indian Ocean had stared up, wondering what I was doing in their ocean. We all become proprietary about the sea. But on her second pass, she came too close and she hovered there. I let the mainsheet go an instant before the downdraft hit us. We heeled far over. The jib sheet jammed where it was tied to the tiller and would not come free. I fought to steer us off the wind, but where is off the wind when the wind is coming straight down? I don't know what the men in the helicopter were thinking about all this. Presumably, Aha, see, he *is* in trouble. When I had regained control of the yawl, I turned my face to them. The sound was deafening. Steering with one hand, I pointed at my chest with the other, then made a thumbs up, then motioned for them to back off. After two repetitions of this sequence, they did so.

I do appreciate their interest and concern. *Chidiock* is indeed an unexpected sight on the ocean. She could indeed have been a lifeboat and I could indeed have been in trouble. That there was no one around the one time I would have welcomed rescue when adrift in the Pacific Ocean is irrelevant. But being sunk by a helicopter is one of the hazards of the sea I had never anticipated.

I put the chart of the Indian Ocean away and took out the larger-scale one, named "Jazā 'Ir Az Zubayr to Adan [*sic*]," to plan what I hoped would be the last night of this passage. Between our present position and Aden, the coast fell away in two shallow bights, divided by a point labeled "Ra's Sailān." The wind was blowing directly from the east. I set *Chidiock* on a course of 240°, which if the wind held— as always on this passage, *if* the wind held—would keep us a safe distance off Ra's Sailān, fifty miles ahead, and carry us to within sight of Aden the following morning.

Naturally I slept even more lightly than usual that night. After midnight, the running lights of the tankers to the south of us were matched by clusters of lights from small fishing boats between us and the invisible shore to the north. At 4:00 A.M. I mistook lights that were

The Longest Passage: Landfall   147

in fact on land for fishing boats, an error that upset me considerably when dawn revealed what looked like tall buildings abeam of us. The chart showed the Aden peninsula to be 2,000 feet high. I could not decide whether I was looking at high land ten miles away or at low land a mile away. Without bothering with breakfast, I jibed *Chidiock* and hardened up until we were close reaching across choppy seas toward the buildings. It was wet going, and although the water was warm, I was thoroughly chilled by the time I was close enough to see that I was off a small village at Ra's Sailān. The "tall" buildings were not tall at all. Some of them were not even buildings, but palm trees. It was not a mistake that anyone who has seen Aden could possibly make.

The real Aden peninsula leapt from the waves at 9:00 A.M., a great huge rock, whose top was lost in clouds. Two thousand feet does not sound all that high, but when the land rises in one sheer face, it is spectacular.

The sea turned emerald green as we neared that great rock. White houses clung to one corner of the peninsula and could be seen on the flat land to the north. Aloof stone fortifications stood on peaks where it seemed building anything would have been impossible. Hawks soared

The longest passage, landfall at Aden, February 22, 1982.

from caves eaten into the rock face a thousand feet above the sea.

As usual I had no detailed chart of the port I was entering. This seldom matters with a boat like *Chidiock*, and except for the tugboats Aden presents no problems for any yacht.

Playing gusts and easing around dead spots as the wind swirled and eddied around the high land, we made our way into the harbor. From the chart you would expect the harbor to be on the leeward side of the peninsula, but it is not. The wind flows around both sides of the great rock, often blowing harder inside than outside, and a breakwater has been constructed to protect the main anchorage.

The anchorage is not large, but it was full of ships, almost all flying the Russian flag and tied fore and aft to permanent moorings. I looked around for other yachts, but saw none. A stone building about a quarter mile away had something of an official air about it. As I lowered my mainsail to prepare to beat on under jib and mizzen, a powerboat filled with men in uniform roared from behind a nearby freighter and sped toward me. I pointed to where I had tied and clothespinned to a shroud my "Q" flag (the yellow code flag by which an entering foreign vessel requests exemption from quarantine). The sinister men grinned and laughed and waved. None spoke English, but they indicated that I should toss them a line. I do not like being towed, but could see no way to communicate to them that I would sail to wherever I was supposed to anchor if they would show me the way. So I did toss them a line and they proceeded to tow us more under than across Aden Harbor. Frantic gestures on my part got them to slow down just enough as *Chidiock*'s stern began to disappear beneath the water.

An odd thing happened when I raised my camera to take a photograph of the towing craft. One moment men were all over the boat; the next, they saw the camera and disappeared below. This was my first intimation that cameras are not welcomed in Aden. A few weeks later, in Port Sudan, I learned how lucky I had been; a woman aboard a Canadian yacht told me that she had been jailed and interrogated for four hours when she innocently took some photographs while visiting Aden.

Miraculously, we survived our Arab version of Mr. Toad's wild ride with nothing worse than a broken jib-furling drum and a few dings in *Chidiock*'s topsides. The men in the other craft dropped us off near the stone building and indicated that I should anchor and go ashore.

Eagerly I inflated the dinghy and rowed the few feet to the stone steps. "Stone" is really redundant, for almost everything in Aden is built of stone. There is nothing else.

Towed to anchorage, Aden.

Several men, lounging in the shady interior of what had once been the steamship passenger terminal, watched me tie up the dinghy. I climbed the slippery steps and stood indecisively for a moment. One of the loungers pointed along the wharf toward a soldier holding a submachine gun. I started toward him, wondering what I had gotten myself into.

With those steps I ended the longest open-boat passage of all time: 4,058 miles and forty-seven days since I had last been ashore, in Singapore. As I neared the guard post, the soldier smiled and said, "Welcome to Aden."

13

"She Is Dying"

"Aden est fini."

I did not find many people to talk to in Aden. Most of those I did were cab drivers, transporting me from the anchorage at Steamer Point to the tiny shack housing the telecommunications office three miles away, where I spent parts of three days trying to telephone Suzanne and my grandmother in California. If cab drivers are to be believed, the average South Yemeni is indifferent to his government. "When the British left, the Communists were the only ones organized," shrugged one man. Another, who had lived in Buffalo, New York, for several years, said, "I like America better, but my family is here. I make enough to get by." The "Aden est fini" man, who had been born in what is now Pakistan and who spoke to me in a curious mixture of English and French, continued, "See, fini," and he pointed at the dilapidated buildings we were passing. Aden in February 1982 looked like a city that had not been rebuilt after extensive war damage.

The world had changed dramatically for me between Darwin, Australia, and Bali; now, between Singapore and Aden it changed dramatically again. Aden is a stark landscape of mountain, rock, and sand. Colors are reversed: in Asia the land is green and the sea brown; in Aden the sea is green and the land brown, almost monochromatically so. The people of Aden are taller than Asians, finer boned; the women are fatter, the men thinner, with what appear at first glance to be the hostile, hollow-cheeked, ascetic faces of fanatics. But as I

"She Is Dying" 151

was to discover time after time in Aden, with only a few exceptions, a simple "Hello" or "Good morning" turned those fierce looks into smiles. My interpretation of the appearance of hostility was that it reflected an insecurity left over from colonial days, when an Arab never knew how a European was going to treat him. In writing of Aden, "him" is not just a convenient pronoun. Most of the women in Aden are veiled. The only ones I recall speaking to were in the post office and the bank.

There is another difference between Aden and Singapore. Aden has little to offer, but what it does have, Aden shares; Singapore has much, but what it has, Singapore does not share—sometimes, as in the case of Changi Yacht Club, not even for money. There was no baksheesh, no bribery, no fee of any kind in Aden. Several of the men who seemed to live permanently in the old steamer terminal helped me carry water containers to the dinghy and always refused to accept a few coins in gratitude.

The only ways that Aden disappointed me had to do with goods, not relations with the people. In early 1982 Aden was not a good place for reprovisioning. You could get water from a tap on the landing. I was

Chidiock in Aden.

told that the water came from wells. Despite the arid landscape, no one seemed to worry about wasting it. I also managed to buy some good oranges at the open market one day, but there were none the next. I found good brown bread; some eggs; a place that sold roasted chickens—in my craving for protein, I ate a whole one for lunch; batteries for my radio; cans of soft drinks; and some very second-rate Bulgarian candy bars. But that was about all. The only things Aden has in abundance are poor Arabs; uniformed men carrying weapons; Russian freighters; ragged children playing in empty lots covered with broken glass; rocks; and blackbirds, vast screaming armies of which darken the evening sky.

While cab drivers might mourn the passing of the British Empire, I saw remarkably little evidence that the British had ever been there. A mile-long row of eight-story apartment buildings near the harbor had been built by them, but the buildings hardly looked British. From some flew signs calling for the banning of the neutron bomb, and one of them housed an office, seemingly in as much disrepair as everything else, of the PLO. Occasionally a shopkeeper recalled the British by quoting me a price in shillings, although the official currency consists of the dinar, worth about $3.00 U.S. and the fils, worth one-thousandth of a dinar.

Prices were not low in Aden, although much lower—I was later told—than prices in Djibouti, which was described by a couple on their second circumnavigation as being the most expensive place on earth. The roasted chicken cost me $4.50, and lunch at a hotel, $12.00.

One of the things I had most looked forward to was eating some decent meals ashore; but because there was no tourism in Aden, finding good food proved difficult. The only nonlocal people around were Russians and some Italians who were conducting an offshore survey for oil; and the only acceptable place to eat within walking distance of the anchorage was the dining room of the Crescent Hotel, where the menu was fixed and schizoid, in partial deference to the Italians, but surprisingly not yet to the Russians. One day I had spaghetti and lamb chops; another, lasagna and something called roast beef. If the food was not very good, it was at least a change from ship's stores.

I did manage to stretch my legs by walking a few miles each day through Aden's dusty, twisting streets. Although I had not walked for almost two months, my feet and ankles did not swell up as they have at times in the past when I have first come ashore, so my efforts at exercising at sea may have done some good.

"She Is Dying" 153

And I did manage to wash myself, using the dinghy as a bathtub with water carried from the shore, much to the amusement of the onlookers. Because the weather in the Indian Ocean had not been severe, my skin, except for my buttocks, was not in really bad shape, and responded immediately to fresh water.

On Thursday morning I finally managed to reach Suzanne by telephone. I had become very upset on Tuesday and Wednesday when I called at what was 11:00 P.M. in San Diego and was told that there was no answer. I had believed that the Yemeni operator was not putting the call through properly, for I had never known my grandmother to be out at that hour. It was wonderful to hear Suzanne's voice, until she said, "She is dying, Webb. The cancer has spread."

"How soon?"

"The doctors don't know. It could happen today. It might take a year. She just had a second operation and seems to be getting better."

I thought for a moment. "I would come back, but to leave *Chidiock* here would be to abandon her."

Suzanne answered quickly, "She does not want you to. There is nothing you can do anyway. She will be happier just knowing you've made it across the Indian Ocean safely."

Too soon our time was up. My grandmother and Suzanne were all the family I had. A recurrence of the cancer had been expected since it had first required surgery three years earlier, but my grandmother had been in apparent good health for an eighty-six-year-old woman when I had left San Diego in December. The first of what were to become a thousand ifs plagued me: if I had gone into Galle, I could have flown back from there. Like all the subsequent ifs, it did no good; but I could not dismiss it from my mind.

With that telephone call I had done as much in Aden as I could, except rest some more, and rest did not seem appropriate when my grandmother lay dying. I had been in port for less than three days, but I resolved that if the officials would permit me to clear on the next day, a Friday, the Muslim Sabbath, I would start up the Red Sea.

That night I wrote Suzanne:

> There is so much I want to talk to you about, tell you, ask you. Those few minutes this morning—for me, morning—were hardly enough. I wish I knew exactly when we will be back together, but so much depends on the weather.
>
> At least, as I told myself all across the Indian Ocean, never again will

we have to be apart for so long. Not on this voyage. Not in the rest of our lives.

Lots of men tell women that they would sail an ocean for them. I just did it for you.

14

The Red Sea Backwards

"No. Oh no," I whispered. I could have shouted at the top of my lungs and not been heard above the wind, but for some reason I whispered, almost prayerfully. Then the first of two waves flipped *Chidiock* onto her side.

It was 2:00 P.M. on Monday, March 1, 1982. Since leaving Aden three days earlier, *Chidiock Tichborne* and I had covered 250 miles, most of them backwards, in a passage thus far divided into three distinct phases. Now we were hove to under mizzen 150 miles up the Red Sea. Now I was standing on the side of the centerboard trunk. Now *Chidiock*'s port gunwale was a foot below the surface of the sea. Now the wind was blowing at force 10 and the average waves were ten feet high, but every half hour or so we encountered a set of three to five waves that were between fifteen and twenty feet high. For most of the past forty-eight hours *Chidiock* had ridden these waves without mishap, but now we were in the wrong place at the wrong time. I will never know what caused these waves to break just as they reached us— perhaps some irregularity in the seabed—but break they did, folding in half as violently as if they had reached a shoreline. I thought, Well, at least I'll have something to write about; everybody likes it when I almost get killed. The second wave picked us up and threw us backwards.

When I had gone to clear with the Harbor Master before leaving Aden on Friday morning, February 26, I had encountered a prime example of Arab mentality. The preceding day, after talking to Suzanne by telephone and learning of my grandmother's illness, I had visited the Immigration office to learn the procedure for departure. The office was next to the police station. I passed the police station during what appeared to be morning muster. As usual a dozen fierce men in uniform glared at me until I said, "Good morning," and then as usual all smiled, nodded, bowed, doffed their caps, and otherwise fell all over themselves to be friendly.

The Immigration office was in ruins, both the building and the interior, which consisted of a large empty room flanked by several tiny rooms stacked to the ceiling with old account books and papers. In one of these rooms I finally found an official, sleeping on a blanket on the floor. When he had come back from splashing water on his face and was sitting officially behind his desk, he asked, "Now what is it that you want?"

"I am going to leave in my boat."

"When are you going to do this?"

"Tomorrow, if possible."

"Of course."

"There is no problem, it being Friday, the Sabbath?"

"No problem."

"What time do you open in the morning?"

"Twenty-four hours. Someone is on duty twenty-four hours."

"And the Harbor Master?"

"The same. You go to his office; it is in the tower on the hill beyond the navy yard. You know the place?"

I nodded.

"You get him to fill out the clearance paper and then you bring it here and we accompany you to your boat and give you back your passport and you are free to go. That is all there is to it."

"What about fees?"

He gave me a superior smile. "No fees."

"None?"

"None," he repeated with satisfaction. The Adenese were justifiably proud of having eradicated the time-honored tradition of baksheesh.

I recalled this conversation in precise detail when the man on the fourth floor of the Harbor Master's office, from which he commanded a panoramic view of the harbor and its approaches, asked politely, "Where are your crew lists stamped by Immigration?"

For a moment I was speechless. "But I was told by Immigration that I didn't need to do anything but come here."

The Red Sea Backwards 157

This reply caused him to pick up the telephone and engage in a rapid conversation in Arabic. When he put down the phone, he frowned.

"Immigration say that you haven't been by there."

"No. Not today. I went yesterday."

His frown became a huge smile as he understood. He waved a hand in a circle in the air. "Oh, *yesterday*," was all he said, but those two words conveyed it all. "Yesterday" was another world, another lifetime, another official, other regulations. What kind of fool would bother with what had been said "yesterday"? I knew when I was beaten, and left for the Immigration office.

Phase 1 of the passage lasted for the ninety-mile stretch from Aden to Bab El Mandeb, the southern entrance to the Red Sea. We covered it in twenty hours of comfortable sailing.

Because of my unscheduled extra visits to government offices, we did not set sail until 10:00 A.M., and noon found us a mile off the refinery on the western side of the harbor. This was the first opportunity I had to check the sextant against a precisely known position, and I took several sights, including a latitude sight at local noon. My trust was re-established when the calculated positions all came out to within a mile of the known one.

Despite pleasant conditions, I did not sleep well that night because we were sailing among several of the Italian ships surveying for oil. They were easy to avoid, since they were running slowly on true east–west courses, but throughout the night one or more of them was always close to *Chidiock* and I was wary.

Saturday morning I felt decadent as I ate a breakfast of brown bread and jam, drank hot coffee, and listened to the Voice of America's morning program. Hot coffee and listening to the radio before sunset are unheard of upon *Chidiock*, but I was feeling expansive. The pilot chart indicated that at this time of year we should have southerlies most of the way to Port Sudan. The February chart showed a 1 percent probability of gales for the waters south of latitude 15° north. We were presently at about 13° north. And the March chart showed no gales at all. Although I had rested in port for less than four full days after forty-seven days at sea, I felt good.

At 10:00 A.M. we sailed between Perim Island and the southwest corner of the Arabian peninsula, entered the Red Sea, and began the brief Phase 2 of the passage.

Arabia looked just as one would imagine it. The western deserts of America have always disappointed me because they are not truly barren; almost everywhere something is growing, even if it is only a tiny weed. But Arabia had the terrible beauty of pure desolation—sand and rock, brown mountains rising inland, medieval forts on two of the hills near the strait, a cluster of huts in what I assumed was a fishing village, for we passed three *Chidiock*-sized boats fishing in the strait.

The sea turned bright green and flattened out. For two hours *Chidiock* sped north; but at noon, when we were off a village called Dhubāb, she began speeding too fast, skating on the edge of control at better than seven knots. I furled the mizzen. A few minutes later I reefed the main. We now had only seventy square feet of sail set. A few minutes later, I untied the jib sheet from the tiller and began steering myself. Phase 2 was over. Phase 3, in which we would have gale-force winds blowing beneath a hard blue sky for three days, had begun.

Sailing was exciting that afternoon as we raced along the arid shore. The wind blew steadily, rather than in gusts, and the sea remained smooth. But as the hours and miles passed and the Red Sea began to widen, the short, steep waves typical of shallow water began to form. The main shipping route, which had been well to the west of us, began to converge with our course because a group of islands forty miles ahead had to be cleared. And the wind increased to forty knots.

At 6:00 P.M., keeping one hand on the tiller, I reached back with the other and undid the shock cord on the mizzen. I was not trying to set more sail, but preparing to heave to. When the mizzen was flattened amidships, I spun *Chidiock*'s bow up into the wind and scrambled for the main halyard. Before I could clear it from the belaying pin, the wildly flailing sail wrapped the mainsheet around the tiller. The sail filled, turning us dangerously beam on to the seas. Two waves crashed aboard. Then the halyard came free, the gaff slid down, order was restored.

In complete darkness I dutifully spooned uncooked freeze-dried chicken stew into my mouth and contemplated our situation. We were about equidistant from the lights of the town of Al Mukhā to the east and the running lights of ships to the west. Each was about five miles away. The sea itself was not threatening. *Chidiock* was riding the waves —which were still small—safely; but she was going backwards too fast. Judging our speed was difficult. I thought it might be as much as two knots. If it was, we would cover more than twenty miles before first light and run great risk of being driven ashore or into the midst of the shipping, which was heavier even than that found in Malacca Strait. The running lights of at least a half dozen ships were always in view.

The Red Sea Backwards 159

For several hours I dozed fitfully as we proceeded stern first up the Red Sea, but at 3:00 A.M. something undefinable made me certain that we were about to be driven ashore. I could see nothing except the distant lights of Al Mukhā to the south. Conditions were far from suitable for sailing, but I felt we had to try to claw offshore.

There is a moment of transition between being hove to and sailing when *Chidiock* is out of control. The instant I eased the mizzen sheet, the bow began to swing off the wind, and I aided its momentum by unfurling the jib. Everything seemed to be all right, until I put the tiller amidships and *Chidiock* jibed. I pulled the tiller hard to starboard and we jibed back, the sails cracking like gunshots as they refilled. I moved the tiller amidships again. Again we jibed and rolled beam on to the waves. I jibed back. More gunshots, more groans from *Chidiock*'s simple rigging. I could not understand what was happening. Had waves caught us and forced the stern around? Was something wrong with the rudder?

As we surfed down waves I could not see, I experimented with the tiller, which was hard over to starboard; when it approached 20 degrees of amidships, the sails threatened to jibe. Neutral helm was so far to starboard that I could not steer from the port side of the cockpit. My weight to leeward caused us to bury the lee rail, but that could not be avoided until after dawn, if then.

For an hour we thrashed our way northwest. Normally one would speak of thrashing to windward; but although our erratic course, caused by the strange position of the tiller and my inability to feel or see the following seas, was a broad reach, we seemed to be fighting against the waves rather than moving with them, and I was using the bilge pump as much as if we were beating. By 4:00 I felt that the land would not be a threat before dawn, so I again hove to.

I did not attempt to sleep, but sat huddled in the cockpit, worrying about when this wind would decrease and wondering what was wrong with the rudder.

As the sun's first rays flowed over the mountains of Arabia, I saw that the waves had doubled in height during the night, and now ranged up to eight feet. My first reaction was, You were crazy to try to sail in such conditions. This was countered by, Would it have been better to have been driven ashore? I would never be able to say why I was so positive we had been in danger of hitting the shore.

Chidiock's rudder is made of galvanized steel and can be lifted up into the cockpit from its slot. Twice so far on this voyage I had bent the rudder shaft on coral, once near Tahiti and once off northern Australia. The first time, the rudder could still be removed normally; but the second time, I had to wait until I reached Darwin, where I removed the tiller cap and dropped the rudder down into the water.

Trusting the mizzen and centerboard to keep *Chidiock*'s bow to the wind, I untied the tiller and tried to pull the rudder up. It would not come. I did not know if the shaft was bent or if the blade was simply not aligned with the slot. I tried to duplicate the angle at which the tiller had been placed to achieve neutral helm during the night. Bracing myself against the yawl's bobbing and rolling, I pulled, heard the *thunk* as the rudder blade caught on the hull, moved the tiller another inch to starboard, and pulled again. Finally I found the correct angle, and to my great relief the rudder came smoothly upward.

The tiller is attached to the rudder by a cap held by a set screw and a tightening screw. The fit is so tight that the cap must be hammered into place. Furthermore, this cap had been on the rudder for almost a year, so it was corroded in place. To remove a cap usually takes me an hour or more of hard labor. But one of the waves during the night had thrown us backwards hard enough to loosen the cap. Once I got the cap off, I was able to remove the rudder and tiller and install the spares. Then I sat and waited, feeling cold, to see what the day would bring.

By noon our situation was becoming untenable. The wind had increased again. I now estimated it as being about fifty knots. The seas had increased to ten or twelve feet high, with higher sets coming through at irregular intervals. Even the ships, several of which had left the shipping channel to swing near *Chidiock*, were making heavy work of it.

With the increase in force the wind had veered a point to the southwest and was again driving us onto the land. We had drifted past several islands during the morning. Now the largest and northernmost, Jazīrat Zuqar, was a mile to the west. The island is 2,000 feet high and steep as well, providing no anchorage, but I thought it might provide a lee. Even more than the night before, these were not sailing conditions for *Chidiock*, but we had to try to get away from the Arabian peninsula and possibly even across the shipping route before nightfall.

I tried sailing under jib alone, but the little yawl handled better when I set the mizzen as well. The lee of Jazīrat Zuqar turned out to be an illusion. Steering demanded both hands on the tiller. Wave after wave roared up and threatened to swamp us. Waves smashed into the cliffs of the island, sending spray high into the air. Waves smashed into the bows and over the decks of southbound ships.

My belief that *Chidiock* is safe as long as we have sea room and/or I am on the tiller was dealt two severe blows by the Red Sea. The first came in the form of a wave that partially capsized us even though I saw it coming, felt it, and fought it.

That wave struck at about 4:00 P.M. By the time I had pumped *Chidiock* out, it was 4:30; I decided enough was enough and remained hove to. Our efforts to get offshore had been somewhat successful. Jazīrat Zuqar was southeast of us. The wind had backed again to the south. According to the compass, we were drifting backwards on course 350°. Tonight's threat would be shipping.

After forcing down another dinner of uncooked freeze-dried food, I settled in to wait out the miserable night. I was wet, and colder than I had been at sea for several years. I recalled hearing over the radio a week or so earlier of 50° temperatures in the Persian Gulf. Somehow I had never thought of cold as being a problem in the Red Sea, although I have lived close enough to deserts to know that they cool off at night. My arms and shoulders and neck were stiff from steering all afternoon. It was, of course, far too wet to take out the radio. I watched the running lights of the ships a few miles away and thought of an old sailor's poem:

> Western wind, when wilt thou blow,
> That the small rain down can rain?
> Oh, that my love were in my arms
> And I in my bed again.

I didn't want a west wind, but the love and bed would have been most welcome.

So that I would be able to react quickly, I slept sitting up. For several hours we seemed to be paralleling the shipping route. At 2:00 A.M. a sound awoke me. I opened my eyes and saw what I at first mistook for a row of street lamps a few feet away. Perhaps I was just so tired that panic could not touch me. Calmly I thought, Those can't be street lamps. But then, what were they? Not even when I realized that they were the interior lights of a ship did I become upset. Her hull was a sheer wall looming less then ten yards away. I was so close that I could not see the bow, but the knowledge that it would have hit us before I had awakened only added to my fatalistic detachment. Close, but no cigar, as a friend used to say. I watched with interest as the stern passed us and the ship plowed on into the night. And then I closed my eyes and went promptly back to sleep.

The year 1982 was a tough one for the reputation of pilot charts of the Red Sea. I fully expected to wake up and find the gale gone. After all, this was March 1 and we were beyond 15° north. But it was not to be. The wind was still blowing at between forty and fifty knots; the waves were still on the average more than ten feet high. The only difference was that now they were smashing into a group of rocks called Jazā 'ir az Zubayr, to the east of us, instead of into islands to the west as they had the day before.

These rocks gave me some interesting information. One of them was shown on the chart to be one hundred feet high. The spray from the waves reached two-thirds of the way up that rock. And it took us just forty-six minutes to drift stern first the two miles that separated two other rocks, giving us a speed of better than two and a half knots. In

Hove to, storm in the Red Sea.

fact, we were averaging closer to three knots, covering about seventy miles a day.

If we had been unlucky to be caught by this gale, we had been lucky to be ten yards west of the ship last night, and lucky again to drift past these rocks at a distance of a few hundred yards without having to try to sail.

The Jazā'ir az Zubayr rocks were the last obstacles for more than sixty miles. The shipping had disappeared, presumably somewhere to the west of us. All morning we remained hove to, speeding north backwards. The gale was bad, to be sure, but I found myself thinking that I was much more tired than I ought to be. Presumably I had not recovered as well as I had hoped from the inevitable deterioration that occurred during the long passage across the Indian Ocean.

At 2:00 P.M. the first of the giant waves capsized us. Then *Chidiock*, now lying on her beam, surfed stern first down the second wave. The moment was unbelievable. I clung to the starboard gunwale as though hanging onto the side of a cliff and watched in awe as the ocean creamed through the submerged port half of the cockpit and clutched at my feet. Again, if we had been unlucky to be caught by those waves, we were lucky that *Chidiock* did not dip her masts into the water, for they would surely have been torn away.

When the wave finally released us, tossing us aside like a toy with which it had become bored, *Chidiock* dropped back onto her bottom. It took a few minutes for me to realize that, incredibly, we were all right. Only the flotation cushions, one bucket, and a chart had been lost. The bucket bobbed nearby. The cushions, one bright red, the other bright yellow, remained visible on distant crests until long after I had bailed and pumped the cockpit dry.

That night the wind finally began to ease, but one more wave partially capsized us. I found myself swimming in the cockpit, grabbed a bucket, and emptied the boat without ever fully waking up.

Tuesday dawn found us hove to against a south wind. Tuesday dusk found us hove to against a north wind. And in between I discovered that we had not escaped our backwards capsize unscathed. When I set sail on *Chidiock* about noon, we accidentally jibed. This time I immediately assumed that something was wrong with the rudder. Neutral helm was achieved with the tiller 15 degrees to starboard of the centerline. I tried to remove the rudder, but soon realized that I would not be able do so so except by sawing through the shaft with a hack saw This seemed excessive. We could continue with the rudder as it was, although in its new position the tiller intruded rudely into my limited living space and I had to readjust the shock cords and jib sheets for self-steering.

I watched myself coming unraveled. I struggled against it, but the frustration was too great. The north wind died Tuesday night, and in Phase 4 we were becalmed for seven days. For the first time ever at sea I felt I might really be going insane.

Hours would pass, sometimes even a full day, during which I would remain outwardly as calm as the wind, but then suddenly I could not take any more and would explode with rage, scream curses at the sky, smash my hand into the gunwale or into my leg, throw something, rant, rave. Then, although I could take no more, I would sit back and take more, for I had no choice. I would search for wind that did not come, gaze at sails that would not fill, stare at a glassy sea without a ripple. There was nowhere I could go. Nothing I could do. I felt completely helpless.

Chidiock was as steady and dry at night as though she were in a secure anchorage, but I did not sleep well and always felt tired. I noted in my log that I was talking aloud to myself, something I have always taken prided in not doing. I was having trouble with simple calculations. Once, I made out the sum of 14 and 24 to be 48, and it then took me an hour to find the error. And my memory was faulty. I could not remember what book I had been reading the day before. Or the name of the boat we had sailed on to New Zealand. Or where I had stowed various things. Again I did not know the exact causes of these difficulties: cumulative stress? dietary deficiency? exhaustion? The causes did not really matter, for I could not do anything about them. Part of me—and that disassociation of myself into two parts was another symptom—watched the process and knew that at sea aboard a boat as small as *Chidiock* it was irreversible.

Only a few noteworthy events marked those seven days: getting a Radio Jerusalem broadcast that reported a nighttime temperature of 48° at the port of Eilat; swimming over the side and discovering that during the capsize not only the rudder shaft had been bent but also the centerboard, a piece of solid 3/8-inch steel; hearing the rumble of a reef, like the sound of a distant train, one night in an area where no reefs showed on the chart; and on another night sailing through a sea thick with millions of jellyfish. The jellyfish were so numerous that at first I thought they were clumps of seaweed or another oil slick. I turned the flashlight on them. The light made them accelerate their graceful undulations. Some were big, fully formed; some were tiny. I watched them intermittently for several hours. In the morning they were gone.

During those terrible seven days, we covered 175 miles, bettering our previous record for futility, set in Malacca Strait, by more than a hundred miles. Since leaving Aden we had made good a total of 533 miles, about half of this distance backwards while hove to.

Phase 5 of the passage began on Tuesday, March 9, when some steady wind at last filled in from the north-northwest. Port Sudan lay 200 reef-strewn miles northwest of us. To be safe, we should have gone on port tack to the northeast for sixty miles and then kept the lights on two atolls, one called charmingly the Hindi Guider, to port. But I was long past caring about being completely safe. On starboard tack we could almost sail the rhumb line to Port Sudan, although we would be in among the reefs. I did not hesitate to remain on starboard tack.

Tuesday afternoon I saw several small sand islands. I rejected the idea of anchoring for the night near them. *Chidiock* was making good progress; there would be some moonlight; and the chart showed enough gaps between reefs so that we stood good odds of not hitting anything. I don't know that I would have made the same decision if I had been rested and in good health, but I was desperate to reach port. On top of everything else, my left ankle had become infected.

Wednesday morning found *Chidiock* wending her way blindly between two reefs, proving that my confidence that I would see them in the moonlight had been misplaced. Wednesday afternoon my left leg became increasingly painful, inflamed, and swollen; the wind increased to twenty-five knots; and *Chidiock* sailed farther into a potential trap.

According to the chart, reefs lay all around us. They were not all connected, but few had lights. I estimated that we were about fifteen miles off the coast of Sudan, near the ancient port of Suakin. Since we would drift if we hove to, the safest plan might be to remain where we were by sailing back and forth all night, and even that plan was not without risk, because of leeway. If we continued onward, we would eventually come upon one of the reefs, and I doubted that at night in those choppy, breaking seas, I would see it in time.

But we could sail on until darkness, and at 4:00 P.M. I saw masts ahead. From a distance, they appeared to be on a large sailing vessel wrecked high on a reef; but as *Chidiock* bashed her way nearer, the large ship turned into four dhows, anchored in the lee of a small arc of coral. With great relief at stumbling onto this unexpected refuge, I steered toward them, anchoring in smooth green water at sunset.

The black-hulled dhows were anchored together fifty yards from me. All seemed to have been there for some time. Huge sun awnings covered them. A couple of children peeked out at me from beneath one of the awnings, but did not respond when I waved. I left at first light the next morning and did not see anyone else. I thought the boats probably belonged to divers or fishermen, but in Port Sudan I was told that it was much more likely they belonged to smugglers who were running whiskey, electronic equipment, or even goats across to Saudi Arabia.

After a quick meal that Wednesday night, in the lee of the reef, I lay down and tried to sleep. Probably because I was running a fever, sleep did not come. For much of the night I lay shivering uncontrollably beneath the tarp.

I do not know which of two reefs, Burns Reef or Shā'ab Tawil, I spent that night behind. Port Sudan lay only forty miles north-northwest of both. In other circumstances I would have expected to reach port the next day, but those forty miles would be directly to windward in what on Thursday again became storm conditions. Good seamanship called for remaining at anchor and waiting for a break in the weather. But good seamanship is not always the decisive consideration. My small supply of antibiotics had been ruined in capsizes. Angry red tendrils were spreading rapidly up my leg.

The seas were vicious—toppling, breaking unpredictably, with white horses everywhere. After an hour I almost decided to turn back, but the dhows and reef had long since disappeared and there was a good chance I would not be able to find them again, so we smashed on. I found myself feverishly thinking that I did not care if I ran *Chidiock* aground; but at the same time I knew that made no sense, for I was not capable of walking across the desert to Port Sudan. Every time a wave doused my infected leg the pain was excruciating.

At noon, almost simultaneously, the water ahead of us changed from black to turquoise and a wave reared up and broke behind us. Instantly I tacked and headed back into safe water. We had just found Towertit Reef.

All afternoon we clawed up the windward side of that reef, which curves the last twenty miles to Port Sudan. *Chidiock* did not have enough power under jib and mizzen to force her way through the

The Red Sea Backwards 167

waves, so I had to reset the reefed main and play the mainsheet continuously by hand. I estimated the wind to be about twenty-five knots, but the waves were up to ten feet high. I later learned that two other yachts, one thirty feet and the other forty-two feet long, were caught by this same wind as they left Port Sudan for Suez. Both suffered broken rigging and torn sails and limped back to the harbor for repairs.

Sunset brought another dhow at anchor behind a patch of coral. Darkness fell when I was a hundred yards from her. Abruptly I could see neither dhow nor reef and did not dare risk sailing closer. With great reluctance and greater sadness, I turned *Chidiock* back into deep water for another shivering and sleepless night.

By dawn my leg was filled with pus and throbbing pain, but I forgot about it for a moment when in the distance I saw a beautiful vision, the top of a grain silo, the tallest building in Port Sudan. We were far enough north so that we were able to sail toward the silo on a close reach.

At 11:00 A.M. *Chidiock*'s anchor splashed down in the crowded yacht anchorage. It was not a moment too soon. I was in the worst shape I have ever been at the end of a passage. A week later my weight was still only 133 pounds, not much for my height of six feet one inch. I was exhausted physically and mentally. The infection in my leg was blood poisoning. I do not know that I could have lasted another day.

Between leaving Singapore on January 5, 1982, and arriving in Port Sudan on March 12, 1982, I sailed more than 4,700 miles in sixty-one days with less than four days' rest in port. The voyage would have been easier if the worst sailing had come at the beginning rather than the end, but it did not. Once again I experienced at first hand the phenomenon that one mile to windward is often harder on boat and crew than tens or even hundreds of miles off the wind.

The contrast between the two passages—from Singapore to Aden and from Aden to Port Sudan—led me to an inescapable conclusion about records. Records can be useful in indicating the edges of human experience, but they are only indicators and are often misleading. They are of interest, particularly to those who do not want to make the effort to explore a subject deeply, because they are easy to compare. But statistics say absolutely nothing about the essence of an experience. My passage of 4,058 miles in forty-seven days in an open boat from Singapore to Aden is a world record and sounds more impressive than my passage of 700 miles in fourteen days from Aden to Port Sudan. Yet the latter was incomparably the more difficult, dangerous, and testing. The truths of the sea, like the truths of the soul, cannot be reduced to numbers.

15

Going Home

Poste Restante in Port Sudan is a haphazard pile of mail thrown carelessly on the corner of a table. Anyone can thumb through it. When I thumbed through it on the morning after my arrival, I did not really expect to find anything addressed to myself, but buried deep in the pile were a telegram and a letter from Suzanne.

I found the telegram first. My chest tightened. Without opening it, I knew what it must say.

> GRANDMOTHER DIED MARCH 5. SUZANNE

I was too late.

Standing in that old colonial building thousands of miles from California, I thought of my grandmother. We were very different in many ways. I did not share her religious views. She had never traveled outside the United States and usually had only a vague idea of where I was and even less of an idea of why I lived as I did. I could not recall her ever reading a book, even mine. And she may unintentionally have destroyed my father, who was her son, by giving him an unrealistic image of himself that he could not sustain in what is called the real world. But she was a kind woman, a woman of exceptional strength and independence and vitality. Blood relationships were important to her, and I was all she had left. I wished that I could have seen her before she died, that she could have had a final opportunity to say whatever she wanted to say to me; but at the moment of her death I had been

Harbor scene, Port Sudan.

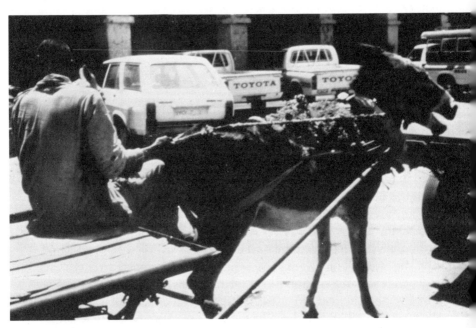

Assorted vehicles, Port Sudan.

Street scene, Port Sudan.

Vegetable merchant, Port Sudan.

becalmed in the Red Sea. In the coming weeks I would miss her even more than I expected.

The letter from Suzanne had been written a few days before my grandmother died. It described how she seemed to be recovering after her surgery and might be able to leave the hospital, although she would require nursing care at home.

"Will you fly back from Suez?" Suzanne wrote. "I need you to hold me in your arms. I have never loved you more than I do now. You are so special."

I stood there surrounded by strangers in that distant land and wanted to cry.

Port Sudan is many things, a number of them probably good, but I saw it only through a miasma of fever, pain, exhaustion, and depression.

Wild camels amble through the few potholed streets, stopping traffic during the day, and flit eerily, like wraiths, from shadow to shadow during the night. Donkey carts are as common as motorized vehicles. Goats chew on garbage and bushes. Blackbirds are everywhere, even perching on the camels and goats. Sun. Sand. White buildings shimmering in the heat. Women in colorful djellabas come down to the harbor and stand gossiping, neck-deep in the water, for hours. A tall people, sometimes beautiful, a blend of black and Arab Africa. The brilliant colors of the open market: bright orange tomatoes, yellow grapefruit, green limes, bloody fly-blown meat, bananas. Vivid blue sky. Sand. Dust. The contrast of black skin and white garments, white eyes, white teeth. Rag-clad members of a sect of desert dwellers who never wash their bodies or cut their hair. Small children standing in the sun all day to sell a few matches or pieces of chewing gum. Men in uniforms, with weapons ready, in front of most government buildings.

But one thing Port Sudan is not is in communication with the rest of the world. You cannot telephone from Port Sudan. You cannot send a telegram and expect it to be transmitted in less than five days. At the suggestion of other sailors I went, in one of the old rowboats that serve as ferries, across the harbor to the ships at the main docks and tried to find someone who would would let me use a ship's radio to telephone California, but I had no success.

A few hours after receiving the telegram and Suzanne's letter, I sprawled beneath *Chidiock*'s tent, roasting hot at midday, and decided to go home.

There were many reasons. The necessity of settling my grandmother's estate was decisive. Had money not been there from that I could not have afforded the trip home. But equally important was the realization that I would be unable to continue the voyage without a period of recuperation and that *Chidiock Tichborne* in Port Sudan was not a good place to recuperate. The food available in Port Sudan is very basic, more suitable for cooking over camel-dung fires than aboard an open boat. There were problems in getting fresh water. I had been able to locate a doctor, who prescribed antibiotics and told me to keep off my leg as much as possible, but I wanted to be closer to medical treatment. And, of course, I wanted to see Suzanne. Life at sea in an open boat is all hard-edged and unyielding. I longed for her gentleness and passion. If I did not go back now, we would have to spend several more months apart. If I did go back, I could rest, take the burden of my grandmother's affairs off Suzanne, and have a good diet and good medical care before I returned in May or June to battle what should be the harder half of the Red Sea—although I shuddered to think of a passage harder than the one we had already experienced. At least, by then the nights would not be so cold.

There are no problems when you arrive in Port Sudan by yacht. You do not need a visa. You can stay pretty much as long as you wish. Everyone is friendly. There *are* problems when you want to leave your yacht there. Brian Mander, one of those generous expatriate Englishmen who have befriended me in many parts of the world, agreed to keep an eye on *Chidiock* if I would anchor her off his office at the British Fisheries Project. But I still had to obtain official permission to leave.

My leg was responding to the antibiotics, but was not helped by my limping from office to office morning after morning to get various papers stamped and signed. One morning I was told to go to the Security office. I was directed to a one-story building surrounded by a fence. The guard at the gate would not let me in. He did not speak English, but directed me to the huge old colonnaded structure that houses the provincial headquarters. There I was sent to a tiny room into which twelve desks had been jammed. Behind one of these desks sat one forlorn soul. I asked him if he had my passport, which had allegedly been sent there by the police, whose approval I also had to obtain. He pointed at one of the empty desks, said, "That man," and resumed shuffling papers.

After ten minutes, various people began filing back in and sitting at various desks and shuffling various papers. But not "that man."

After a half hour, I asked, "Where is 'that man'?"

The man at the next desk shrugged, "At breakfast."

After an hour and a half, "that man" ambled in. When he was comfortably settled behind his desk, I explained what I wanted.

"Oh no," he exclaimed. "This is not the right office."

He led me out to the foyer and pointed at the one-story building from which the guard had turned me away two hours earlier. "You must go over there."

In better times, in better health, I would have accepted this episode as part of the price of the voyage, an example of petty-bureaucratic business as usual, but at that moment I hated him and would gladly have strangled each and every official in Sudan with my bare hands.

That evening I related this experience to a sailor on another yacht. He had a story of his own.

"When I sailed in," he said, "I noticed that one of the lights on Wingate Reef was not working, so I went to the Harbor Master's office to inform them about it. The man there said, 'No. That cannot be.' I said, 'But it is. I just saw it.' He insisted, 'No. If the light were out, someone would have reported it.'"

After three days of trudging about Port Sudan, I finally had all the necessary stamps in my passport; *Chidiock* was safely anchored in eighteen inches of water at the head of the harbor, and everything movable was stored in Brian's apartment; I was ready to catch the evening flight to Khartoum. My leg was still infected. I had developed diarrhea. I still had a fever. But my spirits were soaring. In a few days I would be with Suzanne.

Airplanes and hotel rooms and airplanes. Port Sudan to Khartoum to Athens to Amsterdam to Los Angeles to San Diego. A thousand miles of desert broken by not a single cloud or speck of green; snow on the mountains of Crete; the Parthenon in sunshine; clouds and rain over Europe; pasty-white winter faces in Amsterdam; ice-covered Greenland; patchwork farmland in Canada and the western United States; a clear, smog-free late afternoon in Los Angeles; the familiar lights of San Diego at night.

I could have telephoned from Amsterdam, but thought that since I would arrive in only one more day, I would surprise her. I did call from Los Angeles in the early evening, but there was no answer.

At 9:30 P.M. on Friday, March 19, just one week after I had sailed into Port Sudan, I took a cab from San Diego's Lindbergh Field to what was now our house in Mission Beach. It was odd not to think of the house as my grandmother's. A light was on in the living room, but no one was home.

Exhausted but restless, I thumbed through the mail, took a shower, turned on the television, turned off the television. Finally I heard the back gate open and someone walked across the patio. A key turned in the lock, and I called, "Suzanne?" Dazed, she came into the living room. Her purse fell from her hand. She leaned against the coffee table to keep from falling herself. "What are you doing here?" she gasped. I took her into my arms. She was stiff and wooden. The harbor I had so longed for and so needed was closed to me.

16

A Shipwreck of the Spirit

On May 18, 1982, one day short of two months from the time I had arrived back in San Diego, I stood in the Western Airlines check-in line. There was no one around whom I knew. I saw no friends. No well-wishers. No reporters. No television crews. No Suzanne. I felt sick. I was a hollowness filled with pain. That made no sense, but then nothing made sense any more. On Sunday afternoon, March 21, two days after our reunion, we had had a violent quarrel, and Suzanne had left, and she had never come back.

The line moved forward. I wanted to scream, but remained silent. My heart raced. It seemed to shake my entire body. The floor, the ticket counter, the walls, the terminal building itself, seemed to throb to its pounding. But I remained standing in place. These past weeks had been the worst of my life. I still could not understand. I still could not believe. It was as though I had sailed onto an uncharted reef a thousand miles from the nearest land. How could she write a letter, just two weeks before I saw her, saying she had never loved me more, and then leave? It simply was not possible. But it had happened. The pain was undeniable.

The house was full of gas.

For the first few days I had thought that she was staying with a girl friend, but then I learned that when she had left on Sunday afternoon, she had gone directly to another man. It is one of the oldest of

A Shipwreck of the Spirit   177

sea stories. To ward off suitors while she awaited the return of Ulysses, Penelope continued to weave her tapestry by day and unravel it by night for ten years. Suzanne and I had been apart for less than three months. Times change and so does character, not always for the better.

Had I not been so exhausted, I might have handled the disaster better. The ocean and I had taken me to the edge; Suzanne pushed me over. That statement is merely descriptive. It does not deny my responsibility for my own acts. When I learned that she was with another man, I was devastated. I had sailed toward her for too many miles. My body and my mind had no reserves of strength.

I made my plans two days in advance, sitting in the house I had never had a chance to think of as ours, but not until 5:30 P.M.—when I knew that she must already have left the dental office where she was working and driven past the house, without stopping, to go to him—did I blow out the pilot lights on the heater and the stove and turn up the gas all the way.

I sat in an easy chair in front of the flickering television. It was the night of the NCAA basketball finals and the Academy Awards. The contents of the picture did not reach me. I just watched the flickering.

Neatly arranged on the dining-room table were a will, leaving what I had to my friends, not Suzanne; my poems, which I had that afternoon given the title *Poems of a Lone Voyage;* three keys to safe-deposit boxes; an angry note to Suzanne; a snifter of brandy sitting on a piece of paper on which I had foolishly written, "For the woman I never met"; and a suicide note:

> The sea cannot love, but it does not betray.
> The sea could not kill me; the land and women did.
>
> To those who believed in me, I am sorry that finally the pain was too great.
>
> 3-29-82
>
> *[signature]*

I had made my preparations while sober, taping over the cracks around doors and windows to make the room more airtight; but after four hours of sipping Courvoisier and breathing gas, I was drunk and nearly unconscious. I fell from the chair onto the floor. I began to retch. Layer by layer had been stripped from me. Only the last flicker of life, and what was most fundamental, were left. The desire to die is learned; the will to live, inherent. That will, which has kept me alive at sea, fought not to go under. It forced me to crawl across the dark living room, to fumble blindly with the locks on the door. Several times I fell vomiting back to the floor from a half-sitting position, as I reached for the door chain. Somehow I must have opened it. I lay sprawled, my head and shoulders across the doorsill. Then I was in the Mission Bay Hospital emergency room.

That attempt had several sequelae.

One was that I had medical bills of $646. As I told a friend, with that amount I could have paid for some very high class female companionship, which probably would have been more therapeutic.

Another was my acceptance that I should not die that way, although I continued to believe that suicide can be a rational act. We try to apply reason and will to all other parts of our lives. Only death is left purely to time and chance.

And a third was that despite my decision to go back to sea, my attention was ineluctably drawn to advertisements for guns. One evening I studied an ad in the newspaper for shotguns. Most cost several hundred dollars, but I saw a single-shot model for $49.50. That would do nicely, I thought. After all, I could hardly miss. Then I recalled that I had just closed out a bank account and had more than a thousand dollars in cash. Why, I asked myself, if you are serious about this, are you trying to save money?

With unspeakable sadness I packed some of Suzanne's clothing for her. There was the gold chain we had bought in Tahiti. There a dress from Fiji. The memories poured out. They were so good, so happy, so alive. The best years of her life, she had said time and time again. There was something from Australia. Bali. Singapore. Hong Kong. Macao. We had shared the world. How could she be gone?

Some things that should have been good only made the suffering worse.

April 13 was the first anniversary of our remarriage in Australia. I later learned that like me, she had sat alone that day and looked at photographs of us signing the register in the Cairns courthouse and cried.

The first copy of the first book about this voyage was mailed to me.

A Shipwreck of the Spirit 179

It should have made me happy and proud, but it tore me apart because it was so full of Suzanne. It was even dedicated to her. She cried when I gave it to her.

We spoke on the telephone while she was at work, and we saw one another a few times during her lunch breaks.
She said:
I come so close to coming back.
I am burned out on the voyage.
I love you.
I am proud to have been part of the voyage.
I like going to work every day.
I hate my job.
I want to go back to New Zealand to see my children.
I want us to build a nest.
I will think during the weekend and call you on Sunday. Probably I'll go home with you on Monday after work.
Too much has happened.
The man I am living with is not important and does not matter. [I thought she said this with too much alacrity.]
I can't come back yet.
The magic has gone. [A vestige of my sense of humor caused me to wonder if we would now break for a commercial.]
She said seriously, "All women are bitches."
I asked, "Including you?"
"Including me."
I asked, "Why did you take the cassette of the Sibelius Violin Concerto when you left? You never would have heard of Sibelius but for me."
She replied defiantly, "That's why I want it."
She said, "———— and I went to see *Chariots of Fire* [a movie Suzanne and I had seen together in December] and I spent all the time thinking of you."
But no matter what she said, she did not come back. From the terrible moment she left, I never saw her again except for a few scattered hours. I had to try to save our love by talking to her on street corners and against the demands of her job.

I stood at my grandmother's grave. The grass was wet around the tombstone. I wondered how much her death had affected Suzanne.

Hazel Florence Widen
November 18, 1895–March 5, 1982

In my mind I added:

Suzanne Mary Chiles
March 21, 1976 [the day I met her in Auckland]–March 21, 1982

I was constantly sick to my stomach. Night after night I lay sleepless. I jumped at each ring of the telephone, each car-door opening, each footstep on the sidewalk—thinking, hoping, it was Suzanne.

I had been through the end of love before, but never had it been like this. Always before I had known that the relationship was deteriorating. But Suzanne and I had been happy. I was not just imagining that. None of the people who knew us could believe it had happened any more than I. She had written to a friend, "Long may the happiness last." Everyone thought that Suzanne had been troubled by my grandmother's death—she had by all accounts been wonderful to my grandmother in her last days—and would in time become herself again. But she did not.

When a few weeks had passed without my trying to kill myself again, a friend said, "You have conquered it."

I snapped, "I've conquered nothing. I just lucked out. Or unlucked out, depending on how you see it. All I've done is decide to go back and let the sea kill me or cure me."

Another friend said, "You are not lonely at sea, but lonely in a city full of people."

My friends were tolerant of my temper, for again I snapped, saying, "I have often been lonely at sea." But she was right. At sea I have never been even remotely so lonely as during those endless nights when I lay alone on fresh sheets in a double bed and knew that Suzanne was only a few miles away beside another man.

Often the pain was immobilizing. It was worst in the morning of a pleasant day, when I would just lie there, knowing I had nothing to look forward to that day, no one to share my life with. And it was also bad in the late afternoon, when I would fix myself a vodka and tonic and sit down to watch a news broadcast I did not care about and know that she was driving right by my door on her way to someone else.

Everything reminded me of her. I tried to concentrate on the bad, but I could not forget the good. Children flying kites on Mission Beach

A *Shipwreck of the Spirit* 181

became children flying kites in Bali. A novel set in Australia. A girl who had known mutual friends in Fiji.

I could not accept the fact that Suzanne and I would never walk along a New Zealand country road together again, that we would never make love in the coolness of first light aboard *Chidiock Tichborne*, that she would never wave as I left port or rush into my arms as I entered. It simply was not possible. How could we have been so happy for the past year, obviously happy to one another and to everyone who knew us, increasingly happy since we had remarried in Australia, as she had wanted to remarry for three years? And for the thousandth time, how could I receive that letter, saying she had never loved me more, one week and find her gone the next? How could there be an unopened valentine waiting for me in Djibouti? How could she have told me over the telephone in Aden how much she missed and loved me? How could she say "I come so close to coming back" and never give us a chance to share more than a few harried minutes together? How could I have made the greatest open-boat passage of all time to be with her, only to have her vanish two days after my return?

I reached the head of the line. The girl smiled brightly, took my ticket, checked my luggage, gave me a boarding pass.

I walked into the boarding lounge.

Time did not reduce the pain, although it changed its shape. I did not cry so much. The depression was not so often immobilizing. I was able to start writing. But that was a mixed blessing, for I was writing about sailing toward Suzanne.

I knew I was living too far inside myself. Writing and sailing alone are naturally solitary activities, but when I come ashore I like to be around people, and for six years there had been Suzanne. Because I am alone so much, I had depended so much upon that one relationship, upon the certainty that no matter what the land or the sea did to me, I could count upon her love. I had wanted Suzanne to be my last woman. Now I could not force myself to reach out to others. I felt as though I were trapped at the bottom of a well, gazing up at sunlight far, unreachably far, above me.

Sometimes I looked at a photograph of my father taken when he was five years old. It hung in what had been my grandmother's bedroom. He is wearing a sailor suit, with short pants. When he was in his late thirties, he killed himself.

Sometimes I stood at the back door, looking out at the fig tree and the bougainvillea that dominated my tiny backyard. The fig tree was full of ripe fruit and small birds. The bougainvillea was a cascade of blood-red flowers, covering the garage, spilling over into the alleyway, reaching for the sky. Both were extravagant profusions of blind life.

Sometimes I sat on the beach, looking out at the sea, watching the waves. But often a jogger passed who reminded me of the man Suzanne was living with. She said he was fifty-four years old. I also knew that he was short and permed his hair.

I could not sleep.

As I sat waiting for the boarding gate to open, I could recall only one good night's sleep since the beginning of the year, and that had occurred during the weekend when Suzanne had said she would probably come back the following Monday. I would fall asleep early, at 9:00 or 10:00 P.M. and wake up at midnight, read until 3:00 or 4:00 A.M., then sleep for another hour or two. Or I would go to sleep at 11:00 or midnight and wake up permanently at 3:00 or 4:00. The sea had given me the habit of sleeping lightly, but now the instant I came awake I thought of Suzanne and that thought would keep me awake. I could not control my sleep, but I preferred the nights when I woke up at 3:00 or 4:00, because then I could get up and get dressed and start writing. Often I had a full day's work done by dawn; and with nothing else to do, I would complete a second and third day's work later in the day.

I searched back through my manuscripts for the inventory I had made on my fortieth birthday. Still left were the voyages, books, poems, experience of the world and sea, *Chidiock Tichborne,* pride (tarnished), scars (gaping), Cape Horn, and friends (better even than before). My paintings, which I had found rotting in the garage, and Suzanne were gone. To the question I had asked, Is it enough? I no longer knew the answer. But I supposed it had to be.

Suzanne had taken copies of some of my poems with her. She and I reread "Soft Night," and both of us remarked how not a single word had to be changed. I had not realized until I reread it that exactly ten years to the month had passed since I had lost Mary. I knew that if I fell in love again, I would be very suspicious of March 1992. I retitled the poem, giving Suzanne equal billing.

And I wrote a last poem to her, one that, as I waited for the first of the five airplanes that would take me back to Sudan, she had never seen:

A Shipwreck of the Spirit 183

death is all women
I caress her smooth flanks
there are no other

Unfair, but my feeling at the time.

I remembered what I had written about Suzanne less than a year earlier as I sailed to Bali: "Life on *Chidiock* is often a struggle to impose purpose in a medium of chaotic change, although it might not seem so on this smooth night, and my feelings for Suzanne are one of the few constants in that chaos. She has shared the limitations of an open boat as a home, reduced her worldly goods to a single duffel bag, learned to cook good meals on a camp stove, and endured a succession of potentially final farewells. I think it was Winston Churchill who said that his wife was the sheet anchor of his life. That is what Suzanne has become for me."

Despite the mounting evidence, I could not make myself believe that I had chosen the wrong woman to anchor my life.

I was helped by my friends; by exercise—at one point I was doing three hundred push-ups and sit-ups a day in sets of between twenty and sixty; by the act of writing, which kept me occupied, although full of Suzanne, and was perhaps partially cathartic; by my decision to initiate arrangements to go back to Sudan and let chance and the wall of wind across the Red Sea decide my fate; and by the music from *Chariots of Fire*. For some reason this music partially deadened the pain, made the unbearable barely bearable. I played the cassette endlessly. Ten times. Twenty. Countless times day and night. While I wrote or ate or sat or read. I even carried the cassette player to bed with me and played it against the darkness.

My cherished freedom became a burden. There were limits to how much I could write in a day of twenty waking hours. If I had been planning to stay in San Diego, I would have started looking for a job, not to earn money, but to fill time. Ironically, if I could sell my grandmother's house, I would not have to worry about money for a while. I thought of how primitive life was aboard *Chidiock*, of how I had often told my closest friends that I worried more about money than about the dangers of the sea. Now I would have a little money. I had beds. Clean sheets. Hot showers. A refrigerator. Cold drinks. A car. All the necessities. All the comforts. And I was desolate.

The boarding gate opened. The other passengers and I started to shuffle forward. I thought of the letter I had written to Suzanne two weeks earlier:

Suzanne,

I want you to have this manuscript.

I suppose it has become easier for you not to think about me or see me or share our lives. Probably you will not care, but this is what it has been like for me.

I expect that you are happy, or at least will be content with what —— —— can give you for a while.

I wonder if you ever wonder if you have made a mistake.

After the last two months, I have come to doubt that you are the best woman I've loved; but there is no doubt that losing you has been the most terrible and painful experience of my life.

I am not certain if I am going back to the Red Sea to die. Sometimes I think I will sail out into the middle and then slip away from *Chidiock* and swim until I can swim no longer. I wish it were the open ocean instead of a landlocked sea. And I know that I ought to die struggling, overwhelmed by forces beyond my control. Perhaps that is what is happening, though the forces are not as visible as waves and reefs.

If I live, I know there will be more voyages, more books, more poems, and, hopefully, another woman to love and be loved by; but I have done enough. I have sailed and written truly. Whatever happens, death for me now would not be a tragedy; it might be fulfillment.

W

Suzanne had not yet seen that letter. A few days after I wrote it, I learned that she had flown with the man she was living with—the man who she had constantly insisted "is not important and does not matter," but who did have money—to New Zealand for a month. I learned this indirectly. The last words I had heard from her were "Even if I don't come back, I hope we can be friends," but she had kept her plans from me and had not called to say good-bye.

Perhaps that callousness helped. The Suzanne I loved could never have treated me that way. People did change, I knew—but not completely, overnight. I tried to convince myself that she was unworthy of my love. Probably I was right. But it made no difference.

I took a final look at San Diego from the ground. My home port had become a crucible of pain. Had I really landed at that airport, exhausted but happy, only two months earlier?

As I slowly climbed the boarding ramp, a giant hand was tearing out my guts. I hoped that distance would do what time had not. I knew that what I needed was love, not sailing, but love requires another person. I could confront the sea alone. I would try not to let this betrayal destroy me. I no longer thought that I would swim away from *Chidiock Tichborne*. I would struggle on. I did not know why. It is just what I would try to do.

I tried to say *Resurgam*, but the word would not come.

17

The Shipwreck That Wasn't

May 22, Saturday
Zurich
Dear Ralph and Martha,

I have an hour to kill at the airport. I am going to see a bit of Europe today. The plane goes to Khartoum via Geneva and Athens.

Switzerland has been interesting, though sad. I never before realized how habitually I look in store windows at women's clothes and jewelry to see if something would look good on Suzanne. Also, there seem to be a lot of couples walking around arm in arm, or sitting, holding hands, in sidewalk cafes.

Switzerland is green, misty, orderly, and expensive. During my two-day layover, I have played tourist, visiting museums, riding a cable car up a mountain near Lucerne, and walking beside lakes. A few boats were out sailing. I've never sailed on a lake; one more day and I would probably have rented a boat myself.

The Swiss are physically short. I tower over crowds here as I did in Asia but usually don't in Western countries. A high proportion of Swiss walk using canes. And, if the museums are a true indication, the Swiss have no soul. Efficient bankers and railwaymen do not make great artists.

I stayed at a small hotel near the lake with a good restaurant, featuring Chinese and Indian food as well as continental. One night veal *cordon bleu*, the next a fine chicken curry.

My body has overcome the jet lag and I slept pretty well for me last night. Very odd to be going back through Europe two months later and so much so changed. In the desert tomorrow night and with *Chidiock* the day after. Allah and Sudan Airways willing.

Sincerely,

Will

Port Sudan
May 24, Monday
Dear Ralph and Martha,

I'll probably write this over several days. Two years ago today, I came ashore on Emae Island.

I sailed *Chidiock* this morning, quite slowly, taking almost two hours to move her from the end of the harbor to the yacht anchorage, a distance of only a mile. A combination of a dirty bottom, adverse current, and light wind. *Chidiock* was in good condition, though covered several inches deep in sand, a problem we didn't encounter during the years in the tropics.

I am fortunate to be staying ashore in the apartment of Brian Mander, who watched *C.T.* for me, and thus have access to a shower, air conditioning and iced drinks. Summer in Port Sudan would be nearly intolerable aboard *Chidiock*. The temperature goes above 110° each day.

I don't have much to do in the way of preparation for the passage to Suez. I scrubbed *C.T.*'s interior today and will do the hull tomorrow. The sails need some stitching. Then buy a few provisions, stow, take on water, pay my fees, and leave. Tentatively I'll go Thursday or Friday.

Being here has made me realize just how ill and exhausted I was two months ago. Everything seems sharper, clearer, because now I'm not seeing it through a feverish haze.

Being here has also made me miss Suzanne more. Sailing *Chidiock* brought back too many memories of her. Even rowing the dinghy. I looked at the stern, where she sat as we went ashore in so many harbors, and thought that she would never sit there again. I'm sure you must be tired of this. I certainly am. I wish the pain and sadness would end. I wish I could forget about her.

A deliberate change of subject. In going over the local chart with Brian, I've learned about a number of anchorages in the first hundred miles north and will initially try to stay inside the reef. From then on,

I'll do whatever works. Partially it will depend on my rate of progress. I could anchor almost every ten miles, but that would mean six days to make good one degree of latitude and I have ten degrees to go. Even though there's no one waiting for me, I don't think I want to spend two months getting to Suez.

Wednesday, May 26

I'll mail this tomorrow, but probably won't leave until Saturday. Brian, my host, is a fisheries expert and had to go out on a boat for a few days and won't be back until at least tomorrow; and I can't leave on Friday, Muslim Sabbath, which closes everything here, although it did not in Aden. In any event, it is hard to tear myself away from the air conditioner.

I spent two hours yesterday morning stitching the leech of the jib. I also scrubbed the hull and chipped away at the coral on the bottom while in the dinghy. I'll have to wait until I anchor outside on the reef before scrubbing the bottom thoroughly. The Sudanese use the harbor for everything. They were bathing a donkey near *Chidiock* yesterday.

I've bought most of my provisions, but haven't carried them down to the boat. Brian's Land Rover will make that easier.

The wind has not been strong these past few days, but I don't know what it will be like offshore. I'm giving further thought about inside/outside the reef, and will just make up my mind on the spot.

Other than doing the odd chore on *C.T.*, I've been reading. The best thing has been *Sophie's Choice*. Suzanne read it in Sydney last year just after we remarried.

Unless I add more later, assume that I've sailed on Saturday, May 29.

I will not pretend that I am happy, but I've tried to make a bargain with myself to see this voyage through. If things haven't improved by the time *Chidiock* and I reach San Diego two years from now, I make no promises.

Thanks for being such good friends, particularly during these past two months.

Will

I waved to my local friends, who were sweltering in the shade of a palm tree on Port Sudan's burning shore. As I bent over the anchor

The Shipwreck That Wasn't 189

rode, I thought, This is the first passage I have begun in years without the expectation of being with someone I love at the end. "See you in Cairo," she had said in December. But she wouldn't be there. Then the anchor was coming up through twelve feet of blue water and, as intended, I was too busy to brood further. Not only were there anchored yachts to avoid, and the hulks of two old freighters, but *Chidiock* was surrounded by bathing Sudanese, whose black faces broke into white-toothed grins followed by shrieks of laughter as we glided by, inches away.

We made only five miles that day, but it was enough. The moment *Chidiock Tichborne* was clear of the harbor—not really in the open sea, for we were sheltered by the reef, but at least free of the land—I knew that I would be all right, that I would not deliberately swim away from the boat. The feel of the wind against my skin, the open horizon, the sounds of the low waves as *Chidiock* came alive beneath my hands on the tiller and sheets, all told me that, although I had come from California with no enthusiasm, forcing myself through the necessary motions every step of the way, it had been right to return to the sea.

At the first convenient patch of coral, I anchored, put on my mask and snorkel, and went over the side to clean the boat's bottom. The tiny bits of hard coral were difficult to remove, but the accumulation was much lighter than it had been after I left her in Singapore for a similar period of time.

When the work was done, I let myself drift over the reef, gazing down at brightly colored fish darting from my shadow. I was not happy, but for the first time in months I was not desperately unhappy either.

The next morning at dawn, I raised the anchor and we rode a land breeze to the northeast. All the deliberation about whether to sail inside or outside the reef was irrelevant. Even if conditions were rougher outside, I wanted to get away from the land. What I really wanted was the spacious freedom of the open ocean; but the middle of the Red Sea, I thought—correctly, as it happened—would be freer than the shores.

For three days we beat our way north. The sailing was very wet, but we made better progress than I had expected, covering about one degree of latitude to windward each twenty-four hours. Navigation was limited to dead reckoning. On Tuesday the sun was directly overhead at noon, with a declination of 22°, matching our latitude. In choppy seas, I nevertheless tried to get some sights, hoping only to establish whether we were north or south of the sun; but for the first time in my experience, I was able to bring the sun down to both horizons, which rendered the sights meaningless. One night a loom of lights to the east presumably marked the location of Jiddah. I did not expect ever to see them any closer.

Over any twenty-four-hour period the wind averaged about twenty knots, but it almost never blew at that force. The average came from wind speeds of more than thirty knots for five or six hours in the afternoon and less than ten knots for several hours at night. I was constantly wet, but the nights were much warmer than they had been in March and I was able to sleep reasonably well. As long as we continued to make good progress, I could accept the discomfort.

With the wind steady from the northwest, we remained on a port tack and in a few days were approaching the Arabian side of the Red Sea. On Wednesday morning, before the wind began to blow so hard I couldn't hold the chart, I tried to decide when we should come about. There had been no sign of land except for the lights of Jiddah two nights earlier. I had not seen very many ships, which was odd after the steady procession that had threatened us in March. I put off the decision, hoping that I could get some useful sights that day or at sunset; but the wind was too strong, forcing us down to jib and mizzen for most of the afternoon and not diminishing until well after dark.

In those waters the safest course, in more ways than one, would have been to tack and head west, but I thought we could make it through one last night on port. This was an error in judgment for which I was to pay dearly.

At 2:00 A.M. on Thursday, June 3, 1982, *Chidiock* sailed onto an isolated coral head. She was doing only about two knots at the time. I awoke at the first bump and realized instantly what had happened. The line from the jib sheet caught me as I sat up and reached for the tiller. I pushed it away and struggled from the tarp I use as a blanket. I tried to retract the rudder, but I was too late. The very first bump had bent the rudder shaft. The rudder was already jammed in place. I wondered about the centerboard, but it had pivoted and come up into its slot. I hauled on the pennant to secure it. The wind was light. The sea was almost smooth. Foot-high waves lifted and dropped us. The rudder scraped and groaned a few more times before we drifted free of the coral head and back into silent deep water. That was all. It did not feel like a disaster.

In the darkness I could not see if there was more coral nearby. The

The Shipwreck That Wasn't 191

tiller was jammed far to starboard. Although I had no way of knowing where the rudder blade was, I soon learned that *Chidiock* would sail due west or, with the jib backed, due east. I was not distressed. Only the rudder had been damaged, and rudder damage is not as serious aboard *Chidiock* as it would be on a larger boat. I had a spare rudder. For the rest of the night I would let the little yawl drift slowly west, and at first light I would use the oars to turn her bow east and head for a place marked "Rabigh" on the chart. I had no idea of its size or what I would find there, but surely I could get an anchor down and fit the spare rudder. Quite probably I wouldn't need any help, but if I did, even an auto mechanic could straighten *Chidiock*'s rudder shaft, as one had done in Darwin a year earlier. I had no apprehension about going into Saudi Arabia. At various times in the past I had taken damaged boats into New Zealand and Vanuatu and been treated well; and in the Red Sea area I had encountered no problems in Aden, the capital of a radical Communist country, or in Port Sudan; so why should I have any in Saudi Arabia, which I naïvely thought was the country most friendly to the United States in that part of the world? So perhaps it is, officially.

Thursday, June 3, was a lovely day. Quickly I found that I could control *Chidiock*'s course within an arc of 030° to 060° by how much I backed the jib and how much I let the main and mizzen luff. While I continue to prefer cutter rigs on normal-sized boats, here once again the mizzen proved its value in a boat as small as *Chidiock*.

I thought that we were about thirty miles offshore. I wanted to get as close as possible to that dot on the chart marked "Rabigh," but having no way of knowing which of our limited repertoire of courses would be best, I let *Chidiock* find her own way east. In the light winds of dawn, she sailed 060°, but as the wind increased later, she headed up to 040°.

I could not help comparing this experience as we sailed comfortably at a knot or two with the desperate drift to Emae Island two years earlier. This did not qualify as a shipwreck, but we were disabled. As compared with the earlier experience, this one was almost a catered affair. I was in good health, had ample food and water for more than a month, and knew that we would reach land within the day. My only disappointment was in having to touch land and leave the healing solitude of the sea. I felt almost as though the sea too had rejected me. I spent the morning reading and eating MacIntosh toffee.

Around noon we came across another patch of coral, the first in ten miles of sailing. Luck usually averages out, and aboard a boat the solo sailor must take full responsibility for whatever happens. Undoubtedly there had been times when I had missed disaster by a few feet, such as the incident in March when I awoke to find a ship passing only yards away. I was clearly responsible for *Chidiock*'s hitting the coral head. I could have tacked earlier. But it did seem that we had hit the most outlying, isolated coral head along this stretch of coast.

For the next two hours, my toffee eating was seriously interfered with by the necessity of having to avoid more coral. *Chidiock* is fitted with an oarlock on the transom so that theoretically an oar can be used to steer, but I have not found this method very effective. I kept the oars in their normal locks and turned us by using them as brakes.

When we had escaped from the coral and were again in open water, I fixed myself a bowl of cereal and studied the chart. That I could leisurely do so was proof of the great difference, particularly in a small, open boat, between being hard on the wind and being a few points off it. Although the wind had reached its usual force, *Chidiock*, with her reduced speed and on a close beam reach, was comfortable and dry.

The chart showed an additional band of coral near the shoreline. I hoped to reach it before dark; but as the afternoon wore on and no sight of land appeared, I accepted the fact that we would have to stumble in blindly. Just as the sun set, two lavender mountain peaks appeared to the north of us. I knew that we must be getting close, but the sea ahead seemed endless.

With the coming of night, a glow of lights appeared a few miles south of *Chidiock*'s bow. I could not turn us toward those lights, but we were making leeway in that direction. I kept watch more by sound than by sight. I did not want to have *Chidiock* sail onto more coral, but knew that she probably would. The chart showed the approaches to Rabigh to be infested with reefs. I was not concerned. *Chidiock* was not likely to be further damaged. We just had to get close enough to those lights so that I could row the final leg in the inflatable dinghy.

After midnight the shore became a sound. Somewhere ahead of us waves were breaking. The wind had dropped to less than five knots. Leaving the sails set, I started to row *Chidiock*, trying to keep her parallel to the sound of surf. In that quiet night, the waves sounded huge. It did not seem likely that they could be so, but I began to imagine a slow, heavy swell coming from deep water—the chart showed hundreds of fathoms close to the shore—building into five- or six-foot waves before thumping onto a reef or into cliffs. For the first time I feared that this might turn into a shipwreck after all.

The Shipwreck That Wasn't 193

An hour later the night was shattered by the headlights of a car. I still could not see the shore and rested on my oars to follow its progress. This may be interesting, I thought, as the lights came directly toward us. Is *Chidiock* to be the victim of some hit-and-run Arab, driving of all things not a ship, but an automobile? As the headlights came ever closer, became ever brighter, it seemed as though indeed she might be. I looked over the side and verified that we were still surrounded by water, while presumably the car was still surrounded by land. Nevertheless, the driver still seemed to be intent on running us down. Finally, when the headlights were about fifty yards away, he turned north and sped off. Mentally I thanked him for his help. His headlights had shown that the shore was flat, low, and close, and that the waves were not nearly so big as they sounded.

Although I did not think it would do any good, I crawled to the bow and put out the fifteen-pound CQR on its longest rode, two hundred feet of nylon and thirteen feet of chain. Its effect was to turn *Chidiock* beam on to the surf, so I immediately hauled the anchor back up and returned to the oars.

I tensed as we neared the phosphorescent line. In the surf on Emae Island two years earlier, *Chidiock* had flipped and been dismasted. I did not want her to be further damaged now, and a quick image of her turning over and crushing me formed in my mind. Then we were there, and she remained upright. A two-foot-high wave lifted the little yawl's stern and surfed us forward. The rudder caught on the reef. *Chidiock* started to slue around. The starboard gunwale dipped into the water. I looked for a place to dive clear, but hesitated. A blind dive onto a reef is truly a last resort. A second wave surfed us a few yards farther. A third and then a fourth broke harmlessly behind us. Stern held high by the grinding rudder, *Chidiock* had reached Saudi Arabia.

After a few minutes of rest, I found the can of toffee, and, munching on a couple of pieces, began to consider our situation. Even now I could not see the land, but I knew that it was only feet away. I assumed there was a road along it, although no other vehicles passed. To the north of us stretched only limitless darkness, but about five miles to the south was a string of yellow lights that seemed to be on a pier or jetty, and beyond them was the loom of more lights, presumably of Rabigh.

Clearly, I was going to need some help in getting *Chidiock* off the reef. I could sit where I was and wait for dawn and hope that someone would come along the road and notice me. I could wade ashore and start walking. Or I could get into the dinghy and row to the lights. For a sailor there was really only one choice.

Not knowing when I would be able to get back to *Chidiock*, and having heard many grim tales of yachts in various parts of the world being stripped by the local people, I threw whatever was loose and valuable into the dinghy—the bag of clothes, the bag of food, a container of water, the sextant case, the radio receiver, the Nikonos camera, the bag of valuables.

I know that *Chidiock* is only a thing, made by men from plastic (and as plastic, in coming to an oil-producing country she might have been said to be coming home), but she is an exceptional creation and at times I find it difficult to remember that she is not alive. As I drifted beside her in the dinghy, I saw that she was sitting solidly on the reef, not pounding. Tides in the Red Sea are usually negligible. There seemed to be no reason why she would not be safe or why I would not be able to return to her and continue the voyage. Even though I knew better, I thought, Take care of yourself, little boat. I'll be back soon. But I was wrong. There was a reason. Not a good reason, but a reason. It is called Man.

I had had no sleep that night and only three hours of sleep the night before, but there is nothing like drifting helplessly onto an unfamiliar shore to get the adrenaline pumping and I was not tired. I rowed back through the surf and then maintained a slow, steady stroke just outside the reef.

I was almost content, certainly for the first moments since Suzanne had left and perhaps for the first that year, for while the passage across the Indian Ocean had not been rough, I had felt driven to complete it and push quickly on, mostly to see Suzanne sooner, but partly because the Red Sea worried me and I wanted to get it behind us.

As I rowed, my thoughts started to turn to Suzanne, but I deliberately forced them away. I did not even know where she was. Probably back in New Zealand. At 3:00 A.M. in the darkness of the Arabian night it would be 11:00 A.M. in Auckland. Stop thinking about her if you can, I told myself. And for a while I could. I just lost myself in the rowing and the quiet sounds of the dinghy swishing through the sea and the drops of water falling from the oars and the pleasantly warm night and the distant stars. It was so peaceful.

After an hour I tried to take a break, but we quickly drifted in toward the surf and I had to begin rowing again.

The sun was rising from behind the mountains inland when I reached the string of lights. They were on a concrete breakwater, behind which stood a complex of new buildings connected by a variety

The Shipwreck That Wasn't 195

of pipes and tubes. The whole place was surrounded by a chain link fence and a cluster of prefabricated houses.

It was completely quiet when I stepped ashore and pulled the dinghy up the beach at 5:30 A.M., Friday, June 4, 1982; so I fixed myself a cup of coffee and spread some jam on a few crackers and ate breakfast while I waited.

At 7:15 a bell sounded and men came out of the houses and began to walk sleepily toward the main buildings. I started up the beach. One of them saw me and nudged his neighbor. Both of them stopped, and then, as the others realized something unusual was happening, they all stopped. I had shaved and changed into clean shorts and shirt, but they looked at me as though I had just dropped from the moon.

I said, "Good morning. Does anyone speak English?" I should have known right then that events were going to get out of hand, because after a momentary silence, they all began to speak at once—in what sounded like Italian.

After some histrionic discussion among themselves, they motioned for me to follow them, and we wandered about the buildings until we found an Englishman. His first name was Malcolm, and he actually knew something about my voyage. He was very pleased to meet me. The men were indeed speaking Italian. This was a desalinization plant operated by an Italian company. Yes, he would see that the authorities

Ashore at desalinization plant near Rabigh, Saudi Arabia.

were notified, but since it was the Sabbath he could not be certain that anything much would get done that day. Would I like a fresh-water shower and a cup of tea while I waited?

It seemed that I had just stepped into the shower when Malcolm called, "You had better come out." He sounded nervous. While I was drying off, he called twice more for me to hurry, and when I opened the bathroom door, he whispered, "The police are here."

"Why is that a problem?" I replied in a normal voice.

He handed me a piece of paper and a pencil, "You had better write down your name and passport number and someone we can notify in the U.S." But before I could, an Arab in a baggy khaki uniform appeared in the doorway and angrily gestured at me. "You will have to go," said Malcolm.

"Where?" I asked. But he just shrugged.

I followed the Arab outside. There, another uniformed man pointed a rifle at me, then pointed it at the back of a Datsun pickup truck. I hesitated. He pointed the rifle at me again. I climbed over the tail gate. The two men—what were they? police? soldiers? I would never know—got into the cab. They had not spoken a single word to me.

As the truck sped across the desert, I realized that my life had just passed beyond my control. If it is not a myth that it ever had been in my control.

18

Arabian Prisons: Rabigh Gaol

The Land Rover turned off the highway and stopped in front of a high brown wall topped with barbed wire. "Why are we stopping here?" I asked the driver, but of course he did not understand English any more than I did Arabic, and did not reply. I had thought we were on our way to Jiddah. The last words I had heard in English were, "You will be taken before the Emir and then driven to Jiddah and released to the American consul." Those words had been spoken several hours earlier by an officer, after I had spent the night in what I thought was a police barracks but learned much later actually belonged to the Saudi Arabian coast guard. Since then I had been driven to two other unidentified buildings. At one, where a brand-new Jaguar sedan was parked, I sat in a breezeway while papers were taken into an office and signed by unseen officials. At the other, I sat in a rosewood chair while more papers were signed by a sunken-chested little man. When he gave me the papers, I, believing that they were permission for me to go to Jiddah, foolishly said, "Thank you."

An armed, uniformed guard opened the barred gate. The Land Rover drove through. The gate squeaked shut behind us. I was a prisoner in Rabigh Gaol.

Another guard opened the door of the Land Rover and beckoned for me to get out. As I did so, I asked him, "Why have I been brought here?" He looked at me blankly, then gripped my arm and led me across the courtyard toward a low building. The driver of the Land Rover followed with a clipboard in his hand.

We walked down a dimly lit corridor. The guard knocked on a closed door. When there was no response, he knocked on the next. A muffled voice called something. He opened the door and we saw a man lying on the carpet, as though he had been sleeping. As he sat up, I noticed corporal's stripes on his sleeve. The driver handed him the clipboard. He studied it, then stared at me. I asked, "Why am I here?" He signed the piece of paper on the clipboard. The drive said something in Arabic. All three men looked at me and laughed. The driver left.

The corporal struggled to his feet and walked slowly across the small room and took a ring of keys from the desk. The guard took me by the arm and I was led out of the building and across the courtyard to another wall and another gate. Beyond that gate was an inner yard facing a cell block shaped like an H. The cross arm of the H was barred. Near the gate sat an old wooden table. Behind the table were two more guards, one of them black, the other Arabian. The Arab frisked me, while the black dumped the contents of my knapsack onto the table. From behind the bars about twenty men, mostly Arabs, but including two orientals and several Africans, looked on with interest. The black examined my camera and glanced at the plastic bag that held my passport and ship's papers; it usually also held my money, but I had hidden my traveler's checks and about $400 in cash inside my locked sextant case that morning. The sextant case was still in one of my duffel bags, which I had last seen in the Land Rover. He pawed over a couple of pairs of shorts and shirts and then dropped them onto the dirt.

"Why am I here?" I asked. He looked through me.

From somewhere a thin foam pad appeared and was handed to me. The black unlocked the gate. The other prisoners backed away and I was led to the left wing of the block. We walked to the end of that wing and then back to the first doorway we had passed. There the guards conferred. When they had reached agreement, one of the Arabs pushed me through the doorway into a room and the black pointed from my mattress pad to the floor.

I stood there. "Why am I here? Who is in charge? Doesn't anyone speak English? I want to talk to the American consul."

The four uniformed men turned and walked away.

I looked around. This was my cell. The words were appalling. "My cell." This was not a game. Not a nightmare. I really was locked up in a jail in a small provincial town in Saudi Arabia, and no one in the world except my guards knew I was there. It had all happened too suddenly, too unexpectedly. Only a few minutes ago I had thought I was on my way to the American consul, where presumably this bureaucratic mess was to be resolved. Only yesterday I had come ashore thinking that I would quickly repair *Chidiock Tichborne*'s rudder and that soon, probably by today, I would be sailing up the Red Sea again. Only now did the enormity of what was happening hit me. I really was a prisoner. This really was a cell. Those really were bars on the tiny windows up near the ceiling. I really was locked behind three gates. And no one had said why or how long I would be there or what would happen next.

My cell had no door. My brief glimpse of the other prisoners had not been encouraging. The possibility of homosexual rape entered my mind. I tossed the mattress pad onto the cheap rug on the floor and sat down, using the wall as a back rest.

A few minutes later three of my fellow prisoners came in. These were all Arabs—thin, wiry, unshaven men, wearing heavy white canvas robes. They kicked their sandals off at the doorway and came across and squatted down around me. They stared at me curiously, as one would at an odd animal in a zoo. One of them reached into his pocket and offered me a cigarette. I shook my head no. He said something to the others, then pointed at me and made signs with his hand as though he were drinking from a bottle. I did not understand this and again shook my head. He then held his hands apart as though he were driving a car. Again I nodded no. They looked at me a while longer and then left.

When they had gone I examined my cell. It was about ten by fifteen feet, with a high ceiling. The floor was covered with cheap Arabian carpets, mostly in shades of green and red. The lower half of the walls was painted the color of milk chocolate. The upper half, a pale yellow. Hanging by loose wires from the ceiling was a blue fan that feebly pushed the hot air around. A fluorescent light buzzed incessantly. In one corner were some pieces of oilcloth, and in another was a cardboard box filled with trash. Through the open doorway I could see across the corridor into another cell, where an African, wearing only a pair of tattered shorts, lay sleeping on a foam pad like mine.

I thought, For an hour, this might be an adventure. The hour passed. It was not an adventure. And I started to be filled with despair.

As the afternoon dragged on, several more prisoners came into my cell. Mostly they seemed curious. None was hostile or threatening, except in appearance. Almost all offered me something: bread sticks, cigarettes, oranges, bananas. I tried to decline them all, but everything except the cigarettes was left beside my mattress anyway. Soon I had

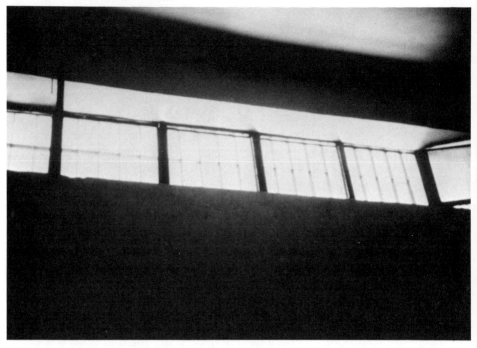

My first cell, Rabigh Gaol.

quite a stack of fruit and bread sticks. Not knowing when, or if, I would be fed, I ate some of the bread. It tasted strongly of caraway.

Many of my visitors made the same gestures of drinking or driving, and I came to understand that they were asking if I had been imprisoned for drinking or for involvement in an automobile accident. My negative nods must have puzzled them less than my attempts to depict by sign language that I had been sailing a small boat up the Red Sea and, damaging the rudder on a coral head, had rowed to shore for repairs.

At about 6:00 P.M. a man came into my cell, took the pieces of oilcloth from the corner, and spread them on the floor. Soon two other men came in, each carrying a huge circular metal tray heaped high with saffron-colored rice topped by some chunks of unidentifiable meat. A tray was placed on each piece of oilcloth. The other prisoners appeared, and I realized that I had been placed in what was usually the eating room.

There were no utensils. Everyone ate with his hands, although not, as in India, with the right hand only. As the men squatted around the trays, they gestured for me to join them. I was reluctant, but I was hungry. I was going to have to eat sometime. If I became ill, I became ill. They made room for me and I reached in and tore off a chunk of meat. Whatever it was, it tasted good. But as I squatted there, I recalled a restaurant Suzanne and I had visited in California that specialized in the novelty of food eaten in this way. If I ever get out of here, I thought, you people have lost a customer.

When we had finished—and there was, as always during my imprisonment, more food than we could eat—one of the men pointed at my greasy hands and motioned for me to follow him. Pausing at the doorway to put on our shoes, we crossed to the other wing of the building, where he showed me a rough concrete room, with wooden stalls on one side that housed toilets and showers. The toilet was a hole in the concrete; one squatted over it and then flushed by pouring in water from a plastic bucket. Along the other wall were a trough used as a urinal and a few water taps. A box of Tide sat on the floor. He sprinkled the powder on my hands and I washed them. Then I nodded to him, said, "Thank you," expecting that he would understand my intention if not the words, and went back to my cell. Paul came in a few minutes later.

Paul is a Somali. He was at the time of my imprisonment in his early twenties, slim, narrow-boned, very black, neatly dressed in long blue pants and a red shirt. I was overjoyed to find that he spoke English. He told me his long African name, which I quickly forgot, but said to call him by his mission name, Paul. He had been educated at a mission and spoke French and Italian, as well as English, Arabic, and Somali.

He said that the other prisoners wanted to know why I was being held. After replying that I did too, I told him my story. Several other men had come into the room, and he interpreted for them. They seemed to look at me with new interest. Many of them smiled. I began to sense the two-class structure of Saudi Arabia's still medieval society. There is the nobility and those associated with them, such as businessmen, and there is everybody else. As a Westerner, I would normally have been included with the upper class, but as a prisoner I was one of them.

Throughout my stay in Rabigh Gaol the other prisoners continued to be kind to me. From Paul I learned that about half of them were in for drinking—not necessarily being drunk, but just possessing alcohol, which is against the tenets of Islam—and the other half were in because of automobile accidents. For either offense they normally served about thirty days, but those accused of drinking were caned before being incarcerated. I witnessed this. The men were beaten through their robes with a cane about five feet long. The blows fell rapidly from shoulders to knees. The men did not appear to be in pain. But often the blows were hard enough to break the cane.

Only two of us had not been charged with drinking or being in an accident: myself and a small, cheerful man, with bright, intelligent eyes, who had killed a man in a knife fight. He was in for six months, following which he would be beheaded with a sword. The six months were to give him time to contemplate his fate. For thievery in Saudi Arabia, the thief's hand is cut off. For adultery, women are still stoned to death.

Knowing the length of their sentences, the other prisoners had settled in more than I ever would. In most cells the size of mine, three or four men lived. They had their clothes, sometimes a copy of the Koran, although I think many of them could not read. They showed great curiosity when I was finally able to get a book of my own, a copy of Michener's *Hawaii* with pictures of whaling ships and Polynesian maidens on the cover. They especially liked the pictures of the maidens. In most cells was a transistor radio, and in some, incredibly, a Sanyo color television set.

I never fully understood the procedure, but I gathered that a prisoner could buy extra food and small luxuries such as soap, and could even rent a television set, if he had money. Until one of the prisoners gave me a fifty-riyal note, which I did not spend and only later learned was worth about $13, I effectively had no money, even though traveler's checks worth a couple of thousand dollars were locked in my sextant case. No matter what American Express tries to tell you, you can't cash them everywhere.

In addition to the money, given to me shyly by an old man I do not recall seeing before or afterward, I was given more food, a pillow, and a sheet. I do not like to accept gifts, but I felt that I was in a survival situation just as much as if I were in a storm at sea and that I should gather whatever resources I could. And I felt too that my treatment by the authorities had made me one of them. Everywhere there is a solidarity of the oppressed.

At 8:00 P.M. Paul told me to come with him to watch the news in English on television. Most programs were in Arabic, but whenever anything came on in English, some prisoner would run down to my cell

Arabian Prisons: Rabigh Gaol 203

and beckon me. Even after I got something to read, I always went. Time dragged. The lights were on twenty-four hours a day. I did not sleep well. And so in addition to the news—Israel's invasion of Lebanon coincided and may have been more than coincidental with my imprisonment—I watched cartoons and a circa-1950 episode of "Lassie," with Arabic subtitles. I deduced the date of this from the women's clothes and the scenes of Los Angeles. California seemed far away. I could not help wondering if I would ever see it again.

The fifteen-minute newscast consisted mostly of home movies of various members of the Saudi royal family greeting visiting dignitaries. "Here is Crown Prince Whatever greeting the minister of education of Ghana." "Here Prince ——— welcomes General ——— of the French Army." "Here, Fujiro ———, head of ——— Industries of Tokyo, which will be constructing the new port of ——— on the Persian Gulf."

Paul acted as interpreter for the prison staff and so had something of trustee status. Apparently he was released the following day; I did not ever see him again, although I looked for him, since he was the only one inside the block with whom I could talk, the only one who could give me any information, however erroneous. His last words to me were, "Don't worry. You will be released tomorrow. No problem."

As I would all my nights in jail, I slept fitfully. The buzzing light was a constant irritation. I would doze for an hour or two and then come wide awake. I still had my watch, so I knew how slowly the hours were passing. In the middle of the night the cell block was quiet except for the sounds of men snoring. At least the temperature dropped at night and became tolerable, if not comfortable. I lay there watching the fan turn, wondering why they were holding me, when I would be released, and, after a while, if I would be released. That first night I thought that my incarceration was just a mistake. "No problem." I would surely be released tomorrow. I looked at my watch. Actually, already today.

On Sunday, June 6, nothing happened. Five times one of the prisoners brought a big brass kettle of tea into my cell. This tea was for all of us, and the other men came in from time to time to pour themselves some. One of them gave me a red plastic glass with white polka dots. The tea was strong and very sweet.

There was no official morning meal, so I was glad to have my bread sticks and oranges and bananas.

The temperature rose with the sun. When the midday meal was brought, the cell was above 110°. This time the trays were heaped with

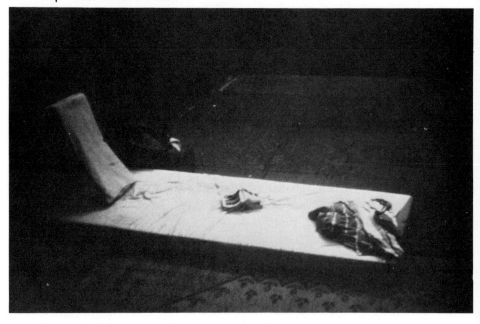

Accommodations in my first cell, Rabigh Gaol.

rice and pieces of chicken. I did not hesitate to eat with the others. On my way back from washing my hands I stopped at the gate and said to the guard, "I want to talk to whoever is in charge." He did not even look at me. I walked slowly to my cell and lay down on my pallet and dozed and wondered and waited.

The evening meal was different—slabs of white goat cheese, pita bread, black olives, and a sweet that tasted like halvah.

On my way back from washing my hands I stopped at the gate and said to the guard, "I want to talk to whoever is in charge." He looked at me but said nothing. I stood in the main corridor for a few minutes and watched some men playing dominoes. Then I walked slowly to my cell and lay down on my pallet and dozed and listened to the fan and wondered and waited. "No problem."

I awoke Monday morning without much hope. Sunday is not a holiday in Muslim countries. Monday is not the start of the work week, but just another day. At about 11:00 A.M. my pulse quickened when a guard appeared in my doorway and pointed at me. I got up and put on my shoes and followed him. The other prisoners smiled and waved to me as we waited for the first gate to open. Their behavior lifted my spirits; perhaps they knew something.

I was led through the second gate and back to the building off the outer courtyard and to the office of the only man in authority in Saudi Arabia who treated me decently. He was in his late twenties, taller than most Arabs, slim, and fairly good-looking. I assume he was the warden of the jail, but I never knew his name or rank. All of the authorities remained shadowy figures. No one ever said, "I am Lieutenant So-and-So" or ". . . Major Such-and-Such." No one ever said, "You are charged with whatever." And certainly no one ever read me my rights. That would have been unthinkable. I had none. But within the framework of what was possible, this man treated me well enough. And he spoke English.

He invited me to sit down. It was a pleasure to sit on a real chair again after several days of living on the floor. He called for cups of tea. It was the same strong, sweet tea served to the prisoners, but it tasted better from a cup. He politely, almost apologetically, asked me all the same questions he knew I had answered at my first place of detention. His office was air-conditioned. My answers were lengthy. He filled in spaces on forms as I spoke. More tea was brought.

After about an hour, he seemed to have completed enough forms. He leaned back in his chair and smiled at me. "Well, there is no problem."

"Then I am going to be released?"

"Oh yes." He seemed pleased to be able to say so.

"When?"

"Ah. Now that I do not know. It is up to Jiddah. A few days. Maybe tomorrow." He seemed downcast at this, but then brightened. "Really. There is no problem."

Perhaps not for you, I thought. "When can I see the American consul?"

This too distressed him. He threw up his hands. "That I cannot say. It is up to Jiddah. I do not have the authority."

A red push-button telephone sat on his chrome-and-teak desk. "Could you not call them on that?"

He seemed shocked, as though I had suggested something obscene. "No . . . I could . . . I mean, it is possible. But I couldn't." He probed in his mind until he found an excuse. "I don't know the number."

"Surely someone in Jiddah could get it for you."

I could feel my life hanging suspended, precariously balanced. In desperation I said, "If you were in trouble in the United States, you would be allowed to see the Saudi consul."

Somehow, perhaps because like all nouveaux riches the Saudis are sensitive about not being civilized, this made the difference. He picked up the telephone, pushed some buttons, and spoke rapidly in Arabic, almost as though he wanted to act before he had time to reflect and talk himself out of it. "There," he said with grim satisfaction. "I have told my friend in Jiddah, who is with the police there, to telephone the American consul."

"Thank you."

"You are welcome. And now you must go back to your room. It will only be for a few more days." He called for the guard.

I stood up. My mind was dazed by the prospect that now, on my fourth day ashore, someone might actually know I was in prison.

His voice broke in on me. "Do you have everything you need?"

"What?"

"Is there anything you need? In your room."

"Oh." I thought for only a moment. "A change of clothes, my razor, my toothbrush, something to read. It is all in the blue knapsack the guards took from me when I arrived here."

He said something to the guard in Arabic; then to me, "You can take your bag to your room. No problem." I noticed he called my cell a room, as though he wished to pretend this was a hotel, not a prison. At the barracks that first night someone had actually said, "You are our guest, not our prisoner."

I thanked him and was led off.

Back in my "room" I went through my knapsack as though it were a treasure chest. In addition to some clean clothes, I found my razor, a bar of soap, fingernail clippers, my radio, a spare pair of eyeglasses, the camera (late one afternoon I surreptitiously took some pictures of the cell), three books, and several pieces of toffee. I felt suddenly rich.

I lost myself in *Hawaii*, and the next two hours passed more quickly than any others during my captivity. At 2:30 P.M. I was surprised when another guard appeared in my doorway and beckoned. I was led back to the warden's office. He was sitting behind his desk, but two other men in business suits were sitting on a couch. "This," said the warden, "is Mr. Fernando Sanchez, the American consul." A Spanish-looking man of about my age stood and shook hands with me. I have seldom been so happy to see anyone in my life. A great sense of relief flooded over me. Now, surely, everything would be all right.

An hour later I was back in my cell, but my spirits were high. The warden had kept his word. His friend had called the American consul. And Mr. Sanchez had immediately dropped everything and driven to Rabigh with a Palestinian interpreter. He and the warden had worked out an arrangement by which Mr. Sanchez would return the next day to see the Emir, and then I would be released to him. "Where would you like to go?" Mr. Sanchez asked.

Resuming the voyage at that point was no longer a possibility. If I did not buy my own ticket out, I would be deported. "Anywhere," I replied. "I have a return ticket from Zurich to Los Angeles, but if you can get me on a flight to anywhere in Europe, I'll take care of the rest."

"There is a British Airways flight to London at 1:00 A.M. every day."

"London will be fine. Anywhere out of here."

I cheerfully ate a piece of toffee. The worst of the day's heat had passed. The temperature in my cell was down to about 100°. One last night in prison. By this time tomorrow I would be free.

Twenty-four hours later I was sitting in exactly the same position, but nothing else was the same. The day that had begun with such great hope had turned into one of ever deepening despair as hour after hour passed and nothing happened. I was ready at dawn, long before anyone could possibly come for me. My knapsack was packed. I even put on my shoes and socks. I was like a kid eager to go to camp.

I had difficulty concentrating on my book as people began to move about in the corridor. Every set of footsteps might be the guard's. But none ever was.

By the time the noon meal was brought, I was disappointed, but still hopeful. I had already learned that usually things do not happen quickly in Arabia. Even if Fernando Sanchez had made an early start from Jiddah, he could easily have been compelled to spend several hours in discussion and tea drinking at some office or other.

By 2:00 P.M. my hope was waning. At 3:00 I went out and asked the guard at the gate if I could speak to the warden. He of course ignored me. At 4:30 my spirits—partially because they had been so high—fell to their lowest depths thus far. The working day was over. Nothing more will happen today, I thought. But what had gone wrong? Why didn't he come for me? Why wasn't I released? Why didn't someone from the embassy at least get some word of explanation to me? What was happening? What was going to happen? When would I be free? I could not read and just sat there despondently asking myself the same unanswerable questions over and over.

At 6:00 I noticed from the corner of my eye someone in the doorway.

Thinking he was one of the prisoners, with the evening meal, I paid no attention to him. Then he came over and poked me with a baton. I looked up. He was a guard. Angry at being ignored, he pulled me to my feet, then pointed at my knapsack and stalked off. I hurried after him. As we waited at the first gate, the prisoners again seemed to know something. Most of them smiled. Many waved and said something in Arabic as we crossed the courtyard. I waved back.

The warden was standing on the steps of the office block, talking to a uniformed man I had not seen before. One of the guards stood beside a white Toyota passenger car parked nearby.

The warden greeted me as though I were an old friend who had been deliberately avoiding him.

"Ah. So there you are. I am sorry that it has taken so long, but now everything has been straightened out. If you will sign these two papers, the driver will take you to Jiddah, where you will see the head detective briefly and then be released to the American consul." I still believe that he thought this was what would happen. He handed me one of the ubiquitous clipboards. The papers were in Arabic.

"What am I signing?"

"Mere routine. They say that you have not been mistreated and that your personal belongings have all been returned to you. Your other two bags are already in the car."

I wrote, "I am unable to read this and sign at the warden's request." And signed my name.

The warden frowned when I returned the board to him, then sighed as though he was disappointed at my suspiciousness.

"Good-bye," he said. "And good luck. We are very sorry if we have inconvenienced you."

Inconvenienced? Yes I suppose being thrown in jail for three days is an inconvenience. But then I recalled that he was the best of the lot and said, "Good-bye."

I got into the passenger seat of the car. Arabian music was coming from a cassette player. Two fluffy orange balls dangled from the rearview mirror.

The prison's outer gate opened. We drove through. The gate squeaked closed behind us. It was just like all the old prison movies. I could have shouted with joy. I was free.

The sun was setting on the Red Sea as the Toyota sped down the modern two-lane highway. Where was *Chidiock Tichborne?* I wondered. And would I ever see her again?

But really nothing mattered just then except that I was free. The wind was wonderfully cool against my face. Inside my cell I had not felt a breath of wind or seen the sun. I breathed deeply. The air did taste better on the outside. The dissonant music blared. I looked at my watch. Only 6:30 P.M. Quite probably I would be on the 1:00 A.M. flight to London and out of this miserable country, but even if I had to stay until tomorrow, it would be all right, now that I was free.

But I wasn't.

19

Arabian Prisons: Jiddah

The loom of the lights of Jiddah. I had seen it from the sea a week earlier. Now I rushed toward those lights on the land.

The two-lane highway became a five-lane freeway as we neared the city. Signs pointed to various exits to the airport. I looked at them longingly. It was only 8:00 P.M., Tuesday, June 8, 1982. I could still make the 1:00 A.M. flight to London. I should have known that it wasn't going to be that simple when my guard got lost.

We turned off the freeway onto a major surface street. With honking horn and flashing lights, the guard fought through three lanes of snarled traffic to a corner. There he asked directions of a policeman, who looked at him with the disdain city dwellers reserve for provincials who don't know their way around. About a mile farther on, we turned onto a side street and stopped before a walled compound. Although I thought I was going in only to complete some brief formality, a muscle twitched in my jaw as we walked through the gate. A few minutes later I felt better as we walked back out. I was not certain exactly what had happened. We had not seen anyone who acted like the "head detective." Presumably we had been told to go somewhere else. We got back into the Toyota and proceeded to go almost everywhere else.

The driver went up side streets and down. He drove along major streets. He went around traffic circles. He even got back onto the freeway. He asked directions at cafes, at small shops, from anyone in uniform—and there were many—and from casual passers-by.

Arabian Prisons: Jiddah

I saw a good deal of Jiddah, a city of about a half million people. The strongest impression was of how much was very new. One-third of the new construction under way in the world at that time was in Saudi Arabia. My wandering guard did not miss the back streets and mazes of some of the remaining old sections of the city, but mostly we drove past new office buildings, hotels, and monuments, and modernistic palaces and mosques. Plate-glass store windows featured the latest in electronic equipment, furniture, clothing—men's not women's—and automobiles. One dealership we passed three times had five Ferraris. On the street, I saw many Jaguars and Mercedes, and several Rolls-Royces.

I have seen the manifestations of all the world's great religions. Protestant churches, Catholic cathedrals, Jewish synagogues, Hindu temples, Confucian temples, Buddhist wats. I have seen American Southern Baptists immerse converts in a muddy river, watched the first wisps of smoke rise from a body in a Hindu cremation on Bali, and heard the muezzin call the faithful to prayer in a pastel Singapore dawn. My own feeling about God is that he does not exist, or he has fallen asleep, or he has lost interest and gone away, leaving us as a small child discards a no-longer-entertaining toy, or he is a sadist. But, on the evidence, he might be Allah. All the other gods just talk, but Allah produces. There is no other reason for such a despicable people as the Arabs to have all that oil.

After more than two hours, the guard finally stumbled upon our destination. This time the wall was higher than any I had yet seen and the two guards at the gate were more heavily armed, one with a submachine gun. Inside the wall stood what appeared to be a modern office building seven or eight stories high, flanked by one-story buildings. The guard motioned for me to get out. He unlocked the trunk and motioned for me to take my duffel bags.

The tall building was dark. We walked across a courtyard to the building on the right. The guard knocked, and we went into an office. Three Arabs, wearing robes, not uniforms, sat near a cheap desk on one side of the room. A single chair was on the other. I was motioned to the chair. The guard started to leave. I said, "I thought you were going to take me to the American consul." The door closed behind him. I said to the three men facing me, "Do any of you speak English?" One of them was middle-aged and had a pitted face. The other two were young. None of them said anything.

We sat there until after 11:00 P.M. They seemed to be waiting for someone who never arrived. Occasionally they spoke a few words to one another. They kept their voices low, as though they did not want me to overhear, but they were speaking in Arabic and need not have bothered. One of them left the room twice. Each time he came back, he shrugged to the others.

At 11:30 they decided they had waited long enough. The oldest one stood up and pointed at me. I no longer hoped to make the 1:00 A.M. flight, but I still believed that I would be released that night to the American consul. I reached for my duffel bags. He shook his head no. I reached for my knapsack. He shook his head no.

The four of us walked across the courtyard to a barred doorway. My heart dropped as the oldest man took a key from a ring attached to his belt.

On the other side of the door was a small entryway, about five by five feet. A metal garbage can sat in one corner, and a bottled-water dispenser in another. A door was in each of the three walls. The center door was made of wood; the other two were of solid steel.

My stomach lurched and then began to contract spasmodically as the guard tried a succession of keys on the right-hand door before he found the one that worked. Something bitter rose to my throat. He gestured for me to go into the cell. I knew it would do no good to ask why, to ask anything. I knew it would do no good to resist. But I could not make my legs move. I could not walk. I could not bear to have another door close behind me. One of the younger guards pushed me impatiently. I stumbled forward. The door slammed. The key clicked. The heavy steel bolt slid home. At least they could not see me as my shoulders dropped and I leaned against the wall. I slid down the wall to the floor. I had thought I was free. What had happened? What was happening? What was going to happen? All the old questions that were to become yet older still. Some of them would never be answered. All I knew was that I had thought I was free, but this place, whatever it was, was worse than Rabigh Gaol.

There was nothing to look at except my cell. By no flight of euphemism could this be called a room. The cell was twelve by twelve feet, with a ceiling about fourteen feet high. From the ceiling hung a blue fan as listless as the one in Rabigh and a flickering fluorescent light that buzzed more noisily. On the floor were cheaper carpets, these in red and blue, more threadbare. They had labels saying they were made in India. Some Arabic graffiti were scribbled on the walls. A plastic bottle was three-quarters full of cigarette butts. It smelled. Eventually I would move it to the far corner of the cell. Until the door opened and someone threw in a mattress pad, a pillow, and of all things, a heavy blanket in a tiger-striped pattern—the temperature in that airless box never dropped below 100° and must often have topped 120°—there was nothing else. The door was solid. Reinforcing ribs had been welded to it. The single window was covered by a solid steel plate. Reinforcing ribs had been welded to it. Both door and window were painted gray. The walls were a dirty yellow. The only air came from gaps of less than an inch at the bottom of the door and at the top of the window. I could not see out of either one, and for days, only my watch and the changing color of those narrow stripes of light would enable me to know whether it was day or night.

I took off my shoes and socks and rolled up the legs of my trousers in a feeble attempt to be cooler, and sprawled hopelessly on the pallet and tried to sleep.

An hour later I was startled by the sound of the door clanging open. Perhaps they have come for me, I thought. But it was only a guard checking to be certain I was still there. I was to be checked in this way every two hours, day and night, at the changing of the guard.

Except to use the toilet hole, I was to be out of that cell for only two periods of about two hours each during the next five days. And each time, when I returned, my situation would be worse.

On Wednesday morning, June 9, I sat leaning against the dirty wall, waiting for something to happen. Surely something would. It had all been arranged. I was to have been released to Fernando Sanchez, the American consul, the night before. Perhaps someone crucial to signing some form or other had been called away by an emergency. Surely there had been only a slight hitch. Last night had been unpleasant because unexpected, but it was over. Today I would finally be set free. After all I had not done anything except come ashore as a distressed mariner.

I was hungry. I had been taken from Rabigh Gaol before the evening meal and had not yet been fed here, whatever here was. It did not seem to be a regular jail. I had not eaten for almost twenty-four hours and missed the pile of bread sticks and fruit left in my cell in Rabigh. Presumably I was closer to freedom here than in Rabigh, but otherwise I almost missed Rabigh. Certainly I had been better off there. Now I was truly a caged animal.

At 11:00 A.M. they came for me. In both Rabigh and Jiddah they came for me only at 11:00 A.M. or 6:00 P.M.; I am sure there must be a textbook on such things.

The direct sunlight blinded me as the guard led me across the courtyard. He kept a firm grip on my forearm. Two armed men were still on guard at the main gate to the compound, and another man with a submachine gun stood at the entrance to the high-rise building.

Inside that building we walked up a flight of marble stairs to the most sumptuous office I was to see. A thick carpet, a modern Scandanavian sofa and chairs, and behind a huge desk of polished ebony, a caricature of a fat, greasy Arab, wearing a white robe and a white headpiece with a band checked red and white like an Italian tablecloth. The fat man was talking on a telephone. We stood until he finished. My guard was very nervous at being in the presence of the fat man. His voice quavered when he answered a question. His hand shook as he saluted. And he gripped my arm more tightly as he led me out and down the corridor to another office. This one was smaller, but still expensively furnished. No one was in this office. The guard directed me to a green upholstered chair in front of a blond wood desk, and then retreated to a chair near the door, from which he watched me suspiciously. The top of the desk was bare except for a single folder, precisely centered.

A while later a man, whom I named Lieutenant Illinois, came in. He could not have been more than twenty-five and was of average height and appearance, but he moved with an assurance and had an air of authority beyond his years that made me believe from the beginning that he was well connected, probably from one of the princely families. He ignored the guard, who leapt to attention and saluted as he swept past, and went to the desk. Without speaking, he began to leaf through the folder. As he did so I noticed that the studs on his robe were pearls and that he wore a gold Rolex wrist watch.

I grew tired of waiting and asked, "Do you speak English?"

Slowly his eyes came up from the papers, as though he were surprised to discover that he was not alone. "A little."

"I want to see the American consul."

He waved one hand vaguely. "Perhaps later." Before I could continue, he said, "I must read these. Then we can talk."

The folder held about a dozen pieces of paper, presumably the records of my interrogations in Rabigh. As he studied them he bobbed his head slowly, like one of those toy dogs people inexplicably put in the rear windows of cars. When he finally looked up again he said, "What is your name?" And I thought, Oh no, not from the beginning.

"Webb Chiles."

"Webb is your first name?"

"Yes."

"That is an unusual name, is it not?"

"You must know America well to know that."

He shrugged modestly, as if to say that knowing America was but one of his many accomplishments.

As the questions continued, I tried to place his accent, finally deciding that he sounded like someone from my native Midwest, however unlikely that might be.

When I answered a question about my religion, he caught the nuance of my saying that I was raised a Christian, rather than that I am a Christian. I said, "You speak English very well. Were you educated in the United States?"

"No," he replied. It was a lie. I'm sure the textbooks on interrogation advise pretending to understand less than you do on the chance that the prisoner will inadvertently say something incriminating.

The questions went on and on. Although the Arabs live in a country with thousands of miles of coastline, those I encountered did not have the least understanding of the sea. Or of the concept of the individual.

"Where did you come from?"

"Port Sudan."

"Where were you going?"

"Suez."

"Then why were you near Arabia?"

"I had to tack against the wind."

"What is tacking?"

He shifted his approach. "When did you leave Sudan?"

"Saturday."

"When did you come ashore?"

"Friday."

"Where were you all that time?"

I had been pleased with my progress to windward and tried to explain that I did not steam at ten or fifteen knots.

"What do you do to earn a living?"

I was experienced enough not to say that I was a writer. I said that I worked on boats, sometimes delivered them.

"Are you married?"

I felt a stab of pain as I said no.

"Do you have a family?"

"No."

This was very suspicious to an Arab. "No parents?"

I did not care to explain that my mother was living but I had not spoken to her for more than fifteen years.

"No brothers or sisters? No children?" He stared at me for a long time before going on.

"Were you ever in the military?"

"No."

"Then where did you learn to sail?"

"I taught myself."

His manner showed that clearly he did not believe this. Individuals did not just teach themselves something in Saudi Arabia. But his next question surprised me. "Do you have permission for this voyage?"

"From whom? You have my clearance papers from Port Sudan to Suez. One does not need permission from anyone to sail around the world; one just does it."

Once again his manner showed that in Saudi Arabia individuals do not do anything without permission. Then, the inevitable, "Why are you making this voyage?"

I did not even attempt an answer beyond a mere "To discover if it is possible."

"Where do you live permanently?"

"On the boat."

"That little boat?"

He resumed. "When did this voyage begin?"

"In 1978."

"Where have you been since then?"

I sighed. "Everywhere."

"Everywhere?"

I had not been in any one place for more than two months in four years. He wrote down the names of all the places as I listed them.

He thumbed through my passport, scrutinizing fifty pages of stamps and visas. "What is this?" he asked suspiciously, pointing to a stamp with Chinese lettering.

"A transit visa for Taiwan."

"You did not tell me that you sailed to China."

"I did not sail to Taiwan. I flew through the capital, Taipei, on my way from and to Singapore when I returned to California last year."

His manner showed that he was not to be fooled so easily. A few pages farther along—he was going from the back of the passport to the front—he paused again: "What country is this?"

I looked. "Vanuatu is a new country. They are islands in the Pacific that used to be called the New Hebrides."

The questions droned on; they were repeated in various combinations, temporarily dropped, then suddenly brought up again. Finally it must have been close to time for his noon meal. He leaned back in his swivel chair. "That is all for now. You must go back to your cell."

"I have not had any food for twenty-four hours."

"An oversight. They will bring you a meal soon."

"Can I have my bags in my cell?"

"What for?"

"My razor, some clean clothes, some books."

"Razors are not permitted in the cells, but I will tell the guard to let you have some clothes and books."

"When will I be released?"

"I do not know. There must be an investigation."

"Of what?"

"You came ashore under suspicious circumstances."

"When can I see the American consul?"

"He has been notified that you are here."

"Where is here?"

The guard pulled me to my feet and led me off.

As we started to cross the courtyard back to my cell, someone called to us from a doorway and I was taken over to a police van painted black, where I was handcuffed to a young Arab wearing Western slacks and shirt. As we were pushed into the back of the van an involuntary "Where are you taking us?" escaped from me, although I knew it would do no good.

The back of the van was dark and incredibly hot, much worse even than my cell. We sat uncomfortably on dirty burlap sacking. My left wrist was cuffed to the Arab's right. When the van bounced over ruts, we were thrown apart and metal cut into flesh. From the street sounds and the stop-and-go motion of the van I could tell that we were still in city traffic.

After fifteen minutes we came to a permanent stop. The lock on the back door clicked and the Arab and I raced each other for the relief of an outside temperature of only 115°.

Three guards convoyed us to a small whitewashed building. Once we were inside, the handcuff was unlocked from the Arab's right wrist and secured to mine.

We were in a cluttered storeroom that evidently served also as a booking facility. I was fingerprinted; then a piece of slate with something, presumably my name, written on it in Arabic was hung around my neck, and mug shots were taken with an old twin-lens Rolleiflex.

I would like to have those photographs. In them I must look worse than I did when I was shipwrecked on Emae Island. I was unshaven and rumpled, and seemed not to have smiled for a thousand years.

No one there spoke English. I did not know if I had been charged with anything, and if so, what the charge was. And as always, I did not know what would happen next. I was almost relieved when, after another suffocating ride in the van, the back door opened onto the courtyard where we had started. At least this was familiar. Only yesterday I had eagerly looked forward to change; now I was becoming wary of it. Whenever things changed, they became worse.

I was called from my cell again at 6:00 P.M. the following day, Thursday, June 10.

During the intervening hours, I had finished reading *Hawaii* and almost finished Balzac's *Cousin Bette*. I wondered what was going to happen. I wondered why I had not heard from anyone at the embassy. If Fernando Sanchez was too busy to come to see me himself, an office boy would have done. Anyone. Just so I knew that I had not been forgotten.

Meals started to appear regularly. I was given a heavy metal tray similar to those in which TV dinners are packaged. I would hear a vehicle pull up outside. The guard would open the door to my cell. I would hand him the tray. He would return it to me heaped high with the same rice and meat, sometimes cheese and olives, served in Rabigh. When I had eaten my fill, I would knock on the door. The guard would unbolt the door to enable me to empty the garbage into the can and then rinse my tray under the lone tap in the toilet room.

The guard with the submachine gun was still on duty when we returned to the main building that Thursday evening, but everyone else seemed to have gone home for the day. Our footsteps echoed hollowly as we walked down the second-floor corridor to Lieutenant Illinois's office. The lieutenant was sitting behind his desk. Without waiting for permission I took the chair I had sat in the day before.

The lieutenant's head bobbed slowly up and down. His attention seemed to be concentrated on a red cylinder, about twelve inches long and five inches in diameter, that he held in his hands. Beside him on another desk lay my chart tube and the Voyageur navigation bag, which I had left aboard *Chidiock*. Obviously someone had brought them from Rabigh. My eyes returned to the cylinder the lieutenant was holding. He turned it slightly in his hands. I was horrified when I saw the label;

the English words printed on it, "Star Flares," did not disturb me, but below them were a number of words printed in Russian. At that moment the lieutenant looked up at me. "What is this?"

"The label says it holds flares."

"Where did you get this?"

"It is not mine."

The lieutenant's manner was friendly, confidential. "But there is nothing wrong with having flares on a boat, is there?"

"No. But I don't carry any."

Now he became frankly disbelieving. "Surely every sailor carries flares."

"I don't. I deliberately do not. I choose to go to sea by myself on a somewhat risky voyage. I do not have the right to expect anyone else to save me if I get into trouble."

"But there is nothing wrong with these, is there?"

"I wouldn't know. I've never seen that canister before."

"But," and he gestured toward the chart tube and the bag, "it was found with your things."

"It could not have been."

"But it was. How do you explain that?"

"You are asking me to explain someone else's mistake. Perhaps it got mixed in with the equipment taken from my boat. All I can tell you is that it is not mine."

He sighed, as an adult would before an obviously lying child, then shook his head as though in pity, moving it from side to side instead of bobbing it up and down as usual. After a long moment he turned to the items on the other desk. To reach them he would have had to stand and take but a single step. Instead, he spoke sharply to the guard, who hurried across the room and handed them to him.

"What is this?"

"That is a tube to hold charts."

"And it isn't yours either, I suppose."

"It is mine."

He unscrewed the end and pulled out a roll of about twenty charts, covering the northern half of the Red Sea and the eastern Mediterranean. He unrolled and studied every chart. When he came to the charts showing portions of Saudi Arabia, he demanded, "Where did you get these?"

"They are U.S. government charts. You can buy them freely in America."

On one of the charts he found in small print a statement that it was based on a British survey of 1922. Triumphantly he pointed this out to me and claimed it was not an American chart. I pointed to the U.S. government seal, but unfortunately that particular seal included the phrase "Defense Mapping Agency."

"You told me you were never in the military."

"I wasn't. Most charts are available to the general public."

He pushed the mass of charts onto the floor and dumped out the contents of the navigation bag. The *Nautical Almanac,* a spray-soaked volume of H.O. 249, dividers, a protractor, some pencils, and a notebook, fell onto his desk.

"What is all this?"

"It is all used to navigate."

"What does 'navigate' mean?"

I sighed inwardly. Explaining myself to other sailors whose native tongue is English is sometimes difficult; explaining myself to these sea-fearing desert dwellers was hopeless. " 'Navigate' is what you do to figure out where you are at sea. You take sights of the sun and stars and use these tables to work out a position."

He studied every page of H.O. 249 and every page of the *Almanac* as though they were code books. I did not want to believe what I was seeing. I did not want to draw the unavoidable conclusion about where all this was leading.

When he had completed his scrutiny, he reached into the desk and pulled out a blue-covered booklet similar to those in which one writes essay examinations in college.

"Now I am going to write out questions in this book in Arabic. Then I will translate them for you verbally. Then you will write out your answers in English. But before we go on, perhaps you would like some tea."

I said I would.

He spoke into the telephone and a servant soon appeared with a tray with a teapot and two cups. As he placed a cup in front of me, I automatically said my only word of Arabic, *Shokrān.*

The lieutenant choked on his tea. "Where did you learn to speak Arabic?"

"I don't. I learned how to say 'thank you' in Rabigh Gaol."

He smirked as though he had caught me out again.

The writing of the questions and answers was a laborious, time-consuming process. I was in no rush. His air-conditioned office was considerably more comfortable than my cell.

The questions were the ones I had answered countless times during close to a week of captivity. About midway through, we came to the question of why I had sailed to the shore. I wrote, "I hit a patch of coral about thirty miles off the coast and damaged the rudder on my boat."

When the lieutenant read this, he asked aloud, "What is a rudder?"

"It is a piece of metal that hangs down in the water and is used to steer the boat."

He shuffled through the papers in the folder until he found a color photograph of *Chidiock Tichborne* at anchor that had been with my passport. "Point out the rudder in this."

"I can't. It is under the water. Toward the stern."

"The stern?"

"About here." I pointed.

He started to set the photograph aside, but then a gleam came into his eyes. "Where was this picture taken?"

"Darwin, Australia."

"Then," he exclaimed with an unspoken *aha*, "what is this flag?" He pointed to a red ensign flying from another boat, in the background.

My heart sank as I realized what he was thinking. It did look like a Russian flag. "That is an Australian Ensign—a nautical . . . a boat flag," I replied wearily.

Nothing more untoward happened until we had almost reached the end of the booklet.

"Now write," the lieutenant said, "where you got the charts and the flares."

"I can write where I got the charts, but not the flares. They are not mine."

"Go ahead and write what you want." His voice demonstrated that what lies I wrote no longer mattered. "You know that canister does not hold flares." He paused, watching my reaction. "It is a bomb."

Food was waiting for me back in my cell, but I could not eat.

Was it really a bomb, or was that statement just another of his ploys? And if it was a bomb, was it there because my run of bad luck was continuing and it had been accidentally placed with my possessions somewhere in transit between *Chidiock* and Jiddah, or had it been placed with my possessions deliberately? If the Saudis wanted to frame me as a terrorist or a spy, my situation was hopeless. I doubt that the rules of evidence in Arabian courts are very stringent. They would not even need to take me to court. They could just keep me locked up indefinitely, as they were already doing. What had seemed days ago to be a tedious bureaucratic hassle had turned into something much more serious and depressing.

The next three days were the most hopeless of my life.

Since Friday was the Muslim Sabbath, I did not expect anything to happen. But Saturday I thought that at least I would be interrogated again. I would have welcomed that or any opportunity to be with someone to whom I could talk and from whom I might learn something of the authorities' intentions. But no one came for me. During those days I never stepped outside. I left my cell only to wash my food tray and use the toilet hole.

Day and night were almost one, distinguishable only by slight alterations in temperature and by the changing color of the tiny slivers of light beneath the steel door and above the steel window. Yellow for daytime. Black for night. Rose at dawn and dusk. The fluorescent light buzzed and flickered. The blue fan turned slowly.

I could do nothing for very long. I would read for a few minutes. Sleep for a few minutes. Think for a few minutes. Pace my cell for a few minutes. Seven small steps brought me diagonally from one corner of the cell to the other. Turn. Seven steps back. Turn. Do push-ups and sit-ups for a few minutes.

I did not talk aloud to myself, but on Friday evening I sat on my mattress and began to sing aloud. I found that I knew many more melodies than lyrics, so I occupied myself for a while with making up my own lyrics. I sang love songs, folk songs, Australian bush ballads; hummed the parts of a few operas, chiefly *Madame Butterfly* and *Carmen;* and even filled the Arabian June night with Christmas carols. At one time the guard must have heard me, for he opened the door and looked in. I did not stop singing. He closed the door again.

Naturally, some of the songs reminded me of Suzanne.

I thought of the day when we were anchored at Vairao, near the southern end of Tahiti, and caught *le truck* to go to the market at the little village of Taravao. I remembered walking along the road together beneath the hot tropic sun. Nothing special happened. We were just happy to be together.

And that memory led to the memory of our stroll a few days earlier through the botanical gardens near the Gauguin Museum. We held hands beneath the stands of giant bamboo and near ponds covered with floating flowers. A green, leafy light fell dimly through the heavy foliage.

And we lay naked, making love, on the tiny white sand beach on Mala later that year. Our own desert island.

Arabian Prisons: Jiddah

And the best time of my life, the best because of her healing love, the weeks at Cook's Beach, New Zealand, after the shipwreck on Emae Island. The pot of soup she kept constantly on the stove. The cool air as we walked among the green hills where sheep grazed, on our way to catch the ferry to Whitianga and a hot meat pie. Gathering pine cones on the beach for the fireplace.

And the night we sat in the top-floor bar at the Sheraton Hotel on the Kowloon side of Hong Kong and watched the lights of the ferryboats plying the harbor far below and the spectacle of the lights that were flung up the hills on Hong Kong Island like drops of spray flung from a breaking wave.

And the afternoon when we went to have lunch in the restaurant on the floating casino in Macao. We were the only Westerners in the room, and the waiter was surprised when we both ordered soup. "Two soup?" he repeated incredulously.

"Two soup," we verified. The soup cost only seventy cents a serving. We expected a cup each. But when one waitress brought a tureen holding about a gallon of soup, we began to understand why he had asked. And when a second waitress brought another huge tureen, we knew. There was soup enough to float *Chidiock*. The Chinese patrons stared at us in open astonishment. What were the crazy Westerners going to do with all that soup? They seemed disappointed when we did not eat it all.

The memories were so good, so painful, so unavoidable in that lonely cell where I had no one else to think about.

It has been a long time since I have believed that justice has much to do with life. Not only had I lost her, but at that very moment she was with another man on the far side of the planet, while I was locked up. In a few months I had lost everything I valued: my grandmother, who was my only family; Suzanne, who was my love as well as my wife; our marriage, which I had wanted to last; *Chidiock Tichborne;* the vision and challenge that was the voyage; access to the solitude of the sea, at times essential to me; and now my freedom. I had nothing left except the dirty clothes I wore. All my dreams had been destroyed. Dispassionately I asked myself, Have I been destroyed too?

Just as she haunted my waking moments, so did Suzanne increasingly fill my brief snatches of sleep. Probably because I knew that she was in New Zealand and because my mind wanted to escape from the furnace in which I lived, I usually dreamed of us together in New Zealand. They were gray-green dreams, dreams the color of winter waves. Dreams of the day six years earlier when we fell in love as we walked on Waiwera Beach. Dreams of sitting, talking, on Eastern Beach, while her children played in the sand.

They were dreams of gray skies and misty seas, of emerald hills and crying gulls; dreams of mountain streams and cold waterfalls, of white, red-roofed bungalows spilling down hillsides; dreams of five-foot-tall wheat-colored fronds bending to the wind; dreams of rain and fog; dreams of waves and walks along damp sand; dreams of love. But the dreams did not last, and always I returned to that burning cell.

The days passed slowly; even the hours and finally the minutes passed slowly. I was overcome by despair. Sometimes that despair was like a wave, flooding over me, pushing me far beneath its surface, where I swam hopelessly, drowning. Sometimes it was like a black panther, stalking me, watching from a tree limb, toying with me, waiting to pounce. Sometimes I wanted to scream in rage and frustration. Once I actually beat my head against the wall. But I stopped. I did not want the guard to come.

The unanswerable questions circled in my mind, but I was not foolish enough to ask why all this had happened to me. And in the end, all the questions became just one: What was going to happen next? I resolved that if they kept me permanently, if I knew that I was going to be imprisoned for more than a year, I would try to escape. If I could reach the coast and steal a boat, any boat, I could cross to Africa. But if escape proved impossible, I would starve myself to death.

They finally came for me at 11:00 A.M. on Sunday. The door squeaked open. The guard pointed at my shoes and socks. I put them on and rolled down my trousers.

I savored the air. Just to be outside again was good. I did not know what to expect, but I felt that something decisive was about to happen.

We walked up to the now familiar second floor, but we did not go to Lieutenant Illinois's office. Instead we turned to the fat man's doorway. The guard knocked. The door opened onto a tableau that will remain forever etched in my memory.

The fat man—I would soon learn that he was a colonel—was sitting behind his desk. Lieutenant Illinois was standing. I would soon learn that he had lied to me about not being educated in the United States. He had in fact graduated from the University of Illinois, where apparently they never use the words "navigate" and "rudder." Perhaps he hadn't lied. He hadn't really been educated anywhere. And to my great

Arabian Prisons: Jiddah

relief, seated on the modern sofa were Fernando Sanchez and the interpreter who had accompanied him to Rabigh.

The instant he saw me, Mr. Sanchez stood and came toward me. "How are you?" he asked.

Despite my relief, I was still angry that no one from the embassy had contacted me for what was now almost a week. "I am all right. Are you going to get me out of here?"

He lowered his voice. "I think so."

"You think so?"

"I am almost certain. There are still some papers to be signed. Some negotiations. I have tried to see you. I have been doing everything I can."

When I heard the full story, I believed that he had. On the day after I had seen him in Rabigh, he had driven back up there to obtain my release. He was told that I had already been transferred to Jiddah, although in fact I had not been. Only a wall separated us, but he had no way of knowing that. He was told to return to Jiddah and wait in his office for me. He waited there until 2:00 the following morning.

He spent most of Wednesday trying to discover where they were holding me. I was not at the Jiddah jail. Finally he was told that I was at the headquarters of Police Intelligence, the Saudi equivalent of the Gestapo. He went there every day, but was not allowed to see me. On Thursday, in answer to his repeated questions as to why I was being held, he was told, "The prisoner had something that looks like a bomb on his boat."

Mr. Sanchez said, "What do you mean it looks like a bomb? You have experts trained by our military. Is it a bomb or isn't it?"

"We will have to see if he admits it is his," was the reply.

On Sunday morning he had received a telephone call from Lieutenant Illinois, who said that there was a possibility I might be released, but that it was up to Mr. Sanchez. Naturally he replied, "What do you mean it is up to me? I don't have him locked up." He was told to come to the headquarters, but when he did so the guard refused to admit him, telling him to come back the next day. At this, Mr. Sanchez demanded to see the colonel in charge. Often such demands are ignored, but this one wasn't.

For over an hour I sat a mute spectator to the negotiation for my freedom. The Saudis suddenly understood English much better than they had. They did not want the word "confiscate" used. They did not like "imprisoned." They threatened to hold me at the deportation center, where aliens are kept chained at ankles, wrists, and neck, for two or three days while a flight out is being arranged.

Finally, mutually agreeable words were found. Papers were signed. While a guard was sent to fetch my duffel bags, Lieutenant Illinois made a lame attempt at self-justification. "Once when I was flying back to college, a full body search was done on me at Kennedy Airport in New York. We have so much. Many people want what we have. We must be very careful. You understand."

I did not say anything.

When we drove through the gate of the compound, I did not experience the great sense of relief that I had felt in Rabigh. I was much more suspicious and cynical. I would not feel free until I was out of this country. I was right.

At the embassy—and this time I was glad to have a guard, a U.S. Marine, lower a barrier behind us—we learned that the Saudi king had died that morning. With him died my chance to be on a flight that day. The airport had been closed indefinitely. On the other hand, had the king died an hour earlier, I would probably not have been released that day, and would have sat in my cell for several more days, unknowing.

I was also given some information by a man who prefers not to be identified. I was told that it is possible that the Saudis, who were displeased with the U.S. government's inability to halt the Israeli invasion of Lebanon, had considered trying to embarrass the U.S. by claiming that an American citizen had been captured in an act of terrorism against the Saudis. He explained that this was only speculation. If it was true, he did not know why they had stopped.

Indeed, he warned me that possibly they had not stopped and I had been released only to be "set up." These last words did little to make me rest easy that night, although I was certainly more comfortable in the apartment of Burnett and Katherine Radosh than I had been in prison. But for me the entire country was a prison.

By Tuesday morning, June 15, the airport had been reopened, and a seat was reserved for me on the Swissair flight to Zurich, scheduled to depart at 1:30 P.M.

Accompanied by a young English-speaking Arabian employee of the embassy, I was at the airport three hours early.

We passed through all the checkpoints in the modern terminal without difficulty, although at each I was more than half afraid that someone was going to rearrest me and find in my duffel bags whatever had been planted there. A weapon, drugs, even a bottle of whiskey would be enough. But it did not happen. And as the departure time neared, my hopes and excitement increased.

Five minutes before boarding was to begin, two armed, uniformed men marched up to me. One of them said something in Arabic and held out his hand. The embassy employee said, "He wants your passport."

I was stricken. "Why?"

He replied in a low voice, "I don't know. But you will have to give it to him. If they take you away, I will telephone the embassy."

Wonderful, I thought; but short of going to war there isn't much the embassy can do if they decide to lock me up forever. I slumped in my chair as I watched the men's retreating backs.

The other passengers walked through the door to the boarding ramp. For one wild moment I considered making a break for the plane. But I knew that was irrational. If they wanted me, they would drag me off the plane.

The last of the passengers climbed up the ramp. I tried to remain outwardly calm, but inwardly I was frantic. To have come so close and be taken away.

The service vehicles pulled back from the aircraft. The rear passenger ramp moved. The rear hatch swung closed. The Swissair employees at the counter were completing forms. One of them ran a total, then glanced speculatively at me. I froze as down the long corridor the uniformed men marched toward me. Their faces were expressionless. Directly in front of me they stopped. I stood up, resigned to going with them. Perhaps they would let me out again someday. One of them held out my passport. I did not wait an instant. I called good-bye over my shoulder to the embassy man and ran to the boarding gate.

My ticket trembled so much in my hand that the Swissair employee had difficulty taking my boarding pass. I dashed up the ramp. The hatch closed immediately, I found my seat. The plane began to taxi to the runway. The engines revved to full power.

I held my breath, trying to sense the exact moment when the wheels left the ground. But not until we were over water, and I knew that if we crashed we would do so into the Red Sea or Egypt—a crash landing in either of these being preferable to a safe landing inside Saudi Arabia —did I know I was truly free. And this time I really was.

As the pilot made an announcement in several different languages about our altitude and cruising speed to Zurich, I stared down at the waves far below me. *Chidiock Tichborne* was down there somewhere, presumably still tied to a coast guard dock in Rabigh. I would never see her again. I regretted that she would remain in a place I so hated. In nearly 20,000 miles the sea had not been able to stop us, but then there is nothing at sea to compare with the horrors of the land.

The voyage is over, I thought, as the Swissair jet sped north. I will have to build a new life. There is not much of the old one left.

I was wrong. Back in California twelve days later, I found within myself the answer to the question I had asked in prison. I had not been destroyed yet. I would continue the voyage. Somehow.

I will sail on. Somehow.

20

Poems of a Lone Voyage

I
Longing

for years he drowned
the voyage in his mind
and wore the women
like clothes of water

the sea is thin today
I can see between the drops
above the waves the white birds call
and down through them
I fall

1966

her laughter is so far from me
it does not seem I ever knew it
odd for I am not even sad
only tired of imagining

I spend my days beside the sea
waiting until I can be free
though now I doubt that can be
think of me

I am already dead
to everyone I knew
and every place I've been
I am already dead
think of me

some afternoon off Berkeley
as you sail across the bay
look down into the water
and think of me
I am not there
to think of me
and as you kiss him
think of me
did I love you
think of me

and though you never knew me
and though I am now surely dead
someday when I am deader
think of me in the evening
when you are alone and quiet
think of me

yet even as I ask it
I am somehow pleased to know
that I might as well ask sea gulls
eating fish contentedly
to think of me

1967

mist, sea mist
mist of the sea mist of me
within this arid cell I breathe you
and,
for a moment,
before my execution,
I am whole again

                       1967

leaves of men of leaves
rustle in the wind
and blow away
in my autumn mind
I rake them with my thoughts
into neat cerebral patterns
once again

leaves of men of leaves
lie on the cool green grass
of clairvoyant glass
breaking beneath my feet
into neat cerebral patterns
without end

leaves of men of leaves
fall from the fallen trees
far from the falling trees
catch in the falling breeze
my mind deceives
into neat cerebral patterns
once again

1967

darkness
not the confident searching blackness
of the glistening crow you loved
or the alien nights in harbor
when I see their hands upon your body
but the dark desolation of the sea
and of my father's death

I did not seek the light too avidly
and what I found, you brought.
if only I could believe again
in angels of light and darkness
or in myself or light or you

not love, for it dies
or light, for I do
but dark peace: absence of pain:
freedom from desire and doggerel

there is less darkness in the sea
than in me
I am one with darkness

1970

sophistry of mind
reality beyond
  so words fail

words fail to describe
how I fell in love with you
  not you: I do not know you
  but with a potential
  exponential
  theoretical
  you
  or,
  more sadly,
  a real you
  that cannot be
  for me
  and not love, because . . .
  and not fell
you see, words fail

words fail
  but is it their fault
  or do I fail words
  fail to find the images
  of my unchanging solitude
  subtly changed by you
    (wind in sails
    white triangles arching out
    and up
    beyond
    my mind

      wind against skin
      bare chest and arms
      hair of Medusa
      hair of a clown

      wind on waves
      spray and foam
      surgical bow
      twelve thousand pounds
      of eager sloop
      balanced
      trembling through the tiller
      to my finger tips

      wind beneath sun
      wind on mind on wind
      wind blowing through my mind
      wind of my life
      sacrilegious wind
      prosaic wind
      nothing more than wind
      or less
      but wind
      until I think of you and forget
      momentarily
      the wind)
   that can capture those too vivid moments
   my body remembers
   though words fail

words fail
   spontaneity not calculation
   intensity not duration
   being not control

words fail
   or have I used the wrong words
   could I have promised to love you when you are old
   could anyone else and mean them as I use the words
   but when you are old remember
   I could have loved you now

        is love then only lust
        no, but
        words fail

words that belong to sane men fail
for I am mad beyond the mind
    would a sane man still remember you
    or write these words
    or live my life
do words fail
because you are merely sane

words fail to bring you to me
or to enable me to forget
and though words fail
still I have hope
a little hope
little hope
in time

                            1971

Soft Night: 1972, 1982: Mary, Suzanne

    march 13
    is my first sane night
    knowing you are with him

    your car and his
    and the light in his apartment
    precisely unheroic symbols
    of the greatest pain I've known
    but I drive home
    with only remote sadness
    you have been—
    no
    have torn yourself
    from me
    at last

    a photograph of my first wife
    taken last Christmas
    portrays no one I ever knew
    an attenuated woman
    tired
    tense
    with a soft child
    and softer husband

in five years
will you be no more
to me
or to yourself

the same soft night
finds me naked
standing in the dark sloop
my face above the main hatch
my eyes upon the moon
imagining that moon
on another night
five years from now
when I am past Cape Horn
and you are lying beside a soft man
or the same soft man
that this soft night
finds you beside
surely softer then

what fatal flaw allows you to lie there
to choose his weakness to my strength
his mediocrity to my genius

you have sided with the masses
and wallow in the herd
with those who can only gape
and chatter and imitate
who have no souls
who are not men or women
and never were alive
what tragic flaw
in this sweet night
when you could have been
so much more

define a man, then, by that
against which he must strive:
against men for wealth and women
and the envy of men?
but none of them are men.
against what
if not this dark fierce night

and the wind and sea
against the myth
he must become
and his own will

you were a woman
more than any I have ever known
perhaps that is the way I made you
perhaps what is left of what I taught you
of what you truly were
makes it easier for you
to feel superior
within the herd.
but what a loss.
what tragic fatal flaw
has made you choose
to spend the night beside
the soft naked insipience
has made you sail
upon the bay
and not the ocean
to retreat
to a soft death
frightened and secure.
hide then, with them.
descend into his trough
until at last you forget
—if you remember now—
that you ever were alive
and that you are not all
you might have been
once were

your degradation will not be mine
the wind still blows
and the ocean waits
to measure and to slay me
no matter what you do
or become.
but in what will you take pride
in such a life
or in this night

glowing through the night
his soft white belly rises in an obscene arch
looms softly like a moon
beyond which your face
—all but your eyes:
  why do they stare
  what do they see
  or remember vaguely
is eclipsed
yet hovers
itself a moon
rising from the shadow
of his graceless form

images flow up from me
into the night
and once more
no
as always
I am alone and free
while you become a remora
to the softly rotting carcass
you caress
and kiss
and rub against.
let it
  poor thing
  but it is your own
take pride in you
for you were more
are still
but will not long remain
can you take pride in it?

not for you the vivid joy of greatness
and of life
for you
   the pastel
   diluted
   smiles and aches
   the long pointless wait for death
for you
   not to become more
   but ever less
for you
   there will be no dawn
   from this soft night

                1972

Grey Days

I've grown to like grey days
days when the sky is low
and cats'-paws only rarely touch the water
days when the south breeze is light
and I can sit with silence on the gentle sloop

it was a sunny day
when my grandfather died
we took him to the hospital the night before
lung cancer
but no one told him

he was a tiny man
in every way
but still I liked him well enough

he died so badly though
not in pain
but weakness
whimpering for more time
for more life
pitiful truly
a child again
had he ever been more
among nurses
probably kind
but after all it is only a job to them

it must not be that way with me I vowed
if chance does not kill me first
one grey day when I am old
but not too old
—that is the trick:
to give up a few good years to death
before it is too late—
I will wait for a grey day
when the sky is low
and I am as calm as the wind
a day like today
with a slight breeze from the south
I'll cast off the mooring lines
and ghost on down the bay

for three days I'll sail west
and on the fourth, I'll open the seacocks and drown
alone, unknown, unburied, and I hope,
still calm

romantic, you say, foolish and why?
you would not ask if you'd seen my grandfather
die

1972

II
Being

Southern Ocean
inhuman sea
cold and violent
comfortless
merciless
as you should be

the wind that would be
is not
without an albatross
the ocean
or me

but what is a generation to an albatross
and where do they go to die
do their bones litter the ocean floor
or do they sail on
feathered wrecks
stormtossed upon the waves

the wind that is
blows against my face
brutally
an indifferent lover
blows into my skin
enters my fingers
flows through my body
more essential than blood

1975

Iphidamas
   no one who has ever read the Iliad
   has remembered you
   until me

raised by a loving family
your father a king
you married
but left for the glorious war
before you had lain with your bride
and in your first combat
Agamemnon killed you

that is all
Homer gave you perhaps twenty lines
blew life into you
marched you into battle
had you slain
meat butchered by heroes

the first time I read the Iliad
even I did not notice you
but the second
during my "honeymoon"
ghastly word
in Chicago in 1962
with a woman from whom I am long divorced
your brief life made me wonder
what happened to your virgin bride

how soon did she forget
and you
   did you have time for regret before you died
   or was the thrusting sword too quick

you could not even know
that Homer would sing of you
   however briefly
and that in 3000 years
I at last would be touched by your death

but if you had known
I wonder
if that would have been enough

1975

I am thirty-three
seventy days alone at sea
four thousand miles from port
boat damaged
voyage abandoned
Cape Horn unpassed
dream unfulfilled

I am thirty-three
and I am becalmed

1975

Die alone, Jean Gau,
as you lived
the wild cells turning your body to water.
Any return to the sea,
even a cancerous death,
is better than remaining ashore
where there is no place
for those of us who voyage alone.

1975

consumed by my voracious dream
and wanton storms that rage
without, within

innocent of hope
surfeit of despair
I heal myself

for me, for now
there can be no harbor
not even you

1975

I want the sea
for my unmarked grave
but if I must have an epitaph:

> winds and waves of torment cease
> to become a poem
> of this senseless voyage.
> smile, fool, and sail on

1975

my silence
is like glass blown by an apprentice
flawed and cracked

but now I have learned how to form silence
and next time I will do it right
perfectly

            1975

Le Restaurant Gauguin

Paul,
perhaps you would be amused
to know how well they remember you in Tahiti
a street
a museum
a plaque where you first stepped ashore
a school
even Le Restaurant Gauguin
—in one of the best hotels, of course—
where if you were alive
and you
they would not let you in

1976

Old Man with Blue Bicycle

frangipani
tiare, eight petaled star
canna
bougainvillea
flowers bloom on flowers
litter sidewalks
cover hillsides
even beneath the sea at Venus Point
fish are flowers to the reef

so all the more I noticed him, the old man
riding his bicycle along the waterfront
always riding, never walking
unshaven, wearing a battered felt cap,
ringing a bell angrily
stopping with a shy smile
to search trash cans
once, on a Sunday, he had a single loaf of bread
tucked under his left arm

Tahiti is not a place to be alone
and after a while I was not
but still I wondered about him
whenever I saw him
and wanted to speak
to ask what he did when not riding that blue bicycle
how he spent his nights
and came to be there that way

but my solitude was as great as his
and I convinced myself we spoke different languages
surely he was French
and always he looked frightened

on Maeva Beach
the young girls bloom

frangipani

1976

Tahitian War Dead

on the Avenue Bruat
overhung by trees
a stone monument
to the Tahitians who died
in what we once called
The Great War

what, I thought, could possibly have made
you go so far to die
how odd
how truly foreign
it all must have seemed
after this
Flanders' fields
and mud
and death

three weeks later
I write these words alone at sea
their names
so carefully enscribed
already forgotten
how odd I ever asked
I, too, a glory seeker

1976

titles

upstairs
in a suburban house
a boy steps back from a painting

two flat planes:
one brown—the desert?
one orange—the sky?
two geometric figures:
one reclining triangles;
one squat squares.
diamond headed both,
serpentine
eyeless
unspeaking
unmoving,
for a thousand years unmoved

after a moment's hesitation
he leans forward
and adds a yellow circle

now there is only the title,
he thinks.
Adam and Eve?
Otiose numens?
Parents?

1978

Suzanne's poem

harpooned whale or woman

   ghostlike white flesh
   stretched taut
   filled with sperm
   unmoving

      1978

departure

judge a man, then, by that
against which he must strive
against what
if not this soft night
and the wind and sea
against the myth
he must become
and his own will
the ocean waits
to measure or to slay me
the ocean waits
and I will sail

1978

*Martha's poem
off Arnhem Land*

through the night
on unseen wind
and unseen waves
I sail unseen

sometimes
in deserted coves
I anchor
unseen

soon
I will not be here
to be unseen
and the people ashore
will not be here
not to see me
                    1981

the last island off Sumatra

islands passed
are women unloved
1982

Suzanne's last poem

death is all women
I caress her smooth flanks
there are no other
                 1982

odd
the small signs
that mark the boundaries of love

the clashes of flesh
the sharing of gentle shores
the healing of sea wounds

all come down to
my buying a cassette of the Sibelius Violin Concerto
and the *Valse Triste*
to replace the one she took
when she left

                                        September 23, 1982

a driver's license
a set of keys
some small coins, green with age

the police gave her
what they took from his pockets

a broken body
in midair
falling
broken
before the fall

he was her only son

he was my only father

she never spoke of him

but when she died
herself
of cancer
thirty-three years later

I found them
in her dresser drawer

a driver's license
a set of keys
some small coins, green with age

1982

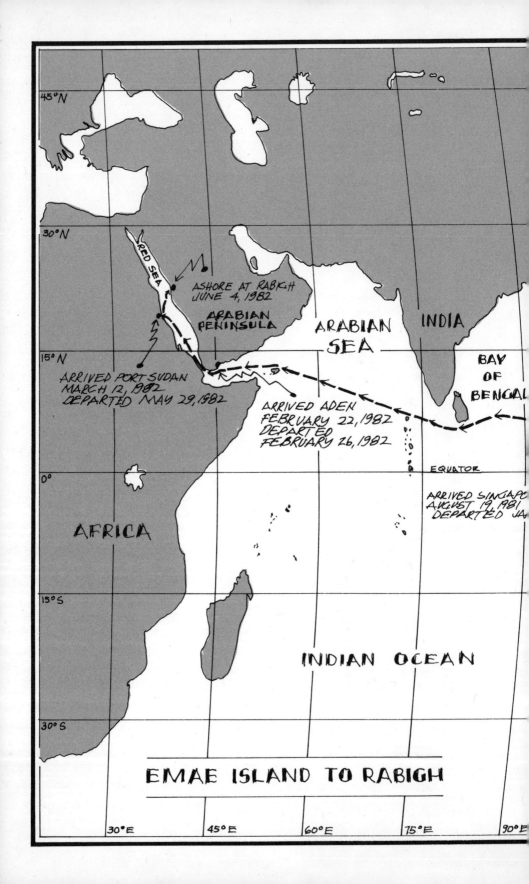